Surviving Thomas Bennet
A Pride & Prejudice Variation

By Shana Granderson, A Lady

CONTENTS

DEDICATION

This book, like all that I write, is dedicated to the love of life, the holder of my heart. You are my one and only and you complete me. You make it all worthwhile and my world revolves around you.

ACKNOWLEDGEMENT & THANK YOU

First and foremost, thank you E.C.S. for standing by me while I dedicate many hours to my craft. You are my shining light and my one and only.

I want to thank my Alpha, Will Jamison and my Beta Caroline Piediscalzi Lippert. To both Gayle Surrette and Carol for taking on the roles of proof-reader and final editing, a huge thank you to both of you. All of you who have assisted me please know that your assistance is most appreciated.

My undying love and appreciation to Jane Austen for her incredible literary masterpieces is more than can be expressed adequately here. I also thank all of the JAFF readers who make writing these stories a pleasure.

INTRODUCTION

**Warning: This book contains violence, although not graphically portrayed. **

Twins are born to James Bennet, his heir, James Junior and second born Thomas. They boys start out as the best of friends until Thomas starts to get resentful of his older brother's status as heir.

The younger Bennet turns to gambling, drink, and carousing. In order to protect Longbourn, unbeknownst to Thomas, James Bennet senior places an entail on the estate so none of his son's creditors are able to make demands against the family estate.

Thomas Bennet was given his legacy of thirty thousand pounds when he reached his majority. He marries Fanny the daughter of a local solicitor in Oxford where Thomas is teaching. He is fired for being drunk at work. He manages to gamble away all of his legacy while going into serious debt to a dangerous man in not too many years.

When James Senior dies, Thomas and Fanny Bennet arrive at Longbourn demanding an imagined inheritance. They find out there is no more for them and leave after abusing one an all roundly swearing revenge.

James Junior, the master of Longbourn, and his wife Priscilla have a son, Jamie, and daughters Jane, Elizabeth, and Mary. Thinking he can sell Longbourn if his brother and son are out of the way, Thomas Bennet murders them and James' wife by causing a carriage accident.

The story reveals how the three surviving daughters are protected by their friends and how they survive the man who murdered their beloved parents and brother. Netherfield belongs to the Darcy's second son, William. There are many of the characters that are both loved and hated from the canon in this story, some similar to canon, a good number of them hugely different, there are also some new characters not from canon.

PROLOGUE

Mr. James Bennet and his wife Beth Bennet owned a reasonably sized estate in Hertfordshire near the town in Meryton, named Longbourn. The estate had been in the family for six generations prior to the current master. They were as happy as any two parents could be, and had been blessed with fraternal twin sons, James, the eldest by about a half hour, and Thomas, his younger brother. Besides their sons, the Bennets had been blessed with a daughter, Jane, some two years after the twins were born.

When the boys were younger, they were inseparable, but as they grew older, resentment took over Thomas when he came to realise that James Junior would inherit everything and that he would only have a legacy. Thomas would hurt his brother when he thought no one was watching and would do everything he could to get his older brother into trouble. Unfortunately for him, his parents were wise to his ways and when he ended up being punished for his misdeeds, his resentment soared to new heights.

At the point the boys were old enough, they were sent to separate schools; both should have gone to Eton and then on to Cambridge, but that was not to be. Due to his behaviour in general, and towards his brother specifically, Thomas was sent to Harrow and Oxford, the first Bennet ever not to attend Eton and Cambridge. No matter how much he railed against his parents' decision, they could not be moved.

At Oxford, Thomas Bennet did well with his studies as he was an intelligent young man, but he had become enamoured with gambling and started to drink heavily. The Bennet twins graduated from their respective universities in 1779. Thomas almost did not graduate; he was lucky to do so regardless of his academic prowess after narrowly escaping being sent down for drunken carousing. When he was one and twenty, his exasperated father released his legacy of thirty thousand pounds to him.

Just after Thomas left with his legacy burning a hole in his pocket, James Bennet Senior placed a strict entail on his estate so that it could not be broken up, could not be sold to anyone who was not a Bennet by blood, and could only pass to the male line. If the male were not a Bennet, he would have to take the Bennet name to claim his inheritance.

He had several reasons for the way the entail was worded; the primary one was that he did not want his younger son's creditors approaching him to collect debts of honour to be paid against Longbourn. The clause that only a male could inherit was placed because an illiterate, unintelligent man, the son of a tradesman by the name of Ned Collins, had compromised his dear Jane for her dowry so he wanted to make sure that Longbourn would not attract fortune hunters. He did what he could to protect his family's land, legacy, and name.

1802

James Bennet Junior was a very contented man; he had married the love of his life, Priscilla, in 1783. When he met her, Priscilla was Lady Priscilla de Melville, the daughter of the Earl of Jersey. He had refused his consent for his daughter to marry a mere country squire; however, as soon as she was of age, she and James were married without the Earl's consent or blessing. Her father disowned her and refused to release his daughter's dowry of thirty thousand pounds. In defiance, his wife had turned her jointure of fifteen thousand pounds to her daughter.

Priscilla never again used her honorary title of 'Lady', and her father never met his grandchildren. Consequently, all of her neighbours in Meryton knew her simply as Mrs. Bennet. She was denied a relationship with her brother Cyril, Viscount Westmore, and was not invited to his wedding when he married Lady Sarah Rhys-Davies, daughter of the Duke of Bedford. Cyril would not go against his father; the siblings had not seen one another again, much to the regret of both. Even after the old earl passed away, Cyril would not go against his father's wishes.

The first child born of James and Priscilla's union in August 1786 was their son Jamie, born a year before James Senior went to his final reward. James Junior had taken over the day to day running of Longbourn some five years earlier. After his beloved father's passing and in the years since, he had taken Longbourn to new heights, even surpassing Netherfield Park's four thousand clear a year.

In January 1788, Priscilla had delivered Jane, followed by Elizabeth in March 1790, followed by Mary, the youngest, in October 1792. By any measure, the Bennets of Longbourn were an extremely happy family. As they grew older, all three of the Bennet daughters became pretty young ladies. Jane resembled her mother, with long blond locks and deep blue eyes, hallmarks of the De Melvilles, while Elizabeth and Mary looked like miniatures of their grandmama Beth, with dark raven-haired tresses and hazel eyes with gold and green flecks.

All four Bennet children were intelligent and well educated. Before Jamie was enrolled in Eton, he had tutors, and most of the time the three sisters would sit in on his lessons. The tutors found this highly irregular at first until they discovered the girls were learning as well as any other boy they had ever taught.

The three girls had a governess, Miss Cecilia Ponsonby, who was helping all three to become very accomplished young women. They could all speak French, Italian, and Spanish like natives and understood and read both Greek and Latin. Musically, they were beyond good on both the pianoforte and the harp, and when the three sang together, the listeners could believe that they were hearing a choir of angels.

While he was studying at Cambridge, James Bennet had met Edward Gardiner, whose father had a highly successful London import-export business—Gardiner and Son—and the two men had maintained a friendship over the years. When it became time for Bennet to start building dowries for his three daughters, he invested his wife's jointure of fifteen thousand pounds with Gardiner and Son and added as much to it as he could each year from the estate's profits. By the current year when Jamie was in his final year at Eton, Jane fourteen, Elizabeth twelve, and Mary who would be ten in October of that year, they each had dowries approaching twenty thousand pounds.

James Bennet's daughters' fortunes were a closely guarded secret for two reasons: Firstly, he did not want any fortune hunters to have a reason to compromise them as had happened to his late sister Jane. Secondly, if there were a disaster that allowed his twin brother Thomas to inherit, given his profligate ways, he did not want his estranged brother to know about the dowries or Jamie's legacy of forty-five thousand pounds. Thomas Bennet would have been even more resentful had he been aware that his father had given his brother five and twenty thousand in addition to the estate which had been the seed of Jamie's legacy. Edward Gardiner had a legal document giving him the sole discretion to approve of his daughters' matches and the release of their dowries if their father was no longer in the mortal world and their brother had not reached his five and twentieth year.

It had been some years since James had heard from Thomas. The last time was after their father's death when Thomas, who had managed to gamble away the entirety of his legacy and go into debt, showed up at Longbourn thinking that he would receive more funds from their father's estate. He and his vulgar wife, Fanny, had been most abusive when it was discovered that there was no more to be gained from James Senior's will.

Thomas had left, screaming epithets at them all, swearing that he would get his revenge for being, in his opinion, cheated out of his inheritance.

~~~~~~~/~~~~~~~

Thomas Bennet had met Francine Lewis, known as Fanny,

the daughter of a solicitor in Oxford not far from the university where he was teaching at the time. They were both selfish and resentful people and married in 1793 as they had relations out of wedlock and Fanny had become with child. Thomas Bennet had begrudgingly agreed to marry her for her dowry of ten thousand that he had promptly gambled away. Their first daughter Kitty (not short for anything, Fanny just liked the name as it was) was born in June 1793, not six months after their wedding. Lydia, who was spoiled by her mother because she looked and acted like Fanny, was born in February 1796.

As Thomas and Fanny did not care to see his brother, other than after his father's funeral, he had no contact with him. It was only when he had tried to wheedle money from his father's estate that he learned of James' marriage and his son. That was another reason for which he resented his brother. He only had two daughters, and silly ones at that. They looked nothing like him, and his wife had not fallen with child again for some reason after Lydia was born.

He blamed everyone, his brother most of all, for his lost legacy of thirty thousand pounds complete. When his father had turned it over to Thomas at his majority, he was begged to invest it, or buy some property or both. That was too much for the indolent Thomas, who believed he would make far more money at the tables.

He won occasionally, but eventually it was all gone, which had necessitated his job at the university. He had a good job but had been dismissed for coming to work in his cups one time too many. After he had frittered away Fanny's dowry, he ended up in debt as his losses mounted.

His desperation and debts had led him to the position he was in now. With the few funds that he had left, Thomas Bennet had hired two thugs to help him. He was waiting with the men at a bend in the road between Longbourn and Purvis Lodge where he knew that his brother, sister-in-law, and all of his family were visiting. However, his men had discovered that the three girls were at home with their governess, but that could not be helped.

He needed Longbourn so he could sell it, pay his debts off, and have money left over to live his life of indolence and dissipation. He was not aware that his late father had set up an entail making his plan to acquire the funds he desperately wanted to fail.

~~~~~~~/~~~~~~~

The Darcys of Pemberley in Derbyshire were an old and very established family in the Ton. There had been a Darcy at the estate since it was awarded to Pierre D'Arcy when he arrived and fought with William the Conqueror. They were one of the wealthiest families in the country; even though they did not have a title, something that had repeatedly been refused over the years.

George and Lady Anne Darcy were a rarity among the Ton; they had made a love match. George had fallen in love with Lady Anne Fitzwilliam and they had married soon after she came out. Her oldest sibling was the current Earl of Matlock, Reginald, whose countess was Elaine, and the middle sister was Lady Catherine, who was married to Sir Lewis de Bourgh, a rich baronet from Kent. They were generally a happy family that enjoyed spending time in one another's company.

The Darcys had four children, the oldest and heir, Alexander Fitzwilliam Darcy, was born in November 1793; he was followed by William Fitzwilliam Darcy in July 1786. Next came Georgiana in December 1791 and lastly, after both parents thought that their time for new babes had passed, Annabeth arrived in September 1795.

In 1801 while William was at Cambridge, George Darcy had met the heir to the Morris estate of Netherfield in Hertfordshire. During their conversation, the man had mentioned that he wished to sell the estate he inherited, as his own estate, a far larger one than Netherfield Park, was in the northern part of Northumberland, not far from the border with Scotland, making the distance too great for him to comfortably manage his secondary estate.

George Darcy had seen an opportunity for William so he

would not have to seek a profession like his older cousin Richard, who would enter the regulars as a lieutenant on graduation from Cambridge. George made an offer that was accepted with the contingency that he wanted to take his sons to see the property and as long as it was as represented, Mr. Darcy would contact Mr. Phillips, the owner's local solicitor, and purchase it for his second son.

Alex was in his final year at Cambridge and William his second when the three Darcys made the trip south during a term break. They had found Netherfield to be exactly as advertised and William had become very excited about the estate that would be his. The three rode the estate and while they were doing so, they met the neighbour, Mr. James Bennet. Hearing that the estate would soon be the property of one of the Darcys, Bennet invited them to dinner at his estate Longbourn that evening.

Dinner was enjoyable for all, but especially for the two Darcy sons who were drawn to the two older Bennet daughters. Jane was still young, but Alex saw traits in her that he found attractive, while William was enjoying a verbal battle, in good spirits, with the second Bennet daughter, who was a little spitfire. He had never met a girl that had been willing to defend her positions with logic as the slip of a girl had done.

George Darcy felt better about William being over a hundred miles south of Pemberley once he came to live in Netherfield Park. He knew William could turn to Mr. Bennet as needed and he and the Bennet son were only separated by about a month in age so William, who did not make friends easily, would by the looks of things have a male friend nearby.

The two were in the same year at Cambridge and by happenstance had not yet met, being at separate colleges. When they returned to their university after the term break was over, they would seek one another out.

The next morning, George contacted the Morris heir's local solicitor, the aforementioned Mr. Frank Phillips, who happened to be the Bennet's legal counsel as well. Mr. Phillips had his client's copy of the provisional sale agreement, and since no terms needed to be changed, the sales documents were signed, and George Darcy handed the solicitor a bank draft and received the deed in William's name.

Three days later the Darcys were back at Pemberley regaling Lady Anne and her daughters with tales of the neighbourhood and the well-bred people that they had met there. George thought that he recognised Mrs. Bennet from somewhere, but he could not place where, so he mentioned nothing about it to his wife.

Life at Pemberley was blissful except for one problem—the son of his late steward—one George Wickham. As a favour to his father who had been a faithful retainer, almost a friend, George Darcy had become godfather to the Wickham son.

When his sons as, well as their cousins Andrew and Richard, started to report George Wickham's vicious propensities, Mr. Darcy's first instinct was to dismiss them as youthful exuberance. He decided, however, to investigate for himself and found that his sons had understated the problem.

The plan had been to send George to university to attain a gentleman's education and then help him get established in a career, either the law or the church. Once the truth of young Wickham's character was discovered, he was called in to the master's study and told that Mr. Darcy had withdrawn his patronage and he was being sent to distant relatives in Devon.

When charm did not work in changing Mr. Darcy's mind, Wickham had revealed his true covetous character and threatened revenge against the Darcys. He had been escorted to Lambton, told never to darken the Darcys' doorstep again, and was given money for the post to Devon and sent on his way.

After Wickham's departure, things had returned to normal at Pemberley.

~~~~~~~/~~~~~~~

Thomas Bennet and his thugs waited until they saw the Bennet carriage leave Purvis Lodge and then they rode to wait near the bend with the steep drop on the one side. They waited until the driver had started to negotiate the turn and started firing in the air. One man charged the horses on his mount and drove the terrified team toward the drop. No matter what the driver tried, there was nothing he could do to stop the momentum of the carriage and horses as they hurtled towards the precipice.

One of the last things that James Bennet saw as he tried to put his body between the wall of the cabin and his wife and son was the evil grin on the face of his brother Thomas as the horses careened over the edge wildly pulling the carriage behind them. No human or animal survived the impact at the bottom of the drop.

A few days later, Thomas and Fanny Bennet and their daughters were travelling through Meryton by *chance*, when they stopped to take a break. They were informed by one of the townsfolk of the tragedy that had befallen James, Priscilla, and Jamie Bennet. Showing complete shock in a Drury Lane worthy performance, the Bennets made their way at all speed to Longbourn.

Thomas felt a sick satisfaction as he saw the black cloth caused by his actions hanging from the gateposts and the black wreath on the front door. He and Fanny would have to play the part so no one would suspect them in the deaths of his brother and his whelp.

They were shown into the drawing room as Fanny looked around, already redecorating in her mind before she reminded herself there was no point as Thomas intended to sell the infernal place as soon as may be. She did not like that the three surviving members of the family were far prettier and better dressed than herself and her daughters.

The new master of Longbourn was shown into the master's study by the solicitor Mr. Phillips, who was already suspicious of the timing of the visit, his suspicions increased when he heard: "How soon may I sell this pile?" Thomas Bennet asked.

"Never," Phillips returned.

"**What do you mean never!**" Bennet yelled. "It is mine, I may do with it as I *like!*"

"That would have been true if your father had not instituted this entail," Phillips handed the fuming man the relevant document.

Thomas Bennet read the document three times over and no amount of re-reading changed the fact that he had murdered his brother for no purpose. "What about what is in the estate accounts?" Bennet grasped at straws.

"Per your brother's will, anything earned before his death will be held in an irrevocable trust; you will have what you earn from today forward," Phillips informed the furious man.

Even in death, his father and brother had cheated him! There was nothing to it. If he and his family were to live, he had to run the estate. "What of the daughters? I will not pay to raise my brother's brats!" Bennet demanded.

"Their pin money will be paid from the trust which also pays for the existing servants, who cannot be discharged. You will receive one hundred pounds per annum per girl for their living expenses, far more than the actual cost would be. They are your wards now with limitations and before you ask, they have small dowries which can never be released to you or transferred to your daughters—even if they meet with an accident. You will have no say in their education.

There will be eyes on you Bennet. I cannot prove it, but my gut tells me you were complicit in the deaths of my friends and young Jamie. If we ever find proof, you will hang. Make sure those innocent girls are *never* hurt." Phillips departed in disgust. Thank goodness the Hills and the other servants would protect the three orphaned girls.

After finding some port to swig down, Thomas Bennet went to inform his wife that their plans had not gone as they expected. She was particularly displeased about the arrangements for the three pretty girls that highlighted both her and her daughters' deficiency in looks. For the first time "Where are my salts" and "My poor nerves" were heard in the halls of Longbourn.

CHAPTER 1

May 1804

The two years plus time had passed since their parents and brother died would have been much harder on the three surviving children of James and Priscilla Bennet had it not been for the intervention and protection of others. The sisters believed that the Phillips, Lucases, Darcys and their extended family, and the Gardiners had been directed by their parents and Jamie in heaven to protect them. Their life would have been horrendous if it were not for those who protected them from the worst of their uncle, aunt, and two cousins.

The new master and mistress had no interest in the estate's running and in any case, did not know how to do so. Thomas Bennet had never seen the value in joining his father and brother when the former had given lessons on the effective running of the estate. Within three years, three of Longbourn's five tenants had left, two of them to Netherfield, and the third had moved to Lucas Lodge, dropping the estate's income below one thousand eight hundred pounds per annum. Mr. Bennet, as the three sisters called him refusing to use any version of the word father or even uncle, seemed to think that the estate would run itself if he sat in the study and read all day while he drank himself into a stupor.

Mrs. Bennet was even worse. At her constant urging, if one of her insipid, vulgar, and very silly daughters wanted what their three cousins owned, it was taken and given to them. Jane, Elizabeth, and Mary had learnt to hide, or remove from Longbourn, anything of theirs that they did not want pilfered, as it was the only way to keep their own possessions.

The Hills had protected them as much as they could. On more than one occasion Fanny Bennet had attempted to dismiss one or both of the Hills and other servants, but she was frustrated to find out that they could not be dismissed without the solicitor Phillips's agreement, as her husband was not paying their wages.

It had not taken said solicitor long to realise that the three girls' pin money would be held by him until they needed something. It had only taken one quarter's money to be stolen from them by Thomas and Fanny Bennet for Phillips to institute the protective measure.

The sisters spent a lot of their time at Netherfield Park, Mr. William Darcy's estate. The three sisters were welcome at his house anytime and had become close with all the Darcys and their extended family. They had been to Pemberley a few times with Miss Ponsonby as companion and chaperone, while Thomas and Fanny Bennet ran Longbourn into the ground.

Mrs. Bennet had been particularly agitated with frequent attacks of her *nerves* for some time as she had failed to become with child again, no matter who the man she had relations with was. She needed a son, or when her husband died the estate would devolve to a cousin, Mr. William Collins. The three sisters had tried, and for the most part succeeded, in keeping far away from her because when she was in a bad mood it would take little for her to lash out at one of them.

The best thing that had happened was when, as if by some miracle, they had returned from a fortnight at Lucas Lodge and found Mr. and Mrs. Bennet gone! It had been mid-June 1804 and had led to much celebration on the estate. Within a month of their departure, the three families of tenants had returned and with Elizabeth, who had a knack for estate management, and the steward, Mr. Giles Hampstead, who used to be an under steward at Pemberley was installed. With William Darcy's help, Longbourn had returned to the level of income it had enjoyed under the late James Bennet Junior.

Mid-April 1802

The three remaining family members of the James Bennet of Longbourn were beyond devastated. One moment they were the happiest of families with six loving members, and then a suspicious accident claimed the life of their mother, father, and brother. Sir William Lucas, the former mayor of Meryton and current Magistrate for the area, had determined that there had been foul play.

Overnight, Jane, Elizabeth, and Mary had gone from being part of a happy, loving family to orphans. Not only that, but strangers had moved into their house and in the short time since their arrival, what the sisters saw was not to their liking. The girls, who would never be without a smile ready to light up their countenances, were changed forever. It was not just the sudden loss of their beloved parents and brother, but the fact that they were now wards of their uncle, who clearly cared not a jot for them.

"What are we to do?" Elizabeth asked through her tears as the three sisters were sitting on a bench under the old willow in the park. In a short time since the unwelcome arrival of the four interlopers, they had learnt that their aunt did not take well to overt signs of mourning their loss or overhearing mention of their parents and Jamie's names.

"We will honour Mama, Papa, and Jamie and be strong. Mr. Phillips told me that he, his wife, and the Lucases are keeping a close watch on what happens here, and we may go to them any-time that we need to," Jane told her crying sisters. "It is time to be strong. That does not mean that we will not mourn our parents and brother, but we will not allow these people to destroy our spirit!" Jane told her sisters defiantly.

"When did you become so strong, Jane?" Mary asked, while tears rolled down her cheeks.

"Because I have no choice, baby sister! I am now the oldest and it does not mean that I will not be overcome by sadness from time to time, but I am determined to do what I need to and make sure that we live as Mama and Papa would have expected us to!" Jane's speech made her sisters feel a little better. They hoped that with time, the pain would diminish somewhat.

Sir William had told them that gunfire was heard right before the accident, as if someone wanted to purposely panic the horses. When he and other men investigated the next day as the bodies were recovered from the gully, they had noticed other tracks indicating horses in the area and one set of hoof prints seemed to go directly toward the spot where the Bennets had gone over the edge of the drop.

Added to that, the Bennets' driver had made the trip between Longbourn and Purvis Lodge hundreds, if not thousands of times. He knew exactly how to negotiate that turn and more than likely could perform the manoeuvre in his sleep. The last thing that drew suspicion was that when the carriage was lifted back up the road pulled by draught horses; it seemed that as his life force drained out on him, James Bennet scratched TH and half of an O or A into the wood inside the cabin with his nails. It was not proof; all they had was suspicion, so as much as Sir William wanted to arrest Thomas Bennet, he had insufficient evidence to do so.

"You know that the profligate brother wanted to sell Longbourn as soon as he set foot on the property before his brother, sister-in-law, and nephew were cold in the ground!" Phillips relayed in disgust to Sir William as they met a few evenings later for an ale at the Red Rooster Inn in Meryton.

"How I wish that I had a reason to arrest that man!" Sir William said in anger. It was rare to see Sir William thus. He was always a jovial, ebullient man. His manner led many to underestimate him. He was in fact a most observant and highly intelligent man. He lived at Lucas Lodge with his wife, Lady Rosina Lucas, his oldest daughter Charlotte, sons Franklin and John, and youngest daughter Maria. They were not a wealthy family, but they were comfortable and wanted for nothing.

"You know, I am holding a letter from Bennet to the Earl of Jersey," Phillips informed Sir William who was one of the few people in Meryton who knew of Priscilla Bennet's antecedents. Along with being far more intelligent than was thought, Sir William was like a steel trap with secrets.

"Would it not be prudent to send it?" Sir William asked.

"I swore to Bennet that I would only do so in an extreme, genuine life or death situation for his survivors if he and Priscilla passed before they came of age. He was a forgiving man, but not for those who hurt his wife. Her father kept her mother from having contact, all because of implacable resentment and his damnable pride. I always thought the son a good man, but even after his father died, he did not reach out to his sister and that hurt her even more. Priscilla was much saddened that her mother passed before her father," Phillips related.

"I can understand that you must follow his wishes. Has Gardiner updated you on the girls' real dowries?"

"He has; they are closing on thirty thousand. The growth will be slower now as there will be no more money from Longbourn to be added to them. Jamie's legacy will be held in trust and divided between the three girls when Mary reaches one and twenty," Phillips informed his best friend.

"All I can say is thank goodness that those two drunks at Longbourn have no idea how wealthy those girls actually are," Sir William opined. Not long after, the two men departed for their homes, for Phillips it was a walk a few doors down on Meryton's main street, and for Sir William it took a short ride on his horse.

~~~~~~~/~~~~~~~

"What is all this blubbering about?" Fanny Bennet spat at her three nieces. "My head hurts. I do not need you three adding to the noise in this home!"

"Mrs. Bennet," recently twelve-year-old Elizabeth spoke up, drawing strength from the conversation with Jane in the park. She was the most outspoken of her sisters. "We have recently lost our beloved parents and brother; can you not understand how it would cause people with normal feelings to be upset?"

Luckily for Elizabeth, Fanny Bennet was a woman of mean understanding and did not understand that she was being insulted. "Do not talk back to me Miss Lizzy! If you do, you will feel the back of my hand. I am the mistress here now and what I say goes! Now go to your chamber and you will not have dinner, none of you!" Fanny Bennet ordered the three girls.

Jane, Elizabeth, and Mary had been moved into one medium-sized chamber that used to belong to Mary. Fanny had given Jane and Elizabeth's chambers to her daughters, who should have been in the nursery.

"I miss Mama, Papa, and Jamie every second of every day," Mary said as she broke down on Jane's shoulder.

"We all do Mary, but as I told you before, Mama and Papa, and Jamie too, would want us to carry on and make the most of our lives. I know for you it is a little more than eleven years, but as each of us becomes one and twenty, we will be free of Mr. and Mrs. Bennet. Mayhap they will drink themselves into an early grave before then! I see clearly why Papa wanted nothing to do with his brother," Jane tried to soothe Mary.

"Does that mean that I will be left here alone after Lizzy turns one and twenty?" A horrified Mary asked.

"No Mary, it does not. Neither Jane nor I will leave this place until you are able to come with us. I promise that if one of us marries before the others are one and twenty, she will take her sisters with her; we will *all* leave together or stay together, but none of us will be here alone with those horrible people," Elizabeth insisted.

"I hoped I would be able to befriend our younger cousins, but they are just like their mother. They are the most vulgar and silly creatures that I have ever had the displeasure of meeting!" Mary stated.

There was no argument from her older sisters. The only thing that all three knew, as far as Lydia and Kitty were concerned, was that they wanted nothing to do with them. Mrs. Bennet spoiled and indulged her daughters; they could do no wrong in their mother's eyes. The three sisters had quickly learnt to avoid the two cousins as they would blame anything, real or imagined, on their older cousins, and Mrs. Bennet would always berate the three sisters.

They wore black in defiance of the mistress of the estate. In her attempt to wipe away any evidence of the previous master and mistress she had ordered the girls not to wear mourning clothes. They had promptly refused, which had led to the first time Fanny Bennet had struck one of the grieving girls.

Fanny did not know how, but the solicitor and the magistrate heard of her actions and warned them that there would not be a warning next time. As much as Fanny wanted to lay into the three girls who thought themselves above her and her wonderful daughters, she would not chance being thrown in the gaol.

~~~~~~~~/~~~~~~~~

A few days later, Fanny Bennet entered her husband's study. He was sporting a black eye and a split lip. "Thomas, what ever happened?" she shrieked.

"It is the debt of honour that I owe. There was no way I could have known my damnable father put an entail on the estate! We must produce a son, Fanny. Otherwise, all of this will be for naught as the estate will fall to some unknown cousin. I have agreed to turn over half of the estate's profits until my debt is paid off," Bennet informed his wife.

"Just how much do you owe?" Fanny wanted to know.

"A little under ten thousand pounds. It will be paid off in six years or so, as there will be interest. I showed the creditor's men the documents from the entail so they know that killing me will get them nothing." Bennet downed a glass of port in one gulp and refilled the large glass. "We are stuck here with those three brats. The one hundred pounds a year for each one for their upkeep is a necessity! We have to keep them alive and well as Phillips will check on them whenever he decides he needs to do so."

"This is not what you promised if we killed that brother of yours and his heir!" Fanny whined.

"Yes, as I told you, I was unaware of the entail. If I had

known about its existence, we would have taken one or more of my dead brother's children and ransomed them instead," Bennet stated with no emotion.

~~~~~~~/~~~~~~~

"Father," said Alex Darcy, who was home for his final Easter break before he graduated from Cambridge. "Have you seen the papers today?" The Darcys, along with the Fitzwilliams from Snowhaven, would normally be at Rosings Park with the de Bourghs for Easter, but with Anne de Bough ill, the annual family holiday had been cancelled. The de Bourgh heir, Peter, was on his grand tour. The family regretted that they would not be in Kent together as they all enjoyed one another's company, but all prayed that Anne would recover soon.

"No, I have not, son; why do you ask?" George Darcy asked his oldest.

"Do you remember the Bennets, Will's neighbours, the ones we had dinner with?" Alex asked.

"Of course I do. Capital people, why do you ask?"

"Mr. Bennet, his wife, and son were all killed in a horrific accident. It says there is speculation that it was foul play but there is no definitive proof!"

"How could anyone be that evil to commit murder so foul? It does not mention those genteel girls that we met, does it, Alex?"

"No father, no word about them, so I would assume that they were not in the conveyance with the rest. What a tragedy, I hope all three are well." Alex was shaken by the news, to have three people dead, one of them Will's age and who he had dined with a month or so earlier.

"William has to be told. He was to rely on Mr. Bennet for guidance; we have no idea what the man who inherited the estate--it says here it now belongs to Mr. Bennet's twin brother; Thomas--is like. When Will finishes his studies, we will spend the first six months with him so that he will feel comfortable in his new role. I am sure that your mother and sister will love seeing his home," George Darcy decided.

Alex found William in the library. It was the part of Pemberley that William would miss most of all when he took up Netherfield's reins. He knew that he could visit Pemberley anytime that he chose, but it would not be the same. Alex handed William the paper, and opened to the page that mentioned the Bennets.

"That is horrendous! And they suspect that it was not an accident; I wonder how the surviving sisters are faring," William speculated. He did not say that he would like to debate more with the little spitfire, Miss Elizabeth, and hoped that she and her sisters would come through the devastation of losing half of their family.

"We will know not until we journey there; mayhap we can ask father if you and I can pay a visit at the end of May for a few weeks when the school year is complete," Alex suggested.

The brothers put the suggestion to their father in his study. "We will all be at Cambridge for your graduation, Alex. Let me check with your mother; if it does not conflict with any plans, then we will all go to Netherfield from the university contingent on your mother's agreement," George Darcy told his sons, "We can be there for a month or six weeks if there are no other plans."

"If Anne is well, then the de Bourghs will be at Cambridge, as will the Fitzwilliams with Richard's graduation. Can we invite them all to come see my estate, Father?" William asked.

"I do not see why not," was their father's response. The three found Lady Anne and her two daughters in the music room.

"We have nothing planned that I know of, George," Lady Anne informed him after he proposed the trip to Netherfield. Georgiana, who was nine, and Annabeth, five, were both very excited about seeing William's estate.

It was decided; the Darcys would arrive at Netherfield around the first day of June.

~~~~~~~/~~~~~~~

Late May, 1802

"Uncle Phillips informs us that the Darcys, whose son owns Netherfield, will be arriving soon," Jane informed Mrs Bennet.

"He is not your uncle and what should I care about who will be at Netherfield," Fanny Bennet shot back.

"He has given us leave to call him thus and he was a good friend of our papa's..." Whatever else Elizabeth was about to say was lost as Fanny struck her on her shoulder.

Even though she was of mean understanding, she had learned the fact that she could not leave marks on the three brats where they could be seen by others. "How many times have I told you not to talk back to me you impertinent brat!" Fanny lifted her hand again but stayed it as Elizabeth's sisters stood by either side of her to protect her.

"You are such a brat, miss high-and-mighty Lizzy," Lydia parroted her mother.

Kitty, as she always did, followed Lydia's lead, even though she was almost three years older.

Fanny Bennet needed an outlet for her frustrations and hitting one of the brats was a way to forget about her problems. Thomas had come to her every night since they had been stuck in this infernal backwater place and her courses had started this very morning! In order to end the entail, she had to produce a son, as much as it was distasteful for her to endure increasing again, it had to be done.

Thomas had promised her that they would take the money left from the sale after his debts were paid and go live in a place like Brighton or Bath where they would enjoy a more varied society. All of that had gone up in smoke because of the infernal entail. Fanny could not understand why she, her husband, and daughters were shunned by the neighbourhood while all seemed to love the three orphans.

Although not a particularly handsome woman, Fanny Bennet was a vain one. She hated the changes that pregnancy wrought on her body. She still had those disgusting reminders of her darling Lydia's birth, with all the marks around her belly. Fanny was somewhat rotund and had blamed that on her two confinements rather than the excess of food and drinks that she consumed.

Luckily for the three sisters, given how much Thomas and Fanny Bennet imbibed, they were often left to their own plans and were able to continue their lessons with Miss Ponsonby, or she would accompany them as they visited neighbours. Mr. Bennet had refused to spend money on masters any longer so, since the objectionable family had taken up residence at Longbourn, there had not been lessons with masters—at least none of which the couple knew.

Fanny Bennet never questioned the girls' desire to visit at Lucas Lodge at least three times a week; she never questioned that it was always Mondays, Wednesdays, and Fridays that the sisters would visit. All she cared about was they were out of the house and she did not have to see them. Occasionally there were other days as well, but always those three. Through Mr. Phillips, it was arranged with Sir William and Lady Lucas that the masters would come to their estate to teach the girls after Bennet had banned masters from Longbourn.

Besides just wanting to help the three, the added advantage was that the two youngest Lucases, John and Maria, benefited from the masters as well, something that Sir William would not have otherwise been able to afford.

~~~~~~~/~~~~~~~

About a sennight later, the three sisters were at Lucas Lodge with their music master when George, Alex, and William Darcy came to call, to letting their neighbours know they had arrived at Netherfield. The three Bennets joined the Lucas family in greeting the new arrivals.

For the still grieving Jane, Elizabeth, and Mary, they felt a kinship to the Darcys as they represented a connection to their parents and brother before that tragic day, no matter how tenuous. The girls were thrilled when they learned that the rest of the Darcy family was at Netherfield that included two daughters near to their own ages. The Darcys also shared that some of their relations would arrive by the morrow.

As the greetings were being made, Mary made the mistake of touching Elizabeth's shoulder, causing her to wince. It was noted by both of the Lucas parents, but they knew that if Eliza wanted to share something with them, she would. They knew Elizabeth tended to climb the old oak tree on the summit of Oakham Mount and she may have injured herself in that endeavour. They would not ask her, as she seemed unwilling to discuss her injury.

"My wife has asked me to extend an invitation for dinner for two days hence, Sir William and Lady Lucas. It is for all members of the family." Mr. Darcy then turned to the three Bennet girls. "I do not want to speak ill of your family, but we did not receive a warm welcome at Longbourn, so I did not issue an invitation to your uncle and his family, however, if you three young ladies are able to attend, you would be more than welcome."

"It is not surprising that Mr. and Mrs. Bennet were not welcoming," Jane informed the Darcys. "I accept on behalf of my sisters," Jane said after seeing nods from both her siblings. "May I ask if you have invited Mr. & Mrs. Phillips?"

"We did," Alex answered, captivated by the strength and beauty that he saw before him.

"Then we will ask Uncle and Aunt Phillips to convey us to your estate," Jane stated. Seeing the questioning look when she mentioned uncle and aunt, she explained how they had begun to address the Phillips thusly and how as the couple had no children she and her sisters were viewed as almost surrogate children.

"Besides the Phillipses, we have invited the Longs and the Gouldings as well," William Darcy shared. He too had noticed the wince when Miss Elizabeth was touched on her shoulder, but he did not know her well enough to ask her about it.

After another fifteen minutes where the Darcy men waxed eloquently about their home in Derbyshire and found out more information about the neighbourhood, they took their leave, looking forward to having good company two days hence.

~~~~~~~/~~~~~~~

On the day of the dinner, Frank and Hattie Phillips arrived just after four to collect the three girls who had become so very dear to them. Thomas and Fanny Bennet were in their cups so they cared not that the responsibility for the three burdens would not be theirs for some hours. Fanny was put out that her *sweet* daughters were not included but accepted that there was no way to bring them to a home where they were neither invited nor known.

The Phillips' carriage arrived at Netherfield Park; they and the three Bennets had been invited to arrive an hour before the Lucases, Gouldings, and Longs to give Georgiana, who was ten, and Annabeth six, time to get to know the three Bennets. Their father believed that the Bennet girls, especially the two younger sisters, would be good friends for his girls.

Lady Anne welcomed the arriving guests warmly and requested to be introduced to them. Once that was accomplished, she introduced the Earl and Countess of Matlock and their two sons, Andrew, Viscount Hilldale, and Richard, who would be joining the dragoons soon after leaving Netherfield in a fortnight.

The girls had never met a peer of the realm before and were somewhat awestruck until they were put at ease noting how down to earth all four Fitzwilliams were. As George Darcy had suspected, it did not take long before the five girls were chatting easily amongst themselves.

"Papa told us after he and our brothers came to see Netherfield how proficient all three of you are on the pianoforte and singing," Georgiana stated. "Anna and I are learning as well. We started with our mother who plays very well and now I learn from a master. I began with him some three years ago and Anna just this year. Please say that you will come to visit me and that we may play some duets?" the normally shy girl asked. Both of her parents noted how quickly their reticent daughter felt at ease with the sisters.

"It will be our pleasure, Miss Darcy," Jane answered for her younger sisters and herself.

"Will you not call me Georgiana, Miss Bennet? I am also called Georgie, although Richard calls me Gigi and I prefer that to Georgie," Miss Darcy offered.

"And please call me Anna," Miss Annabeth added.

"In that case, Gigi and Anna, please call me Jane," the eldest Bennet sister allowed.

"Call me Lizzy; everyone who knows me does," Elizabeth stated.

"And I am just Mary; like Jane, I have no nickname," Mary smiled. She was very happy to have more girls her own age in the neighbourhood.

The other four Darcys and the Fitzwilliams were seated with Mr. and Mrs. Phillips. "I read that the accident that killed the girls' parents and brother was suspicious," George Darcy recalled.

"There is no question there was foul play, and we are all but certain that the current master of Longbourn was behind his brother's murder; unfortunately, he cannot be convicted on speculation, as there is no hard evidence against him," Phillips told angrily. Each time he thought about the man he suspected was behind the murder of his friend and client, he felt the anger boil up all over again.

"Surely not his own brother?" Lord Reginald Fitzwilliam, the Earl, asked in surprise.

Phillips relayed the history of the resentment along with the dissipation, gambling, and drinking of Thomas Bennet. Hearing the information that Thomas Bennet had wanted to sell Longbourn mere days after his brother's death, convinced the listeners that Phillips had more than just a supposition.

"How is it that those poor girls are left to live with the man that more than likely murdered half of their family?" Lady Anne asked, horrified by the thought.

"Unfortunately, my friend James never added a clause in his will as to who would be the guardian of his girls in case both he and his beloved wife perished. As there was no direction from him, they became wards of Thomas Bennet by default. Thankfully, there are some things that I, and Edward Gardiner, are allowed to do to help the girls," Phillips shared.

"Are they related to the Edward Gardiners of Gardiner and Son?" Mr. Darcy asked.

"No, like me, Gardiner is, was, a very good friend of the late James Bennet Junior. Bennet invested with him; the girl's true dowries and the legacy that would have been Jamie's is looked after by his company. Thank God in heaven that the current master and mistress of Longbourn have no idea that the girls have very substantial dowries that are secured, so Bennet cannot access their funds." Phillips did not disclose the amounts, and no one was vulgar enough to ask.

"George, I want to help these poor girls as much as I can," Lady Anne told her husband quietly as they walked into dinner.

The Countess of Matlock had been surreptitiously staring at Jane Bennet along with her son Andrew. As they stood for dinner, Lady Elaine called her eldest to her side. "The more I look at Jane Bennet the more she reminds me of Marie De Melville; they could have been sisters."

"That was what I was thinking when I laid my eyes on her, hopefully Lady Marie will consent to court me when she comes out in February," Andrew agreed with his mother.

"When I mentioned the De Melvilles, there was no sign of recognition from any of the three, so it must be one of those coincidences when perfect strangers look similar to one another," the Countess opined.

Over the weeks that the Darcys were at Netherfield, when the three Bennet sisters were not with their masters, they were at William Darcy's estate with his family. It was just a few weeks after the Fitzwilliams departed to accompany Richard to his induction that Lady Anne and George Darcy were being called, with their permission, Aunt Anne and Uncle George by the sisters.

It seemed that the Bennets of Longbourn cared not a whit

where the three were as long as they did not have to deal with them, so it came to pass that the girls would spend many nights with their new friends in addition to the days.

A few days before the Darcys were to decamp for the North, Lady Anne extended an invitation for Jane, Elizabeth, and Mary to return to Pemberley with them for the summer. The girls accepted with glee, and it was left to Mr. Phillips to inform Thomas and Fanny.

Thomas neither cared, nor realised that the girls were not at Longbourn for the past few weeks. Fanny whined about her daughters being excluded but quickly calmed down when she realised that she would not have to deal with the brats for two months complete.

A few days later, the Darcy carriages departed Netherfield Park with the three girls and their companion-governess, Miss Ponsonby.

CHAPTER 2

For the three sisters, everything about the trip was exciting. They had travelled nowhere besides the Town, so the trip in and of itself was an adventure. Since their parents and brother had been snatched from them, they had found it hard to trust new acquaintances. To them, although they had only met the male half of the family, the Darcys were known from the happy time, a month before their whole world was thrown off kilter.

They mourned their parents and Jamie, and would for the rest of their days, but the time with the Darcy's had begun to bring light back into the three Bennet sisters' lives. They may never be as happy and carefree as they were before that terrible day, but they had begun the long road to recovery as they basked in the warmth and love that was directed at them by caring people.

On the first day of travel, as she thought about how pleasant the Fitzwilliams had been, Jane asked if they had met all of Georgiana's aunts and uncles. Georgiana had explained to her new friends that the de Bourgh family could not join them at Cambridge or afterwards at Netherfield. Her cousin Peter was still on his grand tour and his sister Anne was not well again, so her Uncle Lewis and Aunt Catherine had remained at Rosings Park in Kent to be close to their daughter. There were no more aunts or uncles of which she was aware.

On the last leg of the trip, the second day since departing Hertfordshire, the three Bennets were in the second coach with Georgiana, Annabeth, and Miss Ponsonby. "You will meet our governess, Miss Younge, when we arrive at Pemberley. Her mother was ill, so Mama told her to go be with her family until we return. She is strict but very fair," Georgiana told Miss Ponsonby.

"She *is* strict," Annabeth wrinkled her nose.

"I am sure that if you do your work and heed her, that she is not strict on you is she Miss Annabeth?" the long-time governess asked with a smile.

"S'pose not," Annabeth admitted causing a little laughter among the other four girls as she crossed her arms and huffed.

"We are entering Lambton," Georgiana pointed out, "it is but five miles from here to Pemberley."

"Lambton? Is that not where Aunt Maddie is from?" Elizabeth asked. Jane nodded her head.

"What is your Aunt's family name?" Georgiana enquired.

"Now it is Gardiner, but it was Thatcher before she married Uncle Edward," Jane replied.

"The vicar at the Lambton church is a Mr. Thatcher," Georgiana reported.

"Aunt did tell us that her father is a man of the cloth, did she not?" Mary confirmed.

"I believe that you are correct, Mary," Elizabeth agreed.

"Mayhap we will meet him while we are here," Jane surmised.

"Five miles is even too much for you to walk, Lizzy," Mary stated.

"It is, but as I get older and stronger, that will not be a problem for me in the future," Elizabeth retorted.

"There will be no need to walk; we go into Lambton almost weekly," Georgiana reported.

"Then Gigi, we will make a request to visit him," Jane decided.

"Look," Annabeth pointed excitedly, "it says Pemberley!" she proudly pointed the steel arch over the drive that stretched between the two gateposts as they passed the gatehouse keeper, who doffed his hat to those in the carriages.

Elizabeth was fascinated by the forest that she noted stretching out on the left side of the drive. She could not wait to start exploring the area and especially the forest, there must be some magnificent trees to climb in it. After a mile or two, there was an incline, and as they crested the hill, the three Bennets gaped as they noticed the biggest house that had ever seen in their lives. It made Netherfield look small and that estate's manor house was twice the size of Longbourn's.

"Gigi, Anna, you live in a palace," Mary exclaimed in wonder.

"It is just a home, a large home, but a house, nonetheless," Georgiana responded.

"It is beautiful here!" Elizabeth explained. She had never seen a place that nature had done more for and where the awkward tastes of man had not spoilt what mother nature had designed.

The carriages came to a stop in an internal courtyard and the three Bennets were even more awed at the size of the edifice from close up. It towered above them as they exited the conveyance after a liveried footman had placed the step and opened the door. A kind looking lady and a man standing ramrod straight met the master and mistress of the estate to welcome them home.

"Mrs. Reynolds, the housekeeper, and Mr. Douglas, the butler," Georgiana quietly informed her friends. "Miss Younge," Georgiana inclined her head to point out a younger lady of middling height and light brown hair standing off to the side on the top step just outside of the massive entrance doors.

Per Lady Anne's instructions, Miss Mary Bennet would be in the nursery with Georgiana and Annabeth, while Elizabeth and Jane had elected to share a chamber. The two followed Mrs. Reynolds to a suite in the family wing. There was a sitting room and the biggest bedchamber either of them had ever seen, and in the middle on the wall opposite the bay windows was the biggest bed ever.

Jane and Elizabeth were introduced to a maid who was already busy unpacking their trunks; her name was Peggy, and she was assigned as their shared lady's maid for the duration of stay in Derbyshire.

For the first time since their parents and Jamie's deaths, the sisters felt completely relaxed in a home.

~~~~~~~~/~~~~~~~~

"Where are the brats?" Thomas Bennet asked at dinner one night. His nieces had been gone for a fortnight, and this was the first time he had noted their absence.

"They went to stay with those boring people who live at Netherfield, Papa," Lydia informed him.

"If they are at Netherfield, why have they not been to our home?" Bennet asked as he downed another glass of port. I do not remember seeing them in a few days.

"They are not *at* Netherfield Park Thomas, Lydia said *with*," Fanny corrected her husband. "I was too lenient on those three, I should not have allowed them to go to wherever it is in the north that they have gone."

"You know Mama, I searched their room and could find none of the jewellery that they used to have," Lydia complained.

"Will you not make them share with us, Mama," Kitty whined in support of her younger sister.

"I will help you search after dinner, my beautiful daughters," Fanny promised.

The search of their room, even pulling the mattress from the bed and searching under it, rendered no results and left the three very frustrated. What the greedy, covetous girls could not know, was after the first time that Lydia demanded the cross that their late mother had given Lizzy, followed by Kitty who demanded Jane's, the girls had taken what little jewellery they had and given it all to Uncle Phillips for safe keeping. Neither Kitty nor Lydia actually wanted the crosses, but only desired them because they were not theirs. As soon as they returned to their chambers, they had taken the crosses and cast them aside, so Jane and Elizabeth had reclaimed them and given them to Uncle Frank to place in his safe. Mother and daughters searched through the closet and drawers and could not find any clothing of note. The three sisters had the foresight to pack most of their clothing for the two months they would be gone and whatever they did not take, Mrs. Hill had removed and hidden in her room.

"I will buy you far better things than your cousins have," Fanny Bennet promised, knowing full well that it was a hollow promise. Until the next harvest, she and her family had little to live on given that the estate accounts had been emptied before Thomas had become master.

The more time went by, the more she regretted their ill-conceived plan to murder the three elder Bennets and install themselves at Longbourn. She understood enough to know that their lives had become harder, not easier, and just that day that housekeeper who she could not dismiss had told her that she needed to visit the tenants to help them as needed.

Fanny Bennet had scoffed at the woman. She may not be allowed to get rid of her while the three brats lived in the house, but she could and would choose to ignore her advice. What did a mere servant know about the business of an estate? She completely ignored the fact that as the daughter of an unsuccessful solicitor, she had never set foot on an estate until she and her husband had come to collect the non-existent inheritance when Thomas's father had died. That had been for less than a day and the next time was when she had become mistress some months ago.

While his brother had been a responsible landowner who would not take his estate or tenants for granted, Thomas Bennet was one of the most indolent men one could have the displeasure of meeting. He was always looking for the easy way out, which had led to his gambling, thinking that he would be the one to beat the odds and make his fortune with the minimum effort.

No matter how much he lost, like so many before him, he clung to the belief that he would make it all back, and more with the next hand or roll of the dice. He was an intelligent man when it came to being book smart, however, he had never learnt that the house never loses. When he had frequented a gambling hell in Oxford, he had made the mistake of boasting of his legacy. Consequently, when he was not losing on his own, the dealers helped him along until eventually, he had nothing left. The more he lost, the more he drank; some nights he passed out in his own vomit on the floor of whatever seedy tavern he was drinking at.

Neither he nor Fanny Bennet cared for one another. For her, he was a gentleman's son with a fine fortune and for him, she was someone to warm his bed. Fanny had never felt very satisfied with Thomas's prowess in the bedchamber; more often than not, he could not get his appendage to stand to attention, being as drunk as he was. So Fanny had sought solace in the arms of a few paramours.

She knew that Kitty and Lydia were the results of assignations with other men, and the fathers were not the same for both girls. Each time that she had missed her first courses, she had made sure that Thomas had awoken in her bed for some nights after, so he believed that the daughters born were his.

With Meryton being a small town and Thomas and Fanny Bennet being despised by the populace from servant to estate owners, Fanny had tried to ply her charms once or twice to try and help the begetting of a son along but had been soundly rebuffed each time. Her futile attempts had left her already bad reputation in tatters.

~~~~~~~/~~~~~~~

Frank Phillips sat and stared at the letter to the Earl of Jersey from James Bennet Junior. He had come close to sending it a few times, but each time he had hesitated as he remembered the conversation that he had had with his friend over five years previously.

James Bennet had sat opposite Phillips in the office of his solicitor's practice abutting his house in Meryton. With four children, James had just updated his will and put in place some provisions for his children's protection should the worst come to pass and neither he nor Priscilla were alive to take care of his four children before Jamie reached his majority.

As Phillips remembered the conversation, it hit him that was why James Bennet had not designated a guardian for the girls, he never envisaged a situation where he, his wife, and Jamie would be murdered by anyone, never mind his despicable brother, as Phillips was convinced was the case. After the realisation, he returned to his reverie.

"Phillips, I have written a letter to Priscilla's brother. I will only hand it to you, if and only if, you can promise me on everything that is holy that you will not send it unless and until it is a life and death situation, regarding my children and both myself and my beloved wife are no longer among the living," James Bennet had stated.

"You know I would do anything for you Bennet, I swear on my life, on my honour that I will respect your wishes, no matter what," he had promised.

"I know it sounds like an extreme request, Phillips, but my Priscilla was so badly hurt, first by her father's rejection and cutting her off from her mother and second by her brother. Even after the old Earl died, he kept his distance and did not contact his sister. They used to be so close as children, this made her brother's betrayal even worse than her father's," Bennet explained.

"You did not need to lay this all bare for me, Bennet; I would honour your wishes regardless," Phillips promised.

"Now that you know the whole of it, I am confident if you ever waver, you will remember what I told you and factor that into your decision."

As Phillips remembered the conversation, he acknowledged that Bennet's telling him all had the exact effect that his late friend had intended. Phillips replaced the missive in his safe and locked it.

~~~~~~~/~~~~~~~

The days at Pemberley were the happiest the three Bennet daughters could remember since the day before they received the devastating news that their parents and Jamie had perished in an awful accident. Love infused the very hallways of Pemberley and helped pull the sisters out of the malaise they had been in since the news had been broken to them. Georgiana Darcy's prediction that Misses Younge and Ponsonby would become friends was accurate.

Elizabeth had become an intimate friend of the older Darcy daughter, but Georgiana and Mary had become nigh on inseparable. None of the three Bennets ignored Annabeth and dedicated time to her so that she never felt left out.

After only one day at Pemberley, when Elizabeth could not be found, it became common knowledge not to waste time searching for her before looking in Pemberley's magnificent library first. From the instant that Elizabeth laid eyes on the room, she had gravitated to the library whenever there was no activity planned. It reminded her of the times she used to read and debate books with her dearly departed papa.

James Bennet had dedicated time to all of his children, but for whatever reason, he and Elizabeth had shared an affinity for the written word and debated the meaning of poetry and prose. The debating had started in Elizabeth's eleventh year.

For whatever reason she established a connection with William Darcy over debating on books. He was about seven years her senior, but he never treated her like a little girl. William could not believe this slip of a girl could challenge him so ably in their friendly debates.

One morning, about a sennight prior to their departure, the sisters joined the three older Darcy children for a ride up a bridle path to a crest that overlooked the distant peaks. On their way towards the base of the path, Alexander Darcy noticed a very unwelcome rider on Pemberley's land.

"Wickham, did my father not make it clear that you are not to darken our land again?" Alex challenged as he rode up to George Wickham who was scowling at the Darcy heir.

"I was coming to apologise to my godfather..." Wickham did not finish his sentence.

"After you seduced that girl of fifteen and left her with child, our father disowned you. You very well know he has not been your godfather since the day he banished you from Pemberley," William stated as he, Alexander, and the two footmen who were accompanying the party surrounded Wickham.

"But I am sure…" Wickham tried to say.

"What? That my father will fall for your lies and false charms?" Alexander asked acerbically.

"Surely the memory of my father's service makes Mr. Darcy honour-bound to help me. I am all but penniless," Wickham tried.

"You dare speak of honour when you have none? You had a legacy of two thousand from your father, that was less than two years ago. A prudent man who works and does not expect from others what he does not deserve, could live on such a sum for upwards of fifteen years! Let me guess, you had bad luck at the tables—again!" Alexander took the profligate to task.

Wickham looked away as the man who would have it all while he had nothing hit the nail on the head. It was not his fault that he was dealt bad cards! He did not know what to do. He had less than ten pounds to his name and playing on Mr. Darcy's sympathies had been his last resort. He noticed that Miss Darcy had grown a lot since he had last seen her, and then he noticed the three pretty girls waiting with her. He had no idea who they were and did not care at the moment.

"It is neither my father's fault nor his responsibility to solve problems that you have created for yourself. Leave now or our footmen will restrain you and turn you over to the magistrate for trespassing. Return and there will be no such warning!" Alexander Darcy was not as serious as his younger brother, but he had no time for someone with no moral compass or honour such as George Wickham.

Wickham wheeled his nag, and a stream of invectives were heard as he rode toward the nearest border of the estate, one of the footmen followed closely to make sure that he actually left the Darcys' property.

"What a pleasant man," Elizabeth said sarcastically, as they began the ascent of the bridle path. "He and my Uncle Thomas could be the same person if that man was in his cups all the time."

"He loves to drink," William informed Elizabeth as he rode alongside her. "When we get home, I will ask my father if we may share the story with you and your sisters. Gigi is already aware that he is not a good man. We believe that knowledge is power."

When the riding party arrived at the outlook point, the Bennets understood why the Darcys rode to this point so often. With the peaks shimmering in the distance and everything in-between, the picture that they beheld was a most beautiful one.

On the return to the manor house, Alexander and William knocked on their father's study door before going to their chambers to change. They reported their contact with George Wickham and the warning that Alexander had issued. William requested that he be allowed to share a sanitised version of Wickham's character with the Bennets, just in case they ever came across him again, his father gave his permission.

After they changed, Alexander and William met with the Bennets and told them all they needed to know about Wickham. The remaining days at Pemberley passed quickly, and as much as they did not want to return to Longbourn, the day arrived for their departure. There were hugs and tears exchanged between the Bennet and Darcy sisters with promises to write. Anna-beth was just mastering her letters, and Miss Younge thought it would be good for her to write and receive letters.

The two governesses promised to correspond with one an-other, too. The travellers would drop William at Cambridge for his second to last year, and afterwards Mr. Darcy would accompany the sisters and their governess-companion back to Long-bourn.

As she watched the carriages depart while Alexander consoled his sisters, Lady Anne felt a sadness for the three sisters. She knew that their life was difficult at home and wished that there were more that she could do.

CHAPTER 3

June 1804

T wo years had rolled by since the sisters' wonderful visit to Pemberley. Out of spite, their aunt and uncle had refused permission for them to spend the summer with the Darcys at their estate again, so the Darcys had all come to Netherfield. During that summer, Jane, Elizabeth, and Mary had resided at William's estate for almost three months complete.

They had maintained correspondence with Lady Anne, Georgiana, and Annabeth. The first letter after their return home had been opened by Mrs. Bennet and her daughters, on their first afternoon's lessons at Lucas Lodge, Jane had written from herself and her sisters asking that all letters for them be sent to Lucas Lodge. Mr. Darcy employed an extra courier who was responsible for carrying missives between Derbyshire and Hertfordshire.

Much to their joy, the sisters had spent hardly any time at Longbourn during the last two years. They would spend weeks at Lucas Lodge and with the Phillipses in Meryton. Hattie and Frank Phillips treated them as the children that they had never been blessed with.

Their winters had been split between Gracechurch street and their adopted aunt and uncle, as well as at Darcy House when the Darcys were in Town for the season. Georgiana and Annabeth saw them as sisters, and as much as the three enjoyed spending time with the four young Gardiner children, they loved their time with their sisters of the heart.

During the Easter season of 1803, the Bennet sisters finally met the de Bourghs when they were invited to join the Darcys and Fitzwilliams on their annual gathering at Rosings Park in Kent. They found Sir Lewis and Lady Catherine to be very welcoming. Their son and heir Peter had returned from his grand tour and Alexander Darcy found that he was not the only member of the family interested in Jane Bennet.

Elizabeth at thirteen was four years younger than Anne de Bourgh but they became very close regardless of the age difference. Anne had recovered from the malady that had kept them from meeting sooner, but she did not have the energy that Elizabeth had. At first, she had demurred, but then with encouragement from her new friend, she started walking in the gardens each day with Elizabeth, much to the fear of her mother. Lady Catherine decided to allow it after encouragement from her sisters, Ladies Anne and Elaine, as long as Anne's companion and nurse, Mrs. Jenkinson, monitored the situation carefully.

At first, Anne would only walk for a few minutes before she needed to rest, but then almost miraculously, after a week, each day Anne would be able to walk longer. Mrs. Jenkinson had suggested that they try not giving Anne the daily tinctures and her parents who would try anything to improve their daughter's health agreed, which seemed to accelerate Anne's apparent recovery.

By the time that the parties were ready to depart to London, Lady Catherine had a new favourite person namely Elizabeth Bennet. Anne had a healthy glow about her that had never been seen before and she could walk for more than a half hour before needing rest. Lady Catherine had discharged Anne's doctor as it seemed that everything that he recommended was the opposite of what their daughter needed. The longer Anne went without Mr. Hume bleeding her once a fortnight, the more strength she seemed to gain.

Anne and Lady Catherine, now called Aunt Cat by all three Bennets, were added to the list of correspondents that included Aunt Elaine as well. Lord Andrew Fitzwilliam seeing Jane Bennet after a year was amazed at how much she resembled Lady Marie

De Melville. He had asked Marie if she had any cousins in Hert-fordshire and she had said no. Neither had thought to ask Lord or Lady Jersey.

~~~~~~~/~~~~~~~

The two years had not been kind to the Bennets, even financially. When the first year's harvest was in, the income had dropped close to three thousand pounds due to Thomas Bennet's indolence, so he was only able to pay his creditor one thousand six hundred pounds. By the next year, after losing two of Long-bourn's five tenants in early 1803, the income was two thousand five hundred pounds. Rather than two thousand plus the four hundred he had been short from the previous year he had been expecting, Bennet's creditor was not happy. His man had stud-ied the ledgers, and had seen that Bennet was telling the truth, which was the only thing that had kept the man alive!

Bennet had been knocked about by the creditor's muscle and had come out of it with a broken arm and many bruises and cuts. Now more than ever the three hundred pounds they received coupled with the fact that the salaries of the butler, housekeeper, and the brats' companion were not paid by them was the only thing saving them from financial ruin. In one of his lucid states, Thomas had told his wife that she was not allowed to deny his damned brother's daughters from staying anywhere that was not Longbourn as the more they were not at the estate, the more of the money paid for their upkeep was available for Thomas Bennets.

As he had berated her, he reminded her that her petulance in denying their nieces going to visit their friends wherever it was they lived, could have cost them money they did not have if the friends had not come to stay at Netherfield and the three encumbrances had not stayed with their friends for the sum-mer. He told her in no uncertain terms what he would do if she stopped them being away from Longbourn.

Fanny Bennet had been hit by Thomas before and as much as she hated when the three brats were happy, she was more scared of what Thomas would do to her if she disobeyed him. Kitty and Lydia behaviour had not been acceptable to the stuck ups in the neighbourhood, so they were never invited to go anywhere with their boring cousins. Fanny did what she could to convince them that they were better off without the three in their home.

~~~~~~~/~~~~~~~

It was the day the Darcys were to arrive at Netherfield. Jane, Elizabeth, and Mary, who had been staying at Lucas Lodge for the last month and were usually very attentive to their music master, however on this day most distracted. "*Come mai oggi non vi concentrate sulle lezioni, signorine*?" the master asked in Italian. At the same time that he taught them music, he also spoke to them in his native tongue to polish their language skills.

"Excuse us *Maestro di musica*, it is hard to concentrate when we will see our friends from Derbyshire and Kent very soon," Elizabeth explained.

"*Solo in Italiano*," the master instructed. Elizabeth apologised for her lapse and repeated what she had said in Italian. She knew very well that he understood English perfectly, but since Sir William and Uncle Phillips had told him to, he only conversed in Italian with the sisters.

"*In tal caso, dato che oggi non impari da me, sei scusato per andare ad aspettare i tuoi amici.*" Jane thanked the music master profusely for herself and her sisters for ending class earlier and acknowledged he was correct; it was hard for them to absorb anything while they were so excited.

Even though Jane was already sixteen, she was just as excited as her sisters about the impending arrival of the three families. Jane had become more beautiful than she was the previous year and the same could be said for Elizabeth, who was fourteen, and Mary, who was approaching twelve.

In the year since they had seen the Darcys in Hertfordshire last year, Elizabeth had transformed from an awkward girl of thirteen into a young lady who no longer looked anything like a little girl.

"A note just arrived from Netherfield;" Lady Lucas informed the sisters, "are your trunks packed?"

"They were ready this morning Aunt Rose," the three chorused. Lady Rosina Lucas smiled; she loved the three sisters as if they were one of her own children. Lucas Lodge was smaller than Longbourn, but they had enough chambers to accommodate the three as well as Miss Ponsonby when they were in residence.

"Well then give me a hug. The carriage out front is waiting for you," Lady Lucas instructed.

The excitement bubbled at the surface and all three Bennet sisters had to exercise a good dose of self-control not to squeal with delight. Even Jane, who normally was inscrutable, did not hide the joy that she felt. All three hugged and kissed Aunt Rose on her cheek and made their farewells to Charlotte, John, and Maria Lucas. With a hug to Uncle William, who was waiting with Miss Ponsonby at the door to the coach, the sisters and their companion boarded the coach. It was soon in motion heading toward Netherfield Park.

~~~~~~~/~~~~~~~

Knowing that the three girls were safe at Lucas Lodge and would be at Netherfield later that day, Frank Phillips rode to London to see his good friend and another one of the girls' protectors, Edward Gardiner, at 23 Gracechurch Street.

"What has your man found out about Thomas Bennet?" Phillips asked Gardiner after he had bathed and changed.

"Not as much as we would like to know. He has a creditor that we have not been able to find. If we could, we could buy the debts and use them as leverage over him. Whoever he is, he and his men are very wily. We have followed his men back to London each time they have collected funds from Thomas, but as soon as they reach Seven Dials, they disappear into the maze of streets and alleys within minutes," Gardiner reported.

"We know that there were accomplices the night James,

Pricilla, and Jamie were murdered. It is very frustrating that we have not been able to find any of them!" Phillips lamented.

"I have an idea. I do not know why I did not think of this before!" Edward Gardiner slapped his own forehead. "We should pay a few men to spread the word in Seven Dials that a man is willing to purchase Thomas Bennet's debts, and willing to pay a premium. I bet we will not have to seek the creditor out; he will find me!"

Phillips agreed wholeheartedly, it could work and would allow them to force Bennet to choose between staying at Longbourn or going to debtors' prison. As satisfying as it would be to see Bennet locked away at Marshalsea, their first instinct was to protect the girls by removing the objectionable people from the estate.

Early next morning, five men were tasked with spreading the word around. By that night, one Juan Antonio Álvarez, known to all that knew and feared him as *the Spaniard*, heard someone wanted to buy that useless Bennet's debts from him. With the interest and charges for late payments, Bennet's debts stood at over nine thousand pounds. He would willingly sell the debts, but he had not stayed alive for so many years being incautious. He would use some of his men to carefully investigate and make sure it was not some sort of trap, and this Edward Gardiner would either possess Bennet's debts or he and his family would be killed.

~~~~~~~/~~~~~~~

The three sisters had hardly alighted from the carriages when they were accosted by Georgiana and Annabeth Darcy. The older members of the three families stood by on the stone steps while the girls hugged one another. "Gigi, you are taller than I am!" Elizabeth mock scolded her friend.

"We are *all* taller than you, except Anna and she soon will be as well," Mary said with a deadpan expression.

Georgiana had indeed grown a lot in the last year and resembled her mother even more than the previous year. She was a year younger than Elizabeth but was already noticeably taller. Annabeth at eight had also grown, and although she had dark hair like the men of the family, her facial resemblance to both her mother and sister was remarkable, and she had the Fitzwilliam blue eyes.

Anne de Bourgh approached her friend and hugged her. If one did not know that Anne used to be weak and sickly, they would not have recognised the healthy-looking lady with rosy cheeks approaching Elizabeth. "Lizzy, it has been too long! When may we go walking?" Anne gushed. Like her parents, she knew that her recovery had begun with the impertinent girl from Hertfordshire.

"Anne, you look so hale and healthy! You said that you were doing better in your letters, but the reality far exceeds the picture that I had in my mind," Elizabeth stated as she hugged her friend.

Alexander Darcy had been attracted to Jane Bennet when he had seen her at fifteen, but a year later, he was smitten. It was not just her looks, which were ethereal, but the inner strength that she exuded. He had already told his parents that once Jane Bennet came out in society, he would be requesting a courtship, a decision that his parents heartily endorsed.

William had just graduated from Cambridge; thus, all three families had arrived together after they had proudly watched his graduation ceremony. He was rooted to the spot with his mouth hanging open as he watched Elizabeth Bennet greet his sisters. She was no longer the gangly girl that he remembered from a year ago; she had filled out and was a young lady now. She had always been pretty, but now he could not miss seeing the beauty that she was.

"Are you trying to catch flies?" Captain Richard Fitzwilliam asked. He smirked at his cousin, seeing exactly where his eyes were pointed. Thankfully, Richard had not been sent into battle yet, but it was only a matter of time after the declaration of war against France in 1803. His family hated the idea that he would be going to war sooner rather than later, but they supported his choice of career.

William closed his mouth with a clack. *'How am I going to debate Lizzy when I feel so attracted to her?'* he asked himself. William knew that there were still three to four years to go before he could court Elizabeth and could only hope that when the time came, she would accept him as a suitor. Luckily, Andrew had just begun to court Marie De Melville so he would not be competition and it seemed Peter de Bourgh and his older brother were fixed on the lovely Jane. Richard, although an incorrigible flirt, would not think of taking a wife until he was ready to leave the army.

The Darcys, Fitzwilliams, and de Bourghs welcomed Jane, Elizabeth, and Mary as members of the family. The three girls no longer wore mourning clothes, but rather each wore a pin near their hearts with three small pieces of black ribbon on it. They wanted to keep the memory of their lost parents and brother close to their hearts; each black ribbon represented one of their lost loved ones.

Jane and Elizabeth had often spoken about how different their lives would have been had they been left in the care of the master and mistress of Longbourn. They knew the only reason they were as emotionally strong as they were, was because of the love of all their adoptive aunts, uncles, and their respective families. They did not want to imagine the damage, both physical and emotional, that would have been inflicted upon them had they not had the support system that they did.

"It is so good to see you three looking so happy," Lady Anne said as she hugged her adopted nieces.

"We are overjoyed to be with all of you again Aunt Anne," Jane responded.

"You know we have invited the Phillipses, Lucases, and Gardiners to Pemberley in July," George Darcy told Jane as he hugged her.

"Yes, Uncle George, both Uncle William and Uncle Frank have informed us of that," Jane responded. It was not their father, and no one could ever replace him, but she and her sisters felt fatherly love from the men who had adopted them as their nieces.

"If those despicable people do not allow you to go to Pemberley again this year, then I will march in and take you to Rosings Park regardless of what they say!" Lady Catherine said as she hugged Elizabeth. In Sir Lewis', Peter's, and her eyes, Elizabeth was a hero, and they would do anything within their power to help her and her sisters.

"It is not an issue Aunt Cat; it has been almost a year since Mrs. Bennet has objected. It is the *only* thing that we agree on, that we want to be in each other's company as little as possible," Elizabeth answered after she kissed the tall lady on her cheek.

During their sojourn in Hertfordshire, Peter de Bourgh made the acquaintance of Miss Charlotte Lucas, and the two seemed to seek out one another whenever they were in the same company. Charlotte was only a year younger than the de Bourgh heir, but they seemed to make a connection that neither would have imagined before the meeting.

Charlotte had always believed love had little to do with marriage, but after knowing Master de Bourgh for some weeks, she discovered she was developing tender feelings for him. As much as she noted his attention to her, she tried to protect her heart as they belonged to such different circles, even though her father was a knight of the realm.

Before they were to depart for Rosings, Peter sought out his parents. "Mother, Father, I would like to court Miss Lucas," Peter stated. "I know her parents were in the trade before Sir William acquired his estate, but I believe I am falling in love with her."

"If you truly feel she is the one for you, your father and I," his mother said after a nod from Sir Lewis, "will gladly accept her regardless of her roots, connections, and fortune. My one question, Son, is what of Jane? I thought your affection lay in that direction."

"It was infatuation. I have seen the way that Alex looks at her and I see love in his eyes. That alone would not have made me withdraw, but I see similar looks from Jane directed at Alex. She has never looked upon me with anything but friendship and at the same time, I came to realise I never had any real romantic feelings for her," Peter explained.

"And you have them for Miss Lucas after knowing her for a month?" Sir Lewis asked.

"Yes sir, I do. I find it a pleasure to converse with her on any subject. She has never once asked about Rosings or our fortune like so many debutantes of the Ton do. When she is not with me, I find myself wishing that she were. Those are feelings that I never felt for Jane," Peter responded.

"If that be the case then go to it, Son," Sir Lewis told his heir.

The next day, Peter de Bourgh rode to Lucas Lodge just after breaking his fast and asked Sir William for a private audience with his eldest daughter. Charlotte, who had convinced herself that the disparity in their social standing would be an insurmountable impediment, shed tears of joy as she gladly accepted the courtship. It did not take long for Sir William to bestow his consent and blessing, after which he made the announcement to his family.

Lady Rosina Lucas was so pleased for her daughter, not because her suitor was very wealthy and would one day inherit his father's title, but because she had never seen her daughter so happy before.

The night before at the de Bourghs minus Peter, who would remain at Netherfield with the Darcys to further the courtship, and with the Fitzwilliams departed, there was a celebratory dinner to congratulate the courting couple that was attended by a number of the four and twenty principal families of the area. The Thomas Bennets were, of course, not invited.

~~~~~~~/~~~~~~~

After close to two months of investigating, Juan Antonio Álvarez known as *the Spaniard*, was convinced the offer made by the tradesman was genuine. He would not meet face-to-face with the tradesman. One of the ways *the Spaniard* used to stay safe was that his right-hand man would take the meeting. Always looking to make money, the amount he was willing to sell the debts for was set at ten thousand pounds.

Edward Gardiner was working in his office in his warehouse off Gracechurch Street within walking distance from his home when his head clerk knocked on his door. "There is a Mr. Black to see you sir," the clerk informed his employer.

"I know no Mr. Black," Gardiner was telling his clerk as a big man pushed past.

"Ye wanted ta talk about Thomas Bennet." Gardiner waved his clerk away telling him that he was not to be disturbed.

"How much?" Gardiner asked.

"Ten thousand," the big man returned.

Gardiner was sure that the number was inflated, but he and Phillips had decided to split the cost and this amount was within the limits they had agreed on. "You have all of his signed avowals?" Gardiner asked.

"Right 'ere," the man pulled out a wad of papers from his inside pocket.

"May I see them to verify the authenticity?" Gardiner asked. Phillips had the forethought to send his friend a document with Thomas Bennet's signature on it.

"Some only," the big man replied as he handed Gardiner the top two or three receipts.

On comparison, it was easy to tell they were genuine and Thomas Bennet had signed the avowals. "Let me fill out the draft." Gardiner pulled it from his desk draw, filled out the demanded amount and counter-signed it.

Once he had it in his hands, the big man made sure it was correct in all ways and then handed all of Thomas Bennet's debt receipts over. The draft was folded and placed in the inside pocket where the documents had been in and without a word, the big man exited the office.

Gardiner wrote an express to Phillips, informing him of what had transpired and announcing his pending arrival in Meryton on the morrow.

~~~~~~~/~~~~~~~

At the same time the Gardiner carriage was headed toward Meryton, the Darcys and the three Bennet sisters were departing Netherfield for Pemberley and Peter de Bourgh was at Lucas Lodge requesting yet another private interview with Charlotte Lucas. Peter left Lucas Lodge for Rosings Park a very happy man; he was betrothed to the woman he now knew with certainty that he loved and who had expressed the same to him.

He had but a fortnight before he would see Charlotte again at Pemberley.

CHAPTER 4

"How should we proceed?" Gardiner asked as he handed the avowals to his friend.

"You know that the girls left this morning for Pemberley with the Darcys, do you not?" Phillips asked his friend.

"Yes, I remember Maddie mentioned they would be decamping from the area today. I believe the Lucas family is also travelling with them." Phillips nodded. "Dealing with Bennet will delay our departure north; we should send a missive to the Darcys to let them know we will be some days late," Gardiner suggested.

Phillips composed an express where he informed their hosts of the delay and mentioned it was business with the current master of Longbourn that delayed them. He wrote all would be explained when he and Gardiner arrived at Pemberley.

"How much were his debts?" Phillips asked.

"It cost us ten thousand pounds. The avowals were for a little more than eleven thousand, so evidently Bennet did pay, but his creditor added high interest and late penalties," Gardiner informed Phillips.

"I almost hope he will refuse to leave Longbourn with that family of his; seeing him in Marshalsea for the rest of his life would be some form of justice for James, Priscilla, and Jamie!" Phillips' ire was raised as it always was when he thought of Bennet getting away with the murder of his family.

"I too want justice for our friend and his family but let us hope we can find the men he hired and afterwards we can watch the bastard swing!" Gardiner replied.

"Do you think you could contact his creditor again?" Phillips asked as he was struck with an idea.

"To what end?" Gardiner asked.

"My wager would be that he is a man of many unsavoury connections, and, for a fee of course, he may be able to point us in the right direction of Bennet's accomplices. We could offer transportation rather than the hangman for them if they were to testify against him," Phillips laid out his thinking.

"I believe you have struck on a good idea Phillips, let us hope the miscreants are still alive and have not gotten themselves killed—yet!" Gardiner agreed.

"Time to head for Longbourn," Phillips stated as he summoned his man and instructed him to bring the carriage around.

~~~~~~~/~~~~~~~

In the two years since his attempt to see Mr. Darcy was rebuffed by his sons, George Wickham had not had an easy time of it. He hated to have to work for his money but found no alternative. If only Mr. Darcy had not found out about his dalliances, he would have received a gentleman's education and so many opportunities to be around women with large dowries to make his fortune.

He felt the Darcys had robbed him of his chance of the life that he believed he was entitled to. It was certainly not mucking out stalls as he was at the Golden Bull Inn in a little nowhere town in Devon. Just because he had tried to convince their thirteen-year-old daughter to give him her virtue, the silly chit had gone directly to her parents and informed them! Now he could not go back to his distant relatives as he had been thrown out, which had prompted him to try grovelling at his former godfather's feet.

Returning to Pemberley was not an option; Wickham did not doubt for a moment that as soon as he was seen on Darcy land he would be arrested and transported. That was not something that he was willing to take a chance on. He had to come up with a plan but he just did not know what yet. He was sure with his cunning brain he would think of something to flip his fortunes.

~~~~~~~/~~~~~~~

Miss Caroline Bingley was in a snit, as she often was. Her brother had met Mr. William Darcy at Cambridge and for the two years they were at the school together; she had never met any of his illustrious family or their relatives. She was not interested in the second son, but had convinced herself that if the Darcy heir were to meet her then she would be his choice of wife.

Caroline Bingley was a social-climbing fortune huntress who wanted nothing more than to marry a rich gentleman of the first circles. She had begged her father to send her to an expensive and exclusive seminary in London, but he had refused, and she had been sent to the same seminary in Scarborough as her older sister.

The Bingleys were in trade. Her brother Charles had taken over the Bingley Carriage Works as a partner with their Uncle Paul when their parents were killed in a freak accident. A wheel had snapped for some inexplicable reason, overturning the carriage they were in two years previously. Her father had provided both of his daughters with respectable dowries of ten thousand pounds and Louisa had been able to attract a gentleman of the lower circles whose family had a small estate, Winsdale in Yorkshire, that required an infusion of funds as it barely brought in two thousand pounds per annum.

Her brother-in-law Harold Hurst was the heir, but his father was hale and healthy. At least he owned a small London townhouse he had inherited from an aunt, albeit not in a fashionable area. She had finally browbeaten her sister into requesting her husband host her and their brother at his town home on Wimpole Street for the upcoming season.

No matter how many times she was told by her sister and brothers that a member of the first circles would never consider the daughter of a tradesman as a wife, Caroline knew how it would be—she would become Mrs. Darcy, one way or another! Being in London for a season would be the first step in her plan.

~~~~~~~/~~~~~~~

Phillips and Gardiner were shown to Longbourn's study by Mr. Hill, who did not inform the hated mistress of the guests' arrival. "One way or another we will have Bennet out of here today!" Phillips said quietly to the faithful retainer who had been the first line of defence for the three sisters during the brief periods they had been under the same roof as the despicable pair.

"I did not want to be disturbed!" Bennet growled as he threw back a glass of port. "Phillips, to what do I owe the displeasure of your presence and that of whoever this other man is. Leave now; I have no interest in anything you have to say!"

"My name is Gardiner and I was one of the men charged with looking after my late friend's surviving children that you did not succeed in murdering," Gardiner shot back.

There was a flicker of worry that crossed Bennet's face and it was not missed by either man. He relaxed as he realised that had they any proof, he would already be on his way to gaol. "Say what you must and then leave me be!" Bennet returned, his breath reeking of alcohol even at this hour of the morning.

"Mr. Hill," Phillips called ignoring the hated man. "Please inform Mrs. Bennet that she is required to join us," he instructed.

"Just because you pay his salary does not mean that you may come into my ho..." Whatever Bennet wanted to say was lost as Phillips interjected.

"Just shut up and wait, you wastrel! What we have to say will affect your wife in equal measure," Phillips shared.

Bennet was silenced. He did start to worry again; mayhap he was about to be arrested. How could they know the truth? Phillips had spoken on more than one occasion about his suspicions, but there was never any proof. Had one of the men he had hired talked?

Neither Gardiner nor Phillips missed how the useless man was squirming. They both surmised correctly that Bennet suspected they had discovered his role in murdering his brother, sister-in-law, and nephew. If Phillips did not hear the words of his good friend beseeching him not to send the letter to the Earl of Jersey outside of certain circumstances, he would have done so just to have the pleasure of watching the Earl take care of Bennet.

"What is it Thomas…" Fanny Bennet pushed the book room door open and wobbled into the room, obviously already in her cups. "What are these men doing in our home?" she asked with trepidation suspecting the same thing that her husband did.

"I suggest you sit, Mrs. Bennet," Phillips told her without greeting her.

"What is this about," Bennet demanded again, reminding himself that if they were going to arrest him, he would be in irons already. "I want you two off my property!"

"We are here to give you a simple choice, Bennet," Gardiner stated without emotion.

"What are you going on about, whatever your name is," Bennet sneered feeling a lot more confident.

"We own the debts you had with *the Spaniard,* and we are here to collect. Are you able to pay the ten thousand pounds that you owe us?" Both men had pleasure in seeing both Bennets turn a sickly white.

"How…why…I do not have the funds," Bennet finally realised he was in deep trouble, mayhap he was not on his way to the gallows, but these men had the power to have him thrown into Marshalsea for the rest of his natural life. "What is my choice," a dejected Bennet asked.

"You will sign this document and leave Longbourn and Hertfordshire today and never come back or approach the daughters of the man you murdered. If you break any of the terms of this document, you will be in Marshalsea before you can count to ten," Phillips delivered the first choice with satisfaction as Bennet seemed to age before his eyes. "If you refuse the first option, I have a bailiff and his men waiting outside. As you are not able to satisfy the debts, you and your wife will be on your way to debtors' prison today."

Phillips looked at the shaking woman with disdain. "How

you were stupid enough to sign some of his avowals, I shall never know."

"We have no money; how will we live?" Fanny Bennet finally found her voice.

"That is your problem, not ours," Gardiner said curtly. "There is a little more than four hundred and fifty dollars in the estate account, that is all you will leave with."

"What is your decision Bennet, although you do not deserve to carry that name?" Phillips demanded.

"Is this legal? I thought with the entail the estate could not..." Bennet tried to use the leverage he perceived that he had.

"If you take the time to read the document in your hand, you will see that you are renouncing all claim to Longbourn and anything related to James Bennet's surviving daughters including that from the instant you sign the document, guardianship of the three girls passes to us or anyone we designate.

"As far as the entail goes, we will not be the owners of the estate. It will be held in trust for thirty years or until we receive the notification about your death. At that time, the heir presumptive will be found and the estate will devolve to him as long as he meets the terms laid out in the entail documents," Phillips stated dispassionately.

Seeing he had no leverage and no choice, as Marshalsea for life was not an option for Bennet, he signed the document. Mr. Hill was called in to witness it after both Phillips and Gardiner had affixed their signatures. The reign of Thomas and Fanny Bennet at Longbourn was at its ignominious end.

"We will not be able to look after our daughters," Fanny stated. Although she tried to give the impression that she loved her daughters so much she asked, "How are we to support them with almost no money and no home?"

"You will not be penniless as you deserve to be," Phillips said in disgust. "The only reason that we are allowing you to take the money in the estate account is so you will have something with which to support your daughters."

"Your late father begged you to invest your legacy did he

not, Bennet?" Gardiner reminded the profligate. "You ignored his advice and gambled it all away did you not? Where is your wife's dowry? Also lost at the tables? After throwing away that amount you then went into debt. No wonder you wanted to sell Longbourn! It is time for the two of you to start earning your money, as no one will gift you with anything!"

"Can our girls not stay here?" Fanny pushed.

"You are willing to abandon your own daughters?" an astounded Phillips asked.

"It will be easier without those silly girls," Bennet added.

"Always looking for the easiest way out are you now, Bennet," a disgusted Phillips shot back. He then thought about the fact he and his dear wife Hattie had never been gifted with any children and decided on the spot. "I will write a second irrevocable document which you and your wife will sign giving guardianship of both of your daughters to me. There will be a clause that states that if either of you ever come back to try and claim your abandoned children, there will be the same penalty as if you contravened the terms of the first document you signed!"

"As Thomas said, it will be easier without the two of them," Fanny stated as if she were talking about removing some dirt from her shoe.

"**Noooo**," Lydia screamed as she burst into the study. She had a nasty habit of eavesdropping and until that moment was waiting for her mother to refute the words that had chilled the daughter to her core, but she never did. "How can you leave us behind, you said you love us!" Lydia wailed.

"There is no choice," Fanny said to her daughter, who had always been her favourite with no more warmth than a winter wind.

Phillips rang for the Hills. "Mr. and Mrs. Bennet will be departing Longbourn within the hour and *never* returning. Please have their trunks packed and make sure none of the estate's chattels are hidden in their possessions. Miss Bennet and Miss Lydia will be remaining here for now," Phillips informed the Hills.

For the first time in her life Lydia Bennet was silent, only tears rolled down her cheeks. Her whole world had just shifted on its head and Kitty was still to be told. Her parents stood wordlessly and followed the Hills to their chambers.

"W-w-what will b-b-become of u-us?" a subdued and still crying Lydia asked.

"I promise you and Miss Bennet will be looked after," Phillips told the young girl kindly. At the age of eight, Lydia Bennet had just been abandoned and was in shock. "I ask you and Miss Bennet to await us in the drawing room until your mother and father depart."

"If they care so little for me, they are no longer my parents," Lydia stated emphatically and left the study.

~~~~~~~/~~~~~~~

An hour later the rundown carriage departed Longbourn with the same nag pulling it that had brought the Bennets to the estate. With not enough money to pay a servant, Bennet drove the vehicle himself. Bennet did not stop until he arrived at an inn at the first town in Buckinghamshire. He did not want to take a chance and stop before leaving the accursed Hertfordshire, as he assumed the men who had stolen his estate had men following them until they were out of that shire.

"What are we to do Thomas?" Fanny Bennet wailed as he joined her inside the carriage.

"We will get our revenge, one way or another!" the resentful man declared.

"How Thomas? If we enter that shire again, we will be thrown in gaol!" Fanny moaned.

"I will think of a way without us having to return to the estate or the environs of Hertfordshire!" Thomas boasted. He did not know how yet, but he would not allow his humiliation to stand. To be thrown off his family's estate by a tradesman and whoever the other man was. Gardiner! He would remember that hated name.

He wilfully ignored the fact that all of his woes stemmed

from his actions only. It was so much easier to blame others than accept any responsibility for his own actions. Neither husband nor wife mentioned the daughters they had abandoned nor did they spare them a thought as all they were interested in was their own well-being. Besides, Bennet had over four hundred pounds in bank notes. He was sure to find some games of chance being played at the inn.

~~~~~~~/~~~~~~~

When Kitty Bennet was told she and her sister had been abandoned by their parents, she was inconsolable. She had gotten used to playing the second fiddle to Lydia, but at least she used to get some attention from her mother. At eleven, she had started to question the way that she and Lydia treated their cousins following their parents' lead. When she found out she and Lydia had been abandoned without any hesitation, like her younger sister, any feelings of love she may have felt for her parents was banished from her heart.

Gardiner and Phillips were about to join the girls when the former halted the latter before he opened the door. "Why did you allow them the money if they abandoned their children?" Gardiner asked.

"As I listened to those two disgusting exemplars of human beings, I was thinking how grotesque it is that they were granted children while Hattie and I were not. I intend to speak to my wife and if she agrees we will adopt the girls," Phillips informed his friend.

"Now that we have expelled those two, what about Longbourn, the girls are too young to live here with just their companion," Gardiner asked.

"That will be decided at Pemberley. I just realised I need to write to Darcy. I cannot very well arrive with two extra in my party unannounced," Phillips responded. Gardiner nodded and the two entered the drawing room to find the sisters in each other's arms with Kitty filling the role of older sister trying to soothe her younger sibling.

Phillips explained he needed to talk to his wife before any decisions were to be taken. To that end, he had dispatched his carriage to Meryton to collect his wife. It was not too long before Hattie Phillips arrived. Phillips asked Mrs. Hill to sit with the much-subdued girls while he and Gardiner met with his wife in the study.

The disgusting Bennets were lucky they were away before Hattie Phillips arrived. She was so angry at the callous disregard for their children the couple demonstrated that she agreed with her husband's plan with alacrity. Before they joined the two girls, Phillips wrote an express that was dispatched to Pemberley.

When the three adults entered the drawing room, they found both girls being hugged by the housekeeper as they cried with broken hearts. Once they had calmed some, Hattie Phillips sat on the settee in the spot that had been occupied by Mrs. Hill.

"If you two agree, Mr. Phillips and I would like to adopt you. God never gifted us with children of our own, but now I believe it was part of his plan, so we would be here for you two when you need it most," Both girls nodded their agreement. "Your behaviour has to change; you will need to learn how to behave like proper girls and not the way your mother taught you. With all due respect, she has no clue how to correctly behave in society.

"I will not expect perfection right away, but I do want to see both of you trying to learn. Do you understand?" Both girls nodded. "In return, we will love you no less than if you were daughters of our body. We will *never* abandon you!" Hattie told the two girls.

"As we are not sure where we will live once we talk to our friends and your cousins in Derbyshire, we will wait to decide on our living arrangements, so please just bring a change of clothing for the morrow," Phillips instructed.

"Our cousins will not want to see us," Kitty hung her head in shame.

"If you are truly contrite and do not behave the way you used to, the three will surprise you. We have to wait for a reply from our friends before we leave," Phillips told the girls.

The two went up to their chambers almost silently to re-trieve a change of clothing as they were told to do. Soon after, all five were on their way to Meryton where Mr. Gardiner would switch to his conveyance and head home as he, his wife, and children would be leaving for Pemberley on the morrow.

~~~~~~~/~~~~~~~

Three days later, Phillips received a response:

July 7, 1804

Pemberley

You are <u>all</u> invited!

Darcy

The following morning the Phillips carriage departed for Derbyshire.

CHAPTER 5

Madeline Gardiner had seen Pemberley from the outside before when she had joined her parents, siblings, and friends at the annual harvest ball the Darcys opened to all in the area. She had never been inside, so when Mr. Douglas, the butler, led them toward the drawing room where the family awaited them, she was as much in awe of the surroundings as her husband and children.

"Papa, is this a palace?" Lily, their oldest who was nine asked.

"No dearest." her mother answered. "It is but a large home, not a palace dearest."

The one thing both Gardiner parents noted was, although everything that they noticed was of the highest quality, there were no ostentatious or gaudy furniture or decorations. One could tell that the Darcys were wealthy, but it was not thrown in one's face with overt displays of wealth. Everything they saw so far was to make the house liveable.

"Papa, will there be ponies to ride like you told us?" Eddy, who was seven, asked.

"I am sure that if Mr. Darcy said so, there will be, Eddy," Gardiner reassured his son.

The Gardiners were shown into the drawing room where the Darcy family waited to welcome them to Pemberley. Both Gardiner parents noted that their estimation of comfort over display held true in the drawing room. After the greetings, the four Gardiner children were shown up to the nursery by Anna-beth and Miss Younge.

"If we may impose before we go and change, would you mind if the Bennet sisters were summoned? There is much that needs to be discussed and it affects them directly," Gardiner requested.

"Gigi," George Darcy claimed his daughter's attention. After making her preference of nickname clear, no one called her Georgie any longer. "Please ask Jane, Lizzy, and Mary to come join us."

"Sir William and Lady Lucas should be here too," Maddie Gardiner pointed out. As Georgiana was leaving to fulfil her task, she was told to go play with her younger sister and the Gardiner children after she had summoned the requested people.

It was not long before those summoned were seated in the drawing room and looking expectantly at Edward Gardiner. "Thomas and Fanny Bennet have left Longbourn forever." Gardiner told all—from the acquiring of the debts—to the day of departure. When he got to the part about the other Bennets abandoning their daughters, there were gasps of disbelief that any parent could do such a horrendous thing. When Gardiner mentioned the amount that had been laid out to purchase the miscreant's debts, George Darcy decided that once Phillips arrived, he would ask to be allowed to contribute and take some of the financial burden, or all of it, from the two other gentlemen, as he had more than enough for many lifetimes.

"What will become of Longbourn now?" Jane asked.

"We will decide the way forward together once the Phillipses arrive. You three," Gardiner gestured to the three sisters, "will be here for the discussion as it affects you directly. The material point is that none of you will have to suffer Thomas and Fanny Bennet in your home ever again."

"As glad as I am about those people being banished from our home, I wish that Mama, Papa, and Jamie were still with us," Jane articulated as some tears ran down her cheeks. She did not become maudlin about her lost family as much as she did right after they were taken from her and her sisters, but every now and again she would be hit with a wave of sadness as she thought about them. It was not just her; Elizabeth and Mary would have similar feelings from time to time, especially when there was no activity to distract them.

"They will always be within your hearts," Aunt Anne comforted her, and put her arm around Jane and hugged her as Jane rested her head on her adoptive aunt's shoulder.

"Kitty and Lydia will need much help," Elizabeth stated. Seeing the looks from her sisters, she continued, "It is my belief that they were influenced by that horrible woman who purported to be their mother. Just think what would have become of us if we did not have so many around us who loved us and supported us. What would have become of us if we had not been protected and were left at the mercy of Mr. and Mrs. Bennet?" Elizabeth asked.

"Lizzy has the right of it," Lady Lucas stated. "We all know how they behaved, but it is my belief the girls who will arrive here with the Phillipses will be vastly altered from the girls you detested to spend time with at Longbourn."

"In that case, we will reserve judgement," Jane said thoughtfully. "I am sorry this has happened to them, but it will never repine us not seeing their parents again."

"That applies to me as well," Mary added.

~~~~~~~/~~~~~~~

The first night of the journey from Hertfordshire, the Phillipses stopped at a comfortable inn that George Darcy had recommended. Evidently, Darcy had contacted the landlord if the welcome the family received was anything to go by. After a dinner of hearty mutton stew and freshly baked bread, they retired to the best suite the inn had to offer. Frank and Hattie shared a bedchamber and Kitty and Lydia shared the other.

"Why did our former parents abandon us like we are some rubbish to be thrown out?" Lydia asked as tears of anger rolled down her cheeks. As angry as she was with her parents, the memories of her mother professing her love, it was even more so —the pain was palpable.

"You know Lyddie, it would have been better if our parents were dead like our cousins' family. They at least *know* why their parents are no longer with them and it is not because it was *too hard* to keep them," Kitty postulated.

"Was there anything they told us that was true?" Lydia asked. Pushed by her mother, she used to be the leader, but now she felt anything but and looked to her older sister for guidance.

It seemed to her that Kitty had grown up overnight and seemed older than eleven. From the first year of Lydia's life, she had been pushed aside by her mother and had learnt the only way to gain any of her mother's love and attention was to emulate Lydia's behaviour. Kitty knew the way they behaved was not acceptable, but she craved the love that her mother denied her, so she had done the only thing she could to gain a certain level of approbation from Fanny Bennet.

"I am afraid we cannot rely on anything they told us. Think about it. The only reason we treated Jane, Elizabeth, and Mary the way we did was because our mother encouraged us to do so. She always told us that we did not have good things like they did because *they* took from *us*. What did they ever take from us? We took their possessions and tried to make them feel less than us! No wonder they could not help being in the same room with us. They did the right thing for themselves which is why I believe they were hardly ever at Longbourn." Kitty opined.

"If what we were told were all lies, then our cousins are good, is that not true?" Lydia asked.

"It is, Lydia, and we have much to apologise for when we see them. I believe it will take a long time before they trust us, even if they forgive us right away," Kitty told Lydia. "We can only hope that they will even be willing to hear our apologies. We have a lot for which to make amends."

"If everything mom told us was not true, are you saying we should behave the opposite of the way that she taught us to act?"

"Yes Lyddie, I am. Look how different we are and it has only been a sennight since we were abandoned; now the scales have fallen from our eyes. Rather than be jealous of what our cousins have, we have to be thankful for what we do have. We were taught to covet; doing so is breaking one of the ten commandments. We need to look to our cousins as exemplars of estimable behaviour." Kitty then added, "Look at our cousins; they behaved with grace no matter how we or mom provoked them and never responded in kind. That is how we need to start behaving."

The two sisters were soon in bed, but it took a while to fall asleep as they had a lot to contemplate.

~~~~~~~/~~~~~~~

The night after the revelation by Edward Gardiner, Mary, who now occupied one of the bedchambers in her sister's suite, joined them on the big bed after they all dressed for bed. "Can you believe those ghastly people are gone?" Mary asked.

"Until we return to Longbourn and see for ourselves, it will be hard for me to believe," Elizabeth stated.

"I was thinking about what Aunt Rose said about our cousins," Jane interjected. "The more I think on it, the more I believe our aunt has the right of it. I know I have been angry with them since they came to Longbourn, but I believe they will need as much help and comfort as we are able to give them."

"It will be good to be at Longbourn again and not worry about having to hide from anyone any longer. I am sure the Hills and the rest of the servants rejoiced as soon as those two left our home," Mary supposed.

"I can well imagine that celebration," Elizabeth giggled. "Whether they had one or not, when we return to Longbourn I suggest a dinner party for our friends in the neighbourhood so they know it is safe to visit our estate once again!"

"On a separate note, Jane, why is Alex always looking at you?" Mary asked innocently.

"That Mary, is because he has a *tendre* for our Jane," a smiling Elizabeth announced.

"Lizzy, do not say that." Jane was blushing a deeper colour of crimson than either of her sisters had ever seen before.

"Do you have tender feelings for Alex, Jane?" Elizabeth enquired. Her sister's heightened colour was all the answer she needed.

"He is everything that a gentleman should be," Jane admitted.

"You come out next year sister dearest, I have a feeling he will ask for a courtship not long after," Elizabeth opined.

"Until Peter asked for a courtship and then betrothal with Charlotte, he used to look at Jane just like Alex did," Mary added.

"True, but our Jane never looked back at him like she does Alex," Elizabeth teased.

"Lizzy!" Jane exclaimed, as the impossible happened and she blush deepened.

"To return to the subject of our cousins, it is my opinion that we should welcome them warmly. Just think how much love and support we needed after Mama, Papa, and Jamie were stolen from us. They will need no less, in fact, in some ways, I believe they will need more," Elizabeth told her sisters.

"In that case, we will welcome them warmly," Jane decided, and Mary nodded her agreement.

Not long after, the girls separated. Now that Mary was out of the nursery, Elizabeth shared her bed. It was not a question of not enough chambers, but it was a transition for Mary, and she would sometimes awaken at night crying after a nightmare about her deceased family. This night all three had pleasant dreams of a Fanny and Thomas Bennet-free Longbourn.

~~~~~~~/~~~~~~~

Being abandoned by their parents had snuffed the innate liveliness from both of Fanny and Thomas Bennet's daughters. On the second day of the carriage ride, they were both in deep introspection about their conversation the previous night. They had barely said a word to one another or the Phillipses after they departed the inn in the morning. Both continued to contemplate their new situation and the reality of their erstwhile parents.

They were polite to the Phillipses and answered when spoken to. The adults, noting the sisters needed some peace and quiet, did not try and push them to talk. Lunch had been a very quiet meal and soon after they began the last leg of the two-day journey.

The atmosphere changed as the coach crested the hill and the great house came into view for the first time. "This is the home of our cousins' friends?" Kitty asked in wonder.

"Yes, my dear, they are rather wealthy, but that does not change the fact that they are warm, friendly, and welcoming people. They did not hesitate to include you in the invitation even after knowing all of the particulars. As Mr, Gardiner arrived before us, they will be apprised of the goings on at Longbourn by now," Hattie Phillips informed her adopted daughters kindly.

"That means our cousins are aware of what has taken place with our former parents?" Kitty asked. Phillips nodded.

"I will not blame them if they think that we deserve what has happened, after the way we behaved towards them," Lydia stated downcast.

"Lyddie, do you remember what we discussed last night?" Kitty reminded her younger sister. Lydia lifted her head to meet her sister's eyes and nodded. "It may take a while for Jane, Elizabeth, and Mary to be friendly toward us, but I do not believe they will revel in our pain."

"Your sister is correct Lydia," Hattie Phillips stated. "There is not a vindictive bone in those girls' bodies."

"Uncle and Aunt, when will you officially adopt us?" Kitty asked with purpose.

"My clerk will have filed the papers with the court by the end of this week and then it will be official," Phillips responded.

"May we change our last names to Phillips?" Kitty asked after getting a nod from Lydia.

"If once the adoption is official, and that is what both of you desire, then of course, yes you may," his voice thick with emotion, Phillips answered.

Before they could have any more discussion on the subject, the carriage came to a halt in the large internal courtyard. To the soon-to-be former Bennet sisters' amazement, their three cousins were waiting for them in the courtyard. Phillips exited first and then helped his wife out who hugged her adoptive nieces tightly. Kitty and Lydia were helped out next and stood awkwardly not knowing what to say to their cousins.

Before they knew it, they were enfolded in a group hug and the tears flowed freely. "W-we are so sorry..." Kitty tried to apologise.

"We will talk later," Jane stopped her. "There will be much to discuss, but for now just know we are here for you." Jane's words echoed by her younger sisters served to highlight how wrong Kitty and Lydia's former behaviour was. Once they dried their eyes, the three Bennet sisters led the arriving party to the drawing room where the Darcys awaited them.

~~~~~~~/~~~~~~~~

"My adopted daughters were most gratified at their welcome. They were afraid they would be judged based on their previous behaviour that had been influenced by that woman," Phillips stated as he joined Gardiner, Sir William, and Darcy in the latter's study.

"No one deserves what has befallen those two," Darcy said in a firm voice. "Now that you are both here, will you tell me how you went about contacting *the Spaniard* and acquiring Bennet's debts? From my information, he rarely meets with anyone directly."

"I did not meet with him, but met with one of his men of *business*," Gardiner responded. He proceeded to detail the meeting for Darcy. "Given the time between putting out the word and the point I was contacted, I am sure *the Spaniard* was having me investigated. He is notoriously paranoid."

"There is one thing I would like to do before we proceed gentlemen," Darcy informed the two and seeing their questioning looks he proceeded. "I would like to cover the ten thousand that you laid out." Seeing the coming protest, Darcy held up his hand to stay his friends. "I was sure you would object, but I have as much interest in those three and their welfare as you do. In addition, without it sounding like hubris, that amount would not even be felt from Pemberley's coffers."

"I too would like to contribute for the same reasons that Darcy stated," Sir William volunteered.

"Now you see what you have started Darcy," Phillips stated sardonically.

"Let us be logical. It matters not who covers the money as long as it is done. Do we all agree on this?" Darcy asked. The three men nodded grudgingly admitting he was correct. "As there would be no impact on my finances, then does it not stand to reason that the money comes from me?"

"Your logic is sound Darcy," Gardiner admitted. "For my part, I was allowing my pride to stand in the way of seeing things clearly."

"Neither can I make a creditable response to your proposal," Phillips conceded. "I too allowed my pride to rule my good sense."

"Then do we have an accord?" Darcy asked. The three other men nodded and he handed Gardiner and Phillips a draft for five thousand pounds each.

"Rather sure of yourself were you not?" Phillips ribbed his friend.

"Not sure, but as I know all of you rather well by now, I had no doubt you would see the logic in my argument," Darcy said somewhat smugly. "Who will manage Longbourn for the girls until Bennet shuffles of the mortal coil or the thirty years pass?"

"One of the things I wanted to ask you, Darcy, was if you knew of a good man to be Longbourn's steward," Phillips asked.

"I do. I have an under-steward here, Mr. Giles Hampstead, who had been training for nigh on five years and I would promote if I had an opening. He has family in Essex, so I am relatively sure that he would take a position in Hertfordshire," Darcy suggested.

"We will interview him, but who would live with the girls? They cannot be alone at Longbourn with just a companion and the servants," Gardiner asked.

"Hattie and I have discussed this," Phillips informed the other three. "We are the only ones of our circle who could move and not be affected. Darcy, you and Sir William have your own estates to manage, and Gardiner, you cannot be away from your business. On the other hand, it would be an easy move for Hattie and me. With Meryton but a mile from Longbourn, I will be able to go into the town as needed, but conversely, with such a trifling distance, I would be able to meet with most clients at Longbourn if need be and our daughters are already living there."

"It does sound like a sound plan," Darcy conceded, "You do not intend to present it to the three sisters as a *fait accompli*, do you?"

"Not at all. We will present it to the sisters and see if they agree," Phillips stated.

The rest of their time was spent talking about Gardiner's and Phillips' efforts to bring Bennet to justice for the murders that they were sure that he had committed. Darcy and Sir William agreed that applying to *the Spaniard* was a logical course of action.

CHAPTER 6

When Lydia and Kitty were directed to the nursery, they accepted it without any complaint. Already having accepted that Fanny Bennet had not been correct in almost anything she had done or told them, they understood when Hattie Phillips explained children did not leave the nursery much before the age of twelve. Kitty was told she had the option to be placed in a bed chamber as she was in her twelfth year, but she chose to stay close to Lydia in the nursery.

One of the nursemaids showed them to one of the small chambers of the main nursery and the girls decided they would prefer to share rather than each have their own room. Once they were washed and changed, they were told their cousins were waiting for them. Jane's maid who served her when she was at Pemberley showed the subdued girls to the sitting room in the suite between the sisters' bedchambers.

"How can you be so nice to us after the way we used to behave towards you?" Kitty asked after the door was closed by the retreating maid.

"Is that the way that you will continue to behave?" Jane asked. Kitty and Lydia shook their heads vigorously.

"Am I correct in assuming your mother…" Elizabeth started to ask.

"That woman is *not* our mother!" Lydia bit out vehemently.

"Let me rephrase my question, did Mrs. Bennet tell you how to behave toward us?" Elizabeth completed her question.

"That is not the way we intend to behave and yes, that woman told us to behave with disdain toward you. She blamed all of her husband's and her failings as parents on you," Kitty explained. "She told us you stole the money that should have been ours to explain why your clothes were so much finer than ours. It was she that not only encouraged, but instructed us, to take anything of yours we could without asking you, regardless of our need."

"Those two who masqueraded as your parents are no longer here to influence you, are they?" Jane asked pointedly.

"No, they are not! On the way here, I spoke to Kitty and we both agree that the woman never loved us and only gave us false affection when it suited her needs," Lydia responded sadly.

"I hear that Aunt and Uncle Phillips are in the process of adopting you," Mary stated.

"Yes, and we have asked to take their name when it is over. We know that even if you were adopted that you would not relinquish the name Bennet as your parents and brother loved you and you them, but we cannot bear to hold the same name as those two who turned tail and ran, abandoning us without a second thought," Kitty told her cousins.

"If that be the case, then I propose we start again and only remember the past between us as that remembrance gives us pleasure," Elizabeth suggested.

"We would like that. Kitty told me we can learn a lot from you and we would like that, if you are willing to teach us," Lydia smiled for the first time since Thomas and Fanny had taken off. The two soon-to-be former Bennets were sure, without intending to do so, their former parents may have ended up doing them a great service. It did not lessen the pain of being abandoned, but it did give them hope for a better future.

~~~~~~~/~~~~~~~

In the fortnight since their eviction from Longbourn and Hertfordshire, Fanny and Thomas Bennet had continued their aimless journey south. Bennet had for the first time in his life a run of luck and their funds were now close to a thousand pounds. They arrived in the town of East Meon in Hampshire.

For the first time since they had married, Fanny Bennet

removed most of her husband's money so that he could not lose it all. She liked the town and found a cottage to rent. To make sure that her husband could not find and misuse the funds, she paid for two years' rent upfront with an option for another two years. She had the forethought to leave a deposit equal to another two years' rent with the landlord in case they stayed beyond the first two years.

Fanny was a lady of mean understanding, but she had reasonable survival instincts. By the time she was done, she had left sizable deposits with the general store, haberdashery, and the dress maker. That way, no matter what her husband did she knew they had some level of security.

For her daughters that she had abandoned, she did not spare a thought. In her opinion, it was done and done for the best. Her life would be better now she only had to worry about herself and, to a certain extent, her husband. The town was three to four times larger than Meryton, so she was sure she would be able to find a paramour or two in the area.

When Bennet discovered the bulk of their money missing, he almost had an apoplexy. When he confronted his wife, she informed him the money was secure, and that this way they would be able to live regardless. He slapped his wife a few times and demanded she return the money to him.

"If you hit me again Thomas, I will walk out and you will never know what I have done with the money!" Fanny threatened as Bennet pulled his fist back. Her exclamation stayed the release of his hand. "We have a cottage, nicely furnished, and it is paid for two years ahead." She did not mention the additional two years being held by the landlord or the funds at other stores. "I have set up accounts and will pay what we owe each month from the money that I have secreted away," she lied. She knew full well that had he been aware of the fact that they had essentially prepaid for a year or more, he would have charged into each store demanding the money. "Let us pack up and move into our cottage."

"You want to stay here?" Bennet asked as he calmed

down.

"It is as good a place as any," Fanny returned. "No one here knows us, so we should be able to pass ourselves off as good people," Fanny cackled. "Who knows, we may be able to separate someone from their funds before we leave here."

"We should lie low for a while. Mayhap you are correct, Fanny; this place will do. I will find a way to make those who stole our house from us pay very dearly!" Bennet threatened. Bennet was essentially a coward. He would not risk being thrown into Marshalsea, so he would have to find a way to take his vengeance from a distance.

~~~~~~~/~~~~~~~

"How could his parents have allowed one such as he to become betrothed to a nobody!" Caroline Bingley spat as she threw the *Times of London* down in disgust.

"I do not have the pleasure of understanding your meaning, sister, of whom do you speak?" Bingley asked trying to keep his patience with his sister and her pretentions.

"Mr. Peter de Bourgh, heir to Rosings Park and cousin to the Darcys. He has been trapped by some nobody's daughter of an unheard-of knight in some backwater town of Meryton in Hertfordshire," came the exasperated reply as if her brother should have known the answer.

"You mean the backwater town my friend's estate is near?" Bingley enquired, knowing that it was true.

"He is only a second son," Miss Bingley sniffed with disdain.

"And you are only the daughter and sister of a tradesman! Who are you to make pronouncements about who is and is not worthy of anything," Bingley shot back.

Caroline Bingley got the pinched look that she always did when something displeased her, and her brother talking about his being in trade was a sure way to engender her displeasure. "If you would do your duty to me, I would have met the Darcy heir and secured him already," she stated, choosing to ignore her brother's statement.

"What makes you think that Alexander Darcy would ever look at you, Caroline? He is the grandson and nephew of the Earl of Matlock and you are a tradesman's daughter of eighteen. From where do you get these delusions of grandeur?" Bingley shook his head. He felt sorry for his sister who was never happy with what she had. He was sure she would not think twice about engineering a compromise to get her way, but he would never force any man to marry his younger sister unless the man desired to do so.

"You...you nincompoop you!" Miss Bingley blurted out as she stood with such force that her chair fell backwards.

Invitations to Pemberley and Netherfield had been received and politely refused. His friend understood the problem that Caroline presented and had explained that his brother's eye was firmly fixed on a lady and nothing Bingley's sister could imagine doing would change that. William Darcy understood why his friend declined the invitations, as Bingley did not want to impose his social climbing sister on the Darcys.

Bingley was gratified they were in Scarborough far away from the eyes of the Ton, whose members would chew his sister up and spit her out and not even blink. Neither he nor Louisa were anything like the youngest Bingley. He prayed his sister would not ruin herself and the family along with her. He would have to keep a tight rein on Caroline to make sure that she did not.

~~~~~~~/~~~~~~~

A few days after the newly formed Phillips family arrived, Jane, Elizabeth, and Mary were asked to attend a meeting in the Darcys' private sitting room. The Darcy, Gardiner, Phillips, and Lucas adults were in attendance as well as Alexander and William Darcy. There was a man that none of the three recognised.

"This man," George Darcy indicated that he should come forward, "is Mr. Giles Hampstead. He is one of my under-stewards and I have put his name forward to be Longbourn's steward. He is here in case any of you girls have any questions for him."

Darcy introduced the prospective steward to the three Bennet sisters.

"If he has your confidence, Uncle George, then we have no need questioning Mr. Hampstead," Jane indicated.

"That he does," Darcy intoned. Mr. Hampstead coloured at the praise from the estate's master. "I believe he is more than ready to take over management of an estate and it is my firm belief that he will bring Longbourn back to the prosperity it enjoyed under your late father."

As usual, the three sisters looked a little maudlin as their father was mentioned. "I have all of Papa's journals where he enumerates his methods for crop rotation and the management of the estate," Elizabeth stated, as she wiped a lone tear from her eye.

"If you will permit me to read them, Miss Elizabeth, I would be most interested in learning from your late father's books," Mr. Hampstead responded respectfully.

"As my nieces have no objection, please come see me this afternoon, Mr. Hampstead, and we will sign your contract. When will you be able to depart for Longbourn? It is in great need of a guiding hand as soon as possible," Phillips stated. He was very pleased the man was interested in the position as he doubted he would have been able to find a man half as good on his own.

"Unless Mr. Darcy objects, I will be able to depart on the morrow," Hampstead replied.

"You are free to go, Hampstead. You have my thanks for your loyal years of service to Pemberley," Darcy informed him.

"When you sign the papers this afternoon, Hampstead, I will furnish you with a letter of introduction to the butler and housekeeper at Longbourn," Phillips informed the steward.

Once the man departed the room and the door was closed, the question of who would be the girls' guardians was addressed. "None of us are your family, but the following is what we propose. Aunt Hattie and I will move to Longbourn and would be your primary guardians. That would mean that Kitty and Lydia would be living at Longbourn with us. Do any of you object to that arrangement?" Phillips asked.

Jane looked at her sisters and each shook their head indicating that they had no objection. "We would be happy to have you and your daughters with us at Longbourn, Uncle Frank and Aunt Hattie. The Kitty and Lydia we have discovered since your arrival at Pemberley are girls that we would like to get to know, so their living at the estate with you is no impediment," Jane answered for all three sisters.

"That is capital," Sir William added. "I hope you do not object that myself, Gardiner, and Darcy will also be named as alternate guardians if, heaven forbid, anything happens to Phillips before you three all reach your majority."

"Why would we object to having our adopted uncles in that position?" Elizabeth asked pertly.

The three had often discussed how lucky they were that they had these people in their lives who went out of their way, when they had no need to, to protect and love them. If not for them, their lives would have been horrific—that is if Fanny and Thomas Bennet had not found a way to get rid of them or worse.

"Are you girls aware that your father had money invested with Gardiner and Sons?" seeing the quizzical looks from his friends, Gardiner clarified. "I recently changed the name. Eddy pointed out to me that as he had a brother, the 'Son' was neither fair nor accurate, hence I added the 's' and made it 'Sons.' Where was I, oh yes. You each have very healthy dowries of over thirty thousand and in addition to that, there was Jamie's legacy of thirty thousand pounds. As protection against fortune hunters, it was set up that both your father and I would have to approve your match to ensure it was one that you chose and that you had not been entrapped for your funds. Given the new reality, I would like to change that to two of the four of us to approve.

"Your father kept secret the truth of your fortunes to keep the fortune hunters at bay; I suggest we continue to do so," Gardiner suggested.

"What is to become of Jamie's legacy?" Jane asked.

"It will be split among you three," Phillips responded.

"We have more than enough," Jane said after conferring with her sisters. "We would like half of the amount split between Kitty and Lydia to dower them and the other half to be kept in a trust to fund for worthy charitable causes that we choose."

"That is extremely generous of you three. Aunt Hattie and I will add funds to make their dowries up to ten thousand pounds each and the funds will be invested with Gardiner and Sons," Phillips said in appreciation on behalf of his new daughters.

With agreement on all sides, the meeting came to a close. As Alexander watched the young lady he loved leave, he knew that even if she only had the dowry of two thousand pounds that was published abroad, she would have been his choice. With Mr. Phillips being Jane's primary guardian, Alexander knew he needed to have a conversation with him sooner rather than later. He followed his father's advice that there is no time like the present, and requested a conversation with the solicitor before he met with Longbourn's new steward. The two remained in the sitting room after the rest of the party left.

"Mr. Phillips," Alexander started.

"So formal today," Phillips ribbed the young man, relatively sure what the subject to be canvassed was.

"Jane will be seventeen in January," Alexander tried to begin again.

"I am well aware of that; do you want to help plan her birthday celebration?" Phillips took pity on the exasperated looking young man. "Go ahead Alex, I will refrain from interjecting."

"Has it been discussed when she will come out?" Alexander asked.

"As a matter of fact, it has. My wife, your mother, and Lady Lucas are planning it for November of '05 as she will only be a month or so shy of her eighteenth birthday, why do you ask?" Phillips inquired of the younger man.

"Will you set a time period from her come out until one can declare himself for her?" Alexander asked hopefully.

"The *one* in this scenario would be you?" Phillips asked already knowing it to be true.

"Yes sir, that would be correct," Andrew returned steadily.

"There will be no imposition other than she be out. As long as you are her choice made freely, then I will support her and not stand in the way, Alex," Phillips informed Alex, who was now grinning from ear to ear. Less than a year and a half to go!

~~~~~~~/~~~~~~~

Mr. William Collins was the curate of a small parish church in the town of Croyde in Devon. Collins was not happy with his lot; he was born for better than being a mere curate! He was, after all, the heir to an estate in Hertfordshire called Longbourn. The problem was he had to wait for the master of said estate to meet his maker before he could claim his inheritance.

Collins was a strange mix of sycophantic servility and arrogance. As it is well known, misery likes company and he had recently made the acquaintance of one George Wickham. At first, he had thought the man to be beneath him, as Wickham was working with the horses at the local inn, until he had heard Wickham's story of being cheated out of his birth right.

As he felt he had also been cheated, ignoring the fact that the terms of the entail established the succession unambiguously, Collins became close to Wickham. He was very susceptible to Wickham's false flattery as it puffed up his ego.

Wickham thought the man to be the most stupid he had ever met and found his company distasteful, but as Collins was now his meal ticket, he made sure to lay the flattery on thickly. The more flattery he spewed, the more the stupid man would puff up with pride. He listened to the story about the estate the man was to inherit and started to scheme and look for ways it could benefit himself. Wickham was convinced of his opinion that Collins was too stupid to run such an estate.

With Collins feeding him and allowing him to have a small room in his cottage, Wickham's days of sleeping in the stables were over and with him not having to spend money to feed himself, he was able to gamble and drink a lot more.

For his part, Collins believed his friend recognised that as a member of the clergy he had a high position in society and was paying him his due respect. Collins was blind to the fact there was no one in the town that had respect for him or liked him for that matter.

~~~~~~~/~~~~~~~

As planned, the de Bourghs arrived at Pemberley and the betrothed couple was joyous to be reunited. The day after they arrived, Peter and Charlotte met with their mothers and informed them that the wedding would be in Meryton in September of that year.

"You do not want a London wedding, my son?" Lady Catherine asked.

"Mother, I would marry Charlotte in the middle of a field if that was what she chose, just like Anne one day will marry from her home; Charlotte wants the same," Peter replied.

"If that is what you want, then it will be so. I do have one suggestion though. We should ask William if we can hold the wedding breakfast at his estate as it is the largest estate in the area, is it not Rose?" Lady Catherine asked.

"You are correct, Catherine, it is. Charlotte, you know Lucas Lodge's size. I think Netherfield would suit very well if William agrees," Lady Lucas said.

The betrothed couple looked at one another and nodded. "I will request William, Mother," Peter de Bourgh stated. Later that day he found his cousin, who agreed to the request with alacrity.

CHAPTER 7

October 1805

Fanny and Thomas Bennet had established themselves in East Meon for almost two years. Bennet had been accepted to the position at the parish school for boys and had kept relatively sober during school hours. Luckily, there was not much opportunity to gamble in the out of the way town whose denizens seemed to frown on the activity.

Even though Fanny was the one to make sure they would have the means to live for some years, she was getting more resentful and restless by the day. She did not waste any thinking capacity on her former daughters. All she cared about was that her life was not as she imagined, and how it should have been if they had been able to sell the estate after Thomas dispatched the three Bennets.

Fanny did not understand how entails worked and she did not care to understand. All she knew was, somehow, they had been cheated and they should have been able to sell what was theirs if they had desired to do so. She had not married a gentleman to be stuck in some nowhere town.

She had found three men she visited regularly. Luckily, she did not become with a child as that would have meant that she would have to sleep with her husband again and that was distasteful to her. She had got rid of two needy children; the last thing she wanted was more of the same.

Fanny was sure her husband was not aware he was being cuckolded. She was almost correct. However, Bennet, on one of his drunken binges during a term break at the school where he taught, was passed out outside of a tavern a few miles from the village. He woke up and saw Fanny riding in a cart with the owner of the haberdashery and he did not miss where their hands were on each other.

He did not want his wife anymore, but he certainly did not want any other man to have her. He started to follow her occasionally and one night when he told her he would be at the tavern outside of the town, he spied his wife being admitted to the cottage belonging to the man he had seen her with.

The next day he entered the parlour and dining room combination in their rented cottage. "Were you at home last night Fanny?" Bennet asked nonchalantly.

"Y-yes I was Thomas w-why do you ask?" Fanny responded nervously, worried that he knew what she was doing. She knew he would not allow that kind of blow to his ego to pass.

"No reason. You know Fanny, I have been thinking mayhap it is time to move on. Did you not tell me that you paid for four years, complete for the rental of this cottage?" he enquired.

"Well, the truth is that two years is being held on deposit in case we choose to stay here," Fanny admitted, much relieved that he did not seem to know about her indiscretions.

"Let us go see the landlord and tell him that we will leave at the end of the current term, and then we can choose where we would like to go," Bennet suggested.

His wife was so happy he was not asking about where she had been that she agreed without a thought. A few hours later the two returned to their abode, the returned funds in Bennet's pocket. Along with the money he had retained, he now had a little more than three hundred pounds to his name.

Just when Fanny was starting to relax, Bennet pulled his fist back and let it fly with all of his might into his wife's belly. As she rolled on the floor moaning and crying Bennet spat out: "Did you think I will allow you to cuckold me!" As he spoke, he kicked her repeatedly and stomped on her for good measure.

It was only when Fanny Bennet went silent and stopped moving that he realised he had killed the woman. He felt no remorse for killing her, and if he had been less of a coward, he would have sought out her paramour as well, but the man was bigger than him. Bennet packed hastily, took everything of value from the home including the little bit of jewellery that Fanny had owned. He hired a horse at the inn and was heading south within an hour of murdering his wife.

The body was not discovered for a sennight until someone investigated the smell emanating from the cottage that had become overwhelming.

~~~~~~~/~~~~~~~

Longbourn was once more back to the state that the late James Bennet Junior had brought it. With the steward working closely with Elizabeth, who had an aptitude for estate management, the income was back to over four thousand clear again. The tenants who had left returned as soon as the word spread that Thomas and Fanny Bennet were gone for good.

William Darcy spent a lot of time at Longbourn and visits were reciprocated. For some reason, Alexander found many reasons to visit his younger brother at Netherfield Park, which ultimately led to many hours at Longbourn. His preference for Jane Bennet was not a secret and he cared not who knew it, especially as a few months earlier during her summer visit to Pemberley, Jane had confessed that she felt the same way for him. He became lost in his reverie as he remembered the time that the three sisters had visited Pemberley, and specifically the day of the picnic.

It was a clear summer day that promised to be hot in the afternoon when the three older Darcy siblings rode out with the three Bennet sisters. Miss Ponsonby and Miss Younge were the chaperones along with a footman and groom. The destination was a glen near the little waterfall that was on the tributary of the Derwent river that ran through Pemberley. There was a cool pool of water below the falling water and when the sun hit at the right angle, a rainbow could be seen in the mist created from the water hitting the rocks.

Servants from Pemberley had a table, blankets, and cushions in place when the riding party arrived. Each time that they were at Pemberley the Bennet sisters always found a way to visit the enchanting spot more than once. The table was loaded with enough food to feed double the number that were present.

Alexander had guided Jane to sit on a cushion a little distance from the rest of the party. They could be clearly seen, but no one would hear if they chose to speak, and Alexander was determined to speak. Mr. Phillips had told him that he had to wait until Jane had her coming out to request a courtship or betrothal but talking about his feelings was never embargoed. Alexander returned with plates for Jane and himself.

They ate in companionable silence and after he had retrieved some of the raspberry pastries that he knew Jane preferred, Alexander decided it was time. He was relatively confident that Jane had tender feelings for him. He was about to put his hypothesis to the test.

"Jane, you have to know how I feel about you," Alexander started.

"And how must I know that Alex, have you told me before and I forgot?" Jane teased the man she loved.

"If you are not sure, let me correct that oversight right now," Alexander insisted. Jane nodded her acquiescence as she began to blush deeply. "It is many years now that I have loved you, Jane Bennet. If you feel the same in the smallest measure, tell me and if not, I will forever hold my peace. If, as I pray that you do, you have tender feelings for me, I have to tell you that the day you come out I will be requesting a courtship or betrothal, depending on your preference."

"You would give up so easily?" Jane teased again with an arched eyebrow, something all three sisters seemed to do.

"That is not my preference, Jane. I love you with all that I am, but if that is not what you desire, I will withdraw as your happiness is the most important thing to me," Alexander declared.

"Then it is a good thing that you are the man that I love, Alex; the only man that I could ever imagine sharing my life with," Jane answered.

Alexander thought that he was in a dream, surely that was the only place where his wishes came true. "You love me, Jane?" he asked wanting to make sure he did not dream that she had declared her love for him.

"Yes Alex, I love you. I have done so for more than a year. I thought that my feelings were returned, but until today, I was not sure," Jane assured him.

"I will be there to see you after your curtsey before the Queen. Have you considered how long you would want to court before I request a betrothal?"

"Do we really need a courtship, Alex? Silly me, I thought that was what we had been doing for the last year or so," came Jane's impertinent reply.

Alexander Darcy was so happy he thought that he had died and gone to heaven. When they returned to the manor house, he sought Mr. Phillips out and told him about his discussion with Jane. Phillips did not censure him as Alexander had not contravened his wishes regarding his ward.

Alexander was snapped out of his pleasurable reverie, as William called him for the third time!

~~~~~~~/~~~~~~~

Kitty and Lydia Phillips, now thirteen and ten respectively had recovered a lot of their spirit in the almost two years since they had been adopted by their new mother and father. The best thing that they learnt was what it was like to be in a proper and loving family. They were forever altered from the way that they were when Fanny and Thomas Bennet had been their parents.

Soon after changing their name to Phillips, they stopped mourning the loss of what they had imagined that their former parents were and each and every day they were enveloped in the love they received from the Phillipses, which had healed them. They were no longer vulgar, selfish, or a chore to be around. After their three cousins accepted the sincere apologies proffered by the two, they had been there to help and support Kitty and Lydia as and when needed.

A companion was hired for the three Bennet sisters, a Mrs. Helena Annesley, a gentlewoman who had needed to seek employment after her husband passed and left nothing for her to live on. Miss Ponsonby had become a governess to Kitty and Lydia. They had needed to start almost from scratch, which was no surprise to anyone. Fanny Bennet had not educated them as they should have been.

Kitty could read and write, but poorly, and Lydia could not do either properly. After the first six months of intensive education, both girls were reading and writing as they should and had started to learn French. The same *maestro di musica* who taught their much more advanced cousins agreed to take on the Phillips sisters as he enjoyed a challenge. Almost two years in, neither were proficient on the piano forte, but their playing was improving noticeably. Kitty was not a singer, but Lydia was a natural; her voice blended very nicely with her cousins'.

It was discovered that Kitty had a natural talent as well. She had an excellent eye for sketching and painting. Her father hired a master for her and she progressed from strength to strength. She was particularly talented in drawing and painting people. She did not need her subject to sit for her. As long as she had seen them well at least once, she could reproduce the person almost perfectly.

Lydia was still in the nursery, the only one at Longbourn still there, but she accepted that she still had two to three years before she would be assigned a bed chamber alongside her sister and cousins.

~~~~~~~/~~~~~~~

September of the previous year had seen the wedding of the former Charlotte Lucas and Peter de Bourgh. Meryton's Saint Alfred's church had been overflowing, as the Lucas family was one of the principal families in the area. With the de Bourghs,

Fitzwilliams, Darcys, and a number of their friends attending as well, one would be able to understand why the church was so full.

After a month's wedding trip, the two had arrived back at Rosings Park, where Sir Louis and Lady Catherine had assigned the east wing of the house for them to live in relative privacy. All of that privacy had paid off as Charlotte was approaching her final confinement, meaning that Sir Lewis and Lady Catherine would remain at Rosings for the birth of their first grandchild. Anne would travel to London with her companion and escorts and stay at Matlock House with her aunt and uncle.

All traces of the sickly girl were gone. With regular exercise, proper meals, and never touching the poison that her former doctor prescribed, she was as hale and healthy as any young lady of one and twenty. She was looking forward to spending time with Elizabeth, who had started her on the road to recovery some years previously.

~~~~~~~/~~~~~~~

Bennet rode as far south as he could before he rested his horse in Winchester. He spent a night at an inn in the town and headed toward the coast and Southampton at first light the following morning. He rode around the town for a while and found a house that was advertising room and board. He followed his murdered wife's example and rented a room under the name James Collins.

He was amused that he had appropriated his dead brother's name and that of the presumptive heir of Longbourn. He found a card game and won a little but then gave it all back. For once in his life, once he started to lose, he left the game only a pound or two worse off than when he had sat down.

Knowing that he needed to earn some money, he applied for and was accepted to the position of tutor to Mr. Eagleton on the estate of Bliss Hill just outside of the city. He was sorry he had paid his rent in advance as he would have been able to reside on the estate for free, but unless he found someone to assume his room, the landlord would not refund his money. As it was too much like hard work, Bennet just gave up on the four and twenty pounds and moved to Bliss Hill.

~~~~~~~/~~~~~~~

William found Elizabeth Bennet, at almost sixteen, quite the most handsome young lady of his acquaintance. He envied his older brother, who would propose to Jane Bennet next month as soon as she entered society. He had more than two years to cool his heels until the Bennet sister he was falling in love with would be out.

William, even as a second son, was seen as a target for the matrons of the neighbourhood and their unmarried daughters. Knowing that he owned Netherfield and he had increased his profits to almost five thousand per annum was more than enough for any of them.

A month earlier was the first local assembly that Elizabeth had attended and William Darcy had danced the first and last set with her—the only lady he had honoured thusly. A clear message was sent and received as the mothers and daughters admitted that William Darcy was not interested romantically in any but Miss Elizabeth.

William saw Elizabeth multiple times each week at Longbourn or Netherfield. Mr. and Mrs. Nichols, William's butler and housekeeper, had no doubt that Miss Elizabeth would be their mistress one day.

The rest of the Darcys had arrived days after the harvest ball at Pemberley. They would only be at Netherfield for a few short days as they, along with the Phillips family, Bennet sisters, and Lucas family, were to decamp to London to prepare for Jane's coming out and ball. The Phillips parents would stay with the Gardiners on Gracechurch Street. Kitty and Lydia were invited to join the rest of the young ladies at Matlock House. The de Bourghs had made de Bourgh House, also on Grosvenor Square, available for Sir William and his family.

Given the not-so-secret upcoming proposal, the Bennet sisters were to reside across Grosvenor Square at Matlock House for propriety's sake. If everything went as expected, Georgiana and Annabeth would be with their friends and soon-to-be sisters at the Fitzwilliams' house as well.

~~~~~~~/~~~~~~~

Jane's coming out ball was to be held at Darcy House, so the day after everyone arrived in Town the ladies met with Lady Anne to go over the plans. Ladies Anne, Elaine, and Catherine were sponsoring Jane for her curtsy in front of Her Majesty the Queen, which would be on Monday the fourth day of November.

The ball, hosted by Lady Anne, Hattie Phillips, and Lady Lucas, would be the Wednesday after. Jane had not wanted an extensive guest list, so the ladies had limited the invitations to close friends of the families that were intimate with the Bennet sisters. Due to the exclusive nature of the invitations, many members of the Ton, when encountering one of the Darcys, especially the ladies shopping or the men at their club, would drop not so subtle hints about the ball to no effect.

While the ladies were going over their final plans, the girls were sitting in the music room at Matlock house under the watchful eyes of Mrs. Annesley, Miss Ponsonby, and Miss Younge. "Jane, I cannot believe you will be out in society in a few days," Elizabeth sighed knowing she still had a little more than two years to go before she entered society.

"Methinks our dear sister is waiting for the interview that she will have with Alex after her curtsey," Mary teased.

Jane blushed deeply but did not refute what her sister said. "I am sure the *whole* day will be memorable!" Jane exclaimed.

"Once Alex and Jane are betrothed, I hope they will not wait very long to marry; I cannot wait until we are all sisters," Georgiana gushed.

"And we will be your cousins," Kitty Phillips stated. In the last year, she had become very close with Georgiana Darcy and her cousin Mary. Lydia and Annabeth Darcy had struck up a warm friendship as well.

"We have all been a family for some years now," Anne de Bourgh opined. "My new doctor has pronounced me a normal healthy girl, so I will come out in March with a ball following. By then my sister's and brother's babe will be here and Charlotte will be able to travel once more," Anne informed her friends and cousin.

"The only problem with you marrying Alex is we will not see you nearly as often," Elizabeth expressed. "Gigi and Annabeth will see you far more than I," Elizabeth gave a fake pout.

"Jane will not be the only one who marries a son of Pemberley," Anne teased her friend pointedly.

"Anne!" Elizabeth blushed a deep scarlet from her hairline to the top of her day dress. "I am not yet sixteen!"

"Remind me who William has danced two dances with at each assembly since she came out in Meryton. Lizzy, the *only* young lady he *ever* dances with more than once. And who is it he dances the first and last with each time?" Jane asked, happy to deflect the attention from herself.

"That does not mean anything," Elizabeth said weakly, knowing how what she said sounded.

"You tell yourself that, if it makes you rest easy," Anne said with a twinkle in her eye. It was usually the other way around, Elizabeth the one doing the teasing, so Anne enjoyed the role reversal indeed.

Not long after, the older girls were joined by Annabeth and Lydia, who had completed the duet they were playing, so the talk became of more mundane things.

~~~~~~~/~~~~~~~

George Wickham dreamed of placing his hands around the idiotic William Collins's neck. It was not the man's lack of intelligence that Wickham found grating, but the mixture of pomposity and servility. He treated Wickham like an underling that was far below him. As much as he wanted to rid himself of the man, he was still his meal ticket and he did have a warm bed in which to sleep.

Whenever he could, Wickham would relieve the silly clergyman of some coin so he could indulge in drink and find a game of cards. There was not much in the way of the other type of pursuits that Wickham liked in Croyde. As much as he disliked it, Wickham was well aware that until he had the means to leave the nowhere town, he would have to control his base instincts.

He had no choice; he would have to bide his time and keep pretending to be the adipose man's friend.

~~~~~~~/~~~~~~~

Charles Bingley had some business to conduct in London and had been invited to stay with his friend William Darcy at the Darcy town house. Knowing that Caroline would not be able to control her behaviour among the Darcys, Bingley had begged his sister and brother-in-law to keep the youngest Bingley with them when he travelled to London.

"But Charles, why can I not accompany you to London? I may finally meet the Darcys!" Caroline Bingley whined.

"The trip is for business, and I will stay near Mr. Gardiner's house—you know, near Cheapside and all of my fellow trades-men!" Bingley told the truth, except for where he would reside in London.

"I suppose if you put it like that," she sniffed with disdain. "Why do you have to associate with all of those tradesmen, I do not know!" Miss Bingley got the pinched look of displeasure on her face.

"As you well know, I too am one of *those tradesmen!*" Bingley shot back and left the drawing room before he said what he truly wanted to say to his shrewish sister. Early the next morning, Charles Bingley was on his way to Town.

CHAPTER 8

Charles Bingley arrived at Darcy House the day before Jane Bennet entered society. By the time he had changed and washed, the young ladies residing at Matlock House were present in the drawing room. Bingley was not the first young man to be stopped in his tracks on beholding the three Bennet sisters for the first time. All three were beautiful, but one caught his eye right away. She looked like a blond goddess that had come down to commune with mere mortals like himself.

After William Darcy made the introductions, it took him some minutes to find his voice. Before he spoke, Bingley did not miss the looks of love and adoration that were passing between the Darcy heir and the lady he now knew to be Miss Jane Bennet from Hertfordshire. His friend sat down next to Bingley.

"I had a feeling that you would become a mooncalf over our Jane. Unfortunately for you, she is well on her way to becoming my sister," William Darcy told his friend quietly.

"She is an angel!" Bingley returned in a sotto voice. "If only I had met her before your brother," Bingley lamented.

"Their acquaintance is not new; it is a few years now that we have been extremely close to the Bennet sisters," William shared.

"Where are their parents?" Bingley asked. Even with the knowledge that there could be nothing between him and the lady, it was hard for him to tear his eyes away from the lady that he designated as both a goddess and an angel.

"Their parents are not with us any longer. Before you retire, I will find you and tell you about what happened," William promised.

"I see you are afflicted with the same thing that most men are when they meet my sister," Elizabeth stated impertinently as she sat down next to William.

"Ehm...er...was I staring at Miss Bennet?" Bingley turned red from embarrassment, which only highlighted his flaming red hair.

"Jane will not take umbrage with you, Mr. Bingley, especially when Alex is near her as she sees no one but him," Elizabeth informed Bingley, as William smiled at his friend's embarrassment.

"I thank you, Miss Elizabeth," Bingley returned. "Please know that I was not denigrating yours or your sister's looks; you are all very pretty."

"So, Mary and I are good substitutes as Jane is no longer available?" Elizabeth challenged playfully with an arched eyebrow. Bingley looked horrified that the lady would draw that inference from his words.

"Lizzy! My friend does not know you and is not used to your sense of humour. He thinks you are serious," William stepped in to assist his friend.

"William has the right of it, Mr. Bingley. I was jesting with you, so please take nothing I said as censure," Elizabeth explained as Bingley started to relax after thinking he had just made a monumental gaffe.

"How did you convince your sister to remain in Scarborough?" William asked. Seeing Elizabeth's questioning look, the two explained about Caroline Bingley and her social climbing desires.

"She may believe that I am staying in Cheapside and only meeting with fellow tradesmen," Bingley relayed with a grin.

"Mayhap because that is what you told her?" William returned his friend's grin.

"Your sister truly believes that if she met Alex, he would offer for her?" Elizabeth asked incredulously after assimilating the information that had been imparted.

"I am afraid so, Miss Elizabeth, which is why I have not

brought her with me; she would have embarrassed herself and the family within the first few minutes here. I am afraid that my sister's manners leave a lot to be desired and she is rather vulgar," Bingley owned.

"It would be interesting to meet such a creature. I apologise if I am being impolitic, Mr. Bingley," Elizabeth stated.

"Think nothing of it, Miss Elizabeth; she has been called far worse by my sister Louisa, Louisa's husband Hurst, and myself. Unfortunately, as the baby of the family she was roundly spoilt by my late parents and now believes that all she must do is want something and it will be hers," Bingley related.

Just then Anne de Bourgh and her companion entered the drawing room and Elizabeth introduced her to Mr. Bingley. "You are from Yorkshire Mr. Bingley? I have never been to that county. Mayhap you would be willing to tell me about your home shire?" Anne requested.

William and Elizabeth left Anne and Mr. Bingley chatting amiably on the settee and walked over to disturb the mooncalf looks passing between Jane and Alexander.

"The morrow will be a very big day for both of us, Jane," Alexander opined.

"You think it is big because I am making my curtsy before the Queen, Alex? I have practised many times and been coached by Aunts Anne and Elaine, so I am confident that all will go well on the morrow," Jane teased, knowing exactly what he was referring to.

"Does that mean that I should not seek a private audience with you on the morrow then, Jane? If it is not that important..." Alexander stopped teasing as he received a playful slap on his arm.

"That is an appointment I fully expect you to keep," Jane said with meaning.

"If that be the case, then I will present myself at Matlock House as soon as you return from St. James Palace," Alexander stated.

"It will be my pleasure to receive you, Alex," Jane said almost shyly.

"Are you two planning the rest of your lives?" Elizabeth joked as she sat down next to Jane.

"Not our whole lives, just tomorrow," Alexander replied for both of them.

"Master Alexander, the master requests your presence in his study," the butler informed Alexander.

"Thank you Killion," Alexander took his leave.

"Where is Alex going?" Georgiana asked as she filled the seat that Alexander had vacated.

"Father asked to see him Gigi," William responded.

"I hope he is not in trouble," Georgiana smiled. Both her brothers were the best of brothers one could wish for, and she was sure that whatever her father wanted was nothing to do with Alex being in trouble.

~~~~~~~~/~~~~~~~~

"Sit son," George Darcy indicated one of the chairs in front of his wide oak desk. "Have you resolved to ask for Jane's hand on the morrow, Alex?" he asked.

"I have, Father; we love each other and there is no reason for a courtship when we already know each other's desires. Do you object?" Alexander enquired with concern.

"No, Son, how could I object to you marrying a girl that I already see as a daughter. I ask because you have a choice." George Darcy placed three velvet poaches on the desktop. "There are three rings from the Darcy collection that would all make appropriate betrothal rings." He proceeded to take each one from its velvet bag and place each on top of the bag that it had been in.

Alexander knew which was best for Jane as soon as he saw it. The band was a lighter gold and in the centre of the setting was a large sapphire that he knew would be a perfect match for Jane's eyes. The sapphire was surrounded by a ring of small diamonds. "That one is perfect for Jane," Alexander indicated the chosen ring.

"I had a feeling that you would choose that one. It was your grandmother Darcy's ring. My mother always hoped that either you or William would gift it to your betrothed one day and now her wish has come true," George Darcy allowed memories of his departed mother wash over him.

"Thank you, Father; I am positive that Jane will love it. What about Will's ring when he proposes? Will he be able to choose from the other two?" Alex enquired.

"Those and a few more, so when the time comes for your brother, it will not be an issue," George said as he waved his son away.

Alexander placed the ring back in its bag and placed the ring that he would slip onto Jane's finger into his inside jacket pocket.

~~~~~~~/~~~~~~~

On the day of her curtsy, Jane was awake much earlier than was her wont. If it were just the day of her entry into society it would have been one thing, but this was the day she would be proposed to. She had loved Alexander from almost the first time she had met him when he had dinner at Longbourn with Uncle George and William. She was sad that the people who had been present at that first meeting, Papa, Mama, and Jamie, were not alive to see her accept the man of her dreams. He could have been a poor country squire and it would have made no difference to Jane.

Elizabeth and Mary knocked on her door, a half hour after she woke and she bade them enter. "Will I have to wear a monstrosity like that when I come out?" Mary asked as she indicated the dress with all of its hoops and bows hanging on the door of Jane's walk-in closet.

"Unless there is a new queen who changes the required presentation dress, yes, Sister, you will," Jane smiled. Mary scrunched up her nose showing her distaste for the ungainly gown.

"You will do well, Jane; I am sure that you will not trip when you back away from the Queen," Elizabeth said in support. "You are not nervous about that are you, Janie?"

"No Lizzy, I am not. It is a pity that Aunt Catherine could not be here, but I understand her wanting to be with Charlotte. I believe that Lady Lucas leaves for Rosings today," Jane informed her sisters.

"Sir William will join them later today after your presentation. Alex will apply to him for his consent after Uncle Frank grants his blessing," Elizabeth said.

Jane's lady's maid shooed her sisters out of the chambers as it was time for her mistress to be prepared for her momentous day. There was already a pale blue day dress picked out to change into on Jane's return from St. James as there was no chance she would attend the most important interview of her life in the hooped presentation gown.

~~~~~~~/~~~~~~~

About ten debutantes were being presented the same day as Jane as she waited in an antechamber with Ladies Elaine and Anne. When it was her turn, she was announced by the Lord Chamberlain and then made her walk to the spot before the throne where Queen Charlotte sat. She stopped at the point marked on the floor and made her deep curtsey, holding it for the required time until the Queen gave a little flick of her wrist.

Jane rose out of her curtsey and then began backing away towards the open doors behind her. When the door closed after she passed them, she breathed a big sigh of relief. It was done. She was now an official member of society. "How well you did, Jane," Lady Elaine gushed.

"Thank you, Aunt Elaine; I could not have done this without all the support that I received from yourself and your sisters," Jane replied gratefully.

"I believe that my son is eagerly awaiting my return home," Lady Anne said with a glint in her eye. She could not have chosen a better young lady for her eldest son if she had tried. The Bennet sisters were relatively unknowns among the Ton but that would all change once the announcement of the engagement was seen in the *Times*. There would be much gnashing of teeth as one of the most eligible bachelors was removed from the marriage mart.

"It is a pity the young Lady that Andrew is courting has not been in Town. Her father was thrown from his horse a few months back and it has been a slow recovery, but we received word that he is finally on the mend. The likeness between you and Marie is uncanny," Lady Elaine shared. "They planned to announce their betrothal some months ago, but Marie delayed it until she knew that her father was well once again."

"I look just like my mother; mayhap there is a distant connection there, but Mama never mentioned any family from her side," Jane told her two Aunts.

The carriage arrived before they asked Jane's mother's name. Once they were on the way back to Matlock House discussion of the upcoming expected proposal was the only subject canvassed.

~~~~~~~/~~~~~~~

No sooner had his mother walked through the front door of Darcy House, than Alexander was walking out of it at a brisk pace, just short of running. With his long legs, it was but a minute or two until he was admitted into his Uncle Reggie's house. He was shown into his uncle's study where Mr. Phillips and Sir William awaited him.

"As much as we would like to make you sweat a little, William here needs to get on the road to Kent, so unless you have changed your mind and do not want to ask for our adopted niece's hand you have both our consent and blessing. Just treat her correctly and never harm her!" Phillips admonished.

"Thank you, Mr. Phillips and Sir William, I will treat her as the wonderful lady she is and will spend the rest of my life making her happy," Alexander assured the men.

"Then go to it, young man. I must be off," Sir William informed him after taking Alexander's hand and shaking it.

"Wait here. I will summon Jane," Phillips instructed as he followed Sir William from the study.

It seemed like forever, but a few minutes later Jane glided into the study, leaving the door open a little, looking as beautiful as Alexander had ever seen her. She was smiling a beatific smile and her eyes were showing all the love that she felt for Alexander.

Alexander took Jane's hands in his and dropped to one knee. "Finally, Jane, I am free to ask the question I have been aching to ask for the longest time now. We have declared our love to one another, and I can tell you my love is more ardent today than it was when we first declared our love.

"You are not only the woman I love, Jane Priscilla Bennet, but you are my friend as well. I will spend the rest of my days at your side and not in front of you. In the wedding vows, you vow to obey me, but I will vow the same as we are to be partners for the rest of our days.

"Jane, will you grant my most fervent wish and become my wife? Jane Pricilla Bennet, please marry me." Alexander's eyes were locked on Jane's the whole of his speech and he did not miss the look of absolute pleasure that shone back at him as he completed his proposals.

With gentle pressure, Jane indicated that Alexander should stand. "As we are to be partners, I will not have you kneel before me while I respond," Jane told him lovingly. "I have loved you almost from the first time that I met you at Longbourn when you accompanied William and Uncle George to view Netherfield. There is no other man that I could imagine spending my life with so yes, Alexander Fitzwilliam Darcy, I will marry you and spend the rest of my life loving you," Jane accepted him with glee.

Alexander lowered his head towards Jane and rather than shy away, she tilted her head to indicate her willingness to taste his lips for the first time. When their lips met, the kiss was chaste but they both felt the absolute rectitude of the connection. Their arms wound around each other's waists as they deepened their kisses, both showing the promise of passion to come. They broke apart when there was a knock on the door.

After a moment Phillips entered the study. "Based on the looks I see from both of you I assume that you accepted Alex," Phillips looked at Jane who nodded emphatically while she blushed deeply at almost being discovered kissing her betrothed. "Have you two discussed how long you want your betrothal to be before you marry and where you wish to marry?"

"We have not, Uncle Frank, if it is agreeable to you, could we have this discussion with Alex's parents? I suppose they are waiting for us at Darcy House," Jane requested.

"Jane, I almost forgot," Alexander said as he withdrew the velvet bag from his coat pocket. He took Jane's left hand in his and slipped the ring with its brilliant sapphire onto his fiancée's fourth finger.

"Alex, this is the most gorgeous ring I have ever seen," Jane gushed as the ring sparkled from the sunlight entering the Earl's study from the big window that faced onto the square. Alexander explained who the ring's previous owner was and knowing it was his paternal grandmother's made the ring all the more valuable and special to Jane.

As the three walked into the drawing room, everyone jumped up as soon as they spied the ring on Jane's finger. "Welcome to the family again, Jane," Lord Reggie welcomed her. "You were our adopted niece and now you are to be our niece indeed."

"Please do not have a long betrothal," Annabeth requested, "I cannot wait until Jane, Lizzy, and Mary are my sisters and then Kitty and Lydia will be my cousins!"

"We will do what we can to accommodate your wishes," Alex responded to his youngest sister.

"I could not imagine a better older brother than you Alex," Mary informed him as she hugged Alexander.

"I am very happy to be gaining you and Lizzy as sisters as well Mary," Alexander responded. "And the Phillips girls as cousins. Jane, are you ready to walk to Darcy House to inform my parents?"

"Yes, Alex, I am," Jane replied as she stood to go with Alexander to collect their outerwear.

"May we go with them?" Annabeth requested.

"Let us give them some time with your mother and father alone, Anna; we will see everyone when they come for dinner tonight," Lady Elaine informed her niece.

~~~~~~~/~~~~~~~

"We are so happy to be gaining you as a daughter, Jane," Lady Anne told Jane as she embraced her.

"As I am to be your daughter, Aunt Anne," Jane responded.

"No more Aunt and Uncle, Jane; I would prefer Mother Anne and I think Father George will fit my husband perfectly," Lady Anne requested.

"I echo Anne's words, Jane; we could not be happier. Only a blind man would miss how in love the two of you are. Welcome to the family—as a daughter," George Darcy hugged Jane after his wife had released her embrace.

"Thank you, Father George," Jane replied with pleasure.

"Have you two discussed a wedding date yet?" Lady Anne asked.

"No mother, we have not," Alex replied, "We wanted to discuss it with you first. Neither Jane nor I desire a long betrothal, we have known for a long time, and this is what we both desire," Alexander shared.

"In that case what say you to a month's betrothal? It is not too long, but it will not look rushed either," Lady Anne opined.

"One month is acceptable to me Alex, if you agree," Jane stated.

"I would be happy with tomorrow, but one month it is," Alex agreed.

"Where do you want to marry from, Jane?" Lady Anne asked.

"Now that Longbourn once again truly feels like our home, I want to marry from the estate," Jane decided.

"How does Friday, the sixth day of December, sound to you?" Lady Anne asked as she consulted a calendar. Both agreed it was a fine date.

"I will write to Elliot to start reading the banns at Pemberley," George Darcy told Jane. "Please have your uncle contact Longbourn's rector to do the same."

"As soon as we return to Matlock House, I will request that he send a missive to Mr. Pierce." A few minutes later, the four crossed the square back to Matlock House.

~~~~~~~~/~~~~~~~~

The announcement that dashed the hopes of many a mother and daughter appeared in *the Times of London* the following morning:

> *Mr. George and Lady Anne Darcy are proud to announce the betrothal of their son Alexander Fitzwilliam Darcy to Miss Jane Priscilla Bennet of Longbourn in Hertfordshire.*

As had been predicted, there was much gnashing of teeth and spiteful exclamations while at the same time bemoaning they had not received invitations to the lucky lady's coming out ball the following day.

It would take a few more days for the London broadsheets to reach other parts of the country.

~~~~~~~~/~~~~~~~~

As much as Elizabeth wanted to be at Jane's ball, she knew it was out of the question. She spent the night at Matlock House with the rest of the girls who were not out yet watching the row of carriages that were arriving across the square at Darcy House.

Anne had returned to Rosings that morning after receiving the news that Charlotte had delivered a healthy baby boy, Lewis William de Bourgh, and that mother and babe were both well. The new aunt and her companion had been on the road, not an hour later.

Jane stood in the receiving line between Lady Anne and Hattie Phillips. As much as she wanted her betrothed next to her, it was understood that as it was her coming out ball and not a betrothal ball, it could not be so.

The night went by in a blur. Everyone stopped to bestow

their well wishes for her coming out, but also for her betrothal as they had seen the announcement. The highlight for Jane was dancing three sets with her betrothed. If they had not been told that they could not dance more than three, they would have danced exclusively with one another. Jane led off the first with her Uncle Frank, and then switched to Uncle George for the second dance of the first set.

She danced the second, supper, and final sets with Alex, and no one who saw them together could deny that the couple had made a love match. Although it was Jane's coming out ball, with the Ton waking up to the news of her betrothal to Alexander Darcy, there was a lot of scrutiny of them as a couple. It did not hurt that the betrothal was unequivocally supported by three powerful families that included a peer and a baronet.

By the time Jane collapsed into her bed at Matlock House, it was past five in the morning. She was extremely tired but even more happy. In a month, she would be Jane Darcy.

CHAPTER 9

L ord Cyril De Melville, the Earl of Jersey, was much recovered from his malady and was sitting in the morning parlour in his manor house. He and his family lived on the estate of Broadhurst in Essex. They were a family of five; his oldest and heir, Wesley, Viscount Westmore, was the ripe old age of one and twenty. Next was his daughter, Lady Marie, who was nineteen and who was being courted by Lord Andrew Fitzwilliam, Viscount Hilldale. The baby was Lady Loretta, just turned fifteen. His wife, Lady Sarah, was one of the patronesses of Almack's.

The Earl regretted that his malady of some duration had kept his family from Town. He was sure had Marie and Andrew been more in one another's company, the latter would have made his proposals already. As he was sitting, his ruminations took him to a subject that he thought about more and more as he grew older.

The banishment of his sister, Lady Priscilla, from the family by the late earl, Lord Cyril's father, had hurt both him and his mother to their core. His father had held connections, rank, and fortune above all else and the fact Priscilla had loved James Bennet meant nothing to the old earl. James was a landed gentleman who had some wealth, but that was not nearly enough to satisfy Lord Cyril's father and he had refused his permission when Priscilla was twenty.

As soon as she turned one and twenty, Priscilla left her father's home and married the man she loved. From that day forward, her father banished her from the family and even went as far as to refuse to release her dowry. His father had been furious when he discovered his wife had defied him and gifted Priscilla with the fifteen thousand pounds that had been left under the former countess' control in the marriage settlement. As such, he had no power to stop the money from being transferred to his daughter.

Lord Cyril berated himself as he had many times. Yes, he had made a pledge to his father to never contact his sister again. On her deathbed, his mother had begged him to contact his sister. If she had survived her husband, who she never forgave for separating her from Priscilla, she would have sought her daughter out the very day of his death. But it was not to be. The Countess died some months before a heart ailment claimed her husband.

In grief over losing his wife, yet not willing to get past his pride and admit he had been wrong, before the previous Earl of Jersey died, he had his son reaffirm his oath to not contact his disowned daughter. Always intimidated by the larger-than-life figure of his father, Lord Cyril, still Viscount Westmore, acceded to his father's wishes.

Now more than a decade after his father's death, Lord Cyril was racked with guilt that he had not stood up to his father and had honoured the oath that he took just prior to the previous earl's death. He told himself that his word was his bond. If only he had not made the promise to his father. The truth was that just as he was scared when he made the oath, the same fear stopped him still. He had no idea how his sister would accept him and most of all he feared her reproaching him for his cowardice in failing to stand up to their tyrannical father.

"How are you feeling today, Cyril?" Lady Sarah asked as she entered the parlour with the newly arrived broadsheets from London.

"Much better, Sarah. It seems for once that our doctor is correct; I should be able to return to Town by next year for the next session of the Lords. Anything interesting from London?" he asked with mild interest.

"Actually, there is. Andrew's cousin Alexander Darcy is betrothed." The Earl did not know why his wife seemed hesitant to say more.

"Do we know the girl?" he asked, seeing the uncomfortable look his wife was giving him.

"We may not know her, but there is a chance you know her mother," Lady Sarah told her husband.

"What is her name Sarah?" Lord Cyril demanded.

"Jane Priscilla Bennet," she returned. Her husband's eyes flew open in shock.

All the while dreading the answer, he asked, "Does it mention her parents?"

"It does not. It just says she is from the estate of Longbourn in Hertfordshire," Lady Sarah informed her husband.

"After my father refused James Bennet, there was no discussion of him in the home and I did not meet him as he had courted Priscilla while I was at Cambridge. To my shame, I do not know where they live. It could be a coincidence, or this Miss Bennet could be our niece. If only I had the strength of character to stand up to my father!" Lord Cyril lamented.

"It is never too late, Cyril; I am sure that your sister would welcome it if you were to reach out to her. It may be hard for you because of the oath to your father, but I made no such oath. Will you permit me to write to Longbourn and enquire about her parents?" Lady Sarah suggested.

"So much time has passed, and I am much ashamed for not reaching out to my sister the day my father died as my mother would have. Let me consider this please, Sarah," Lord Cyril requested.

~~~~~~~/~~~~~~~

"HOW CAN THIS BE!" Miss Caroline Bingley yelled as she read the only section that she ever read—the social announcements in the London broadsheet.

"What has you vexed this time, sister?" Mrs. Louisa Hurst asked her troublesome sister. If only she had not allowed Charles to convince her to keep Caroline with them while he was in Town.

"Mr. Alexander Darcy is betrothed!" Miss Bingley spat.

"How could the betrothal of a man who does not know that you exist impact you in any way Caroline?" Mrs. Hurst asked the salient question.

"Do not be so obtuse, Louisa! If Charles had done his duty to me and introduced me to the Darcys, it would be *me* betrothed to the heir of Pemberley now, not some miss I have never heard of with no accomplishments or dowry," Miss Bingley stated in her grating voice.

"Caroline, you are the one who is obtuse," Mrs. Hurst told her outraged sister as she picked up the papers that had been tossed aside in anger. "What makes you think even had the Darcys *wanted* to meet you that Mr. Darcy would have been interested in a tradesman's daughter? Also, there is not a word about the lady's dowry or accomplishments. As I am sure you know no more of Miss Jane Bennet than I do, you have no basis to make your wild assertions. At the very least she is a gentleman's daughter, something you are not!"

"If I had met him, he would have chosen me!" Miss Bingley screeched, ignoring everything that her sister has just said.

"Do you know why you have never met the Darcys, Caroline?" Mrs. Hurst said soothingly.

"Of course I do. Charles refuses his duty to me!" she returned.

"That is not it, Caroline. Charles will not agree to introduce you as you have no clue how to behave as a young lady should. Your pretentions, airs, and graces, your thinking that you are far above your actual status, would make you ridiculous in the eyes of the Ton and your ruin would be felt by Charles and even myself as well," Mrs. Hurst tried to explain even though she was sure that her sister was not able to hear anything that she did not want to hear.

Miss Bingley ignored every word that her sister said because as Mrs. Hurst correctly surmised, it did not fit with what Caroline Bingley believed. "If the heir is not available, then I will have to settle for the spare; you never know what will befall the older brother," Miss Bingley said maniacally.

'*I need to write to Charles. Caroline's delusions are becoming more and more detached from reality,*' Mrs. Hurst told herself. "It has been a trying morning, sister; would you not like to go rest for a little while?" she suggested aloud.

Without answering, Miss Bingley stood and made her way to her chambers. She needed peace and quiet to plot her next strategy. She would show her brother and sister that she too can become a leading member of the *Haut Bon Ton*!

~~~~~~~/~~~~~~~

"That is not fair!" Wickham whined as he read the London papers that announced the betrothal of Alexander Darcy, the man he envied more than any other.

"What is not fair?" Collins asked.

"The son of the family I told you about, that are jealous of me and stole my rightful inheritance," Wickham replied bitterly.

"What about him?" Collins could not understand what his friend was on about again.

"He is betrothed, most likely to some rich woman with a huge dowry, as if the Darcys needed more money!" the envious man retorted.

"Who is his betrothed?" Collins wanted to know.

"Miss Jane Priscilla Bennet of Longbourn in Hertfordshire," Wickham read off the name.

"Longbourn in Hertfordshire!" Collins exclaimed.

"That is what is written," Wickham returned, somewhat confused by the stupid man's reactions.

"Longbourn will be my inheritance after the current master meets his maker. I thought they were a family of no consequence, but they must be wealthy for one of their daughters to make such a match," Collins opined.

"Have you ever met them?" Wickham asked as he started to think of ways to exploit the information.

"No there was a break between my father and the current master, so we do not know each other!" Collins launched into a long-winded explanation of how his dearly departed father was accused of compromising Longbourn's then master's daughter, which Collins's father always denied while forbidding him to ask his mother about the subject.

"That means the estate you will inherit is far more valuable than you suspected," Wickham stated as the avarice in him took over.

"It would seem so," Collins agreed.

"Can you not approach them now?" Wickham probed.

"No. According to the entail, until the present master expires, I have no rights there. Very unfair is it not?" Collins shared.

Wickham was not sure how he would be able to capitalise on this information yet, but he was confident that it would come to him soon enough. Wickham dreamed about separating himself from the hapless clergyman, but nothing better had presented itself yet, so he would have to stick it out. With the knowledge of Collins's inheritance, he would stay where he was and suffer the fool's inanity for as long as needed until he knew how to profit from the situation.

~~~~~~~/~~~~~~~

Thomas Bennet picked up the London papers as his charges were working on their sums quietly. It was then that he saw the announcement of Jane Bennet's betrothal to a Darcy, a family that he knew had almost unlimited resources.

'*Why would a family like that allow their son to attach himself to one with only two thousand pounds to her name?*' he asked himself. Then it hit him! "*They would not! Phillips and that Gardiner man had lied to him! There must be far more dowry than he had been informed! That money should be his!*' Bennet ignored the fact that Phillips had told him regardless of the amount, the girls' dowries were protected and could not be accessed. "*How dare James hide money from me! I will get my due and make them pay!*" Bennet promised himself.

He was not sure how yet, but he would exact his revenge through another. His brother had denied him part of his father's wealth and Bennet had made him pay with his life. He would not risk debtor's prison by returning to Meryton, or Hertfordshire for that matter. Here he was working as a tutor to spoiled boys when he had no need! If only he had known!

Not once in his ruminations of revenge and resentment did he spare a thought for either the wife he had so callously murdered or the daughters he and his late wife had abandoned without a thought. Bennet relied on his intelligence—which he believed was much greater than reality would suggest—to come up with a plan. He ignored the fact he had yet to decide on a creditable plan, and it was approaching two years since his eviction from Longbourn.

~~~~~~~/~~~~~~~

The day after Bingley arrived in Scarborough, his older sister requested a private talk. Bingley was sure the subject would be their younger sister and her behaviour. His expectations were not disappointed.

"What are we to do with her?" Bingley asked in exasperation. "She refuses to listen to any counsel except her own. Do you believe she is a danger to others?"

"I pray not, Charles, but I cannot say that with certainty. If only our parents had not indulged her every whim. They spoilt her, and now we have to live with the consequences," Mrs. Hurst opined.

"Is it time to set her up in her own establishment?" Bingley asked.

"We may have reached that point. Harold and I spoke. We will not have her with us any longer and I know that you will not be able to see your friends as long as Caroline is with you," Mrs. Hurst said resignedly.

"Please have her summoned, Louisa," Bingley requested.

Some fifteen minutes later, Miss Bingley swept into the study in an awful burnt orange creation. "Have you returned to do your duty to me, Charles?" Miss Bingley asked condescendingly.

"In a manner of speaking," Bingley returned cryptically.

"When do we leave for me to meet the Darcys' second son? As the older one is betrothed, I will have to settle for him," Miss Bingley sniffed.

"Have you lost your senses, Caroline! William Darcy knows all about you, and he has *no desire* to ever meet you, never mind anything beyond that. Besides, if I am not mistaken, he has already selected the lady who will be his wife one day." Bingley erred in sharing that opinion with his sister whose shade of red deepened the more he spoke and reached a purple hue with his last statement.

"That is not to be borne!" Miss Bingley screeched in her shrewish voice. "What hussy has entrapped the man that is to be mine. Your inaction lost me the heir, but I *will* have his brother!"

"And how will you achieve your aim, Caroline?" her sister asked with scorn.

"Charles will…" she started to respond and only achieved two words before her brother interjected.

"There are *no* circumstances under which I will inflict you on my friends! I was going to set you up in your own establishment as neither I nor Louisa can abide you being with us. I rather think that I will need to escort you to Bedlam. If I hear one more word on this subject from you, you will be committed to that institution for the rest of your days!" Bingley had finally reached the limit with his younger sister.

"I-I was only joking Charles. If you think that an establishment is best for me, I will accept it quietly," Miss Bingley pleaded. Bingley wanted to believe her more than he actually did, knowing that consigning her to Bedlam would be a final step.

"You will have four to five hundred a year in the form of interest on your dowry. You will have to pay your own bills. If you keep overspending as you have, I *will not* cover your overages. Do you agree to these terms?" Bingley demanded.

Miss Bingley nodded. '*I will show them! They are jealous of me! I will marry a Darcy!*' the delusional woman told herself.

~~~~~~~/~~~~~~~

A fortnight after the Earl of Jersey found out about the betrothal of Miss Jane Bennet to the Darcy heir, he asked his wife to attend him. "For now, I have decided to request that you do not write to the Bennets. When we see Andrew and the Fitzwilliams again next year, we will make some discreet enquiries. I do not want to open us to ridicule if it is not Priscilla's family," Lord Cyril informed his wife.

Lady Sarah honoured her husband's wishes but felt sorry for him, as he was allowing his pride to stand in the way of healing a breach that was long overdue for repair. She decided writing to her friends, Ladies Anne and Elaine, with some questions could not hurt. It was not writing to Longbourn as her husband asked her not to after all.

~~~~~~~/~~~~~~~

Bennet was so disturbed by reading about Miss Jane Bennet's betrothal and the assumptions he made of being cheated out of the money that was his due, that he took to drinking heavily once more. Since he had been on the estate, he had held himself under good regulation, but all of that slipped as he stewed over his perceived wrongs.

His drinking became obvious as he was arriving for lessons later than their scheduled start time. At first, it was not by much, but it soon came to the notice of the estate's master as his boys' governess informed him about the situation. Bennet was summoned into the master's study. When he arrived, he was already in his cups.

"Bennet you are fired, I want you to pack and get..." the man was cut off as Bennet picked up a paperweight on the master's desk and hefted it at him. It caught him with a glancing blow; it was not fatal but enough to knock the man out.

Luckily for Bennet, there had not been much noise. He had the presence of mind to take the strongbox from the desk drawer. The box contained one thousand pounds that he folded and placed in his pocket. Bennet closed the study door and told the butler as he left the house that the master had asked not to be disturbed. He retrieved the money that was left in his room and then made his way to the stables.

The grooms were used to him borrowing a horse, so they did not remark when he asked for a strong horse to be saddled and then rode towards the estate's gates. By the time the master regained consciousness and realised that he had been robbed, Bennet was long gone.

CHAPTER 10

Ladies Elaine and Anne received letters from their mutual friend the Countess of Jersey, but as they were planning the betrothal ball for Jane and Alexander to be held at Matlock House on the six and twentieth day of November, they had little time for anything else. The letter to each was placed in a stack of the non-emergency post to be read after the wedding. The day after the ball the families would all depart for London and decamp to Meryton.

The ball was attended by many more members of the Ton than had been invited to Jane's coming out and had been enjoyed by all. Lady Catherine, Sir Lewis, and Anne de Bourgh arrived in Town a few days before the ball. Little Lewis the second was doing very well, as was Charlotte, as evidenced by the proud grandparent's attendance at the ball.

As she had at her coming out ball, Jane danced three sets with her betrothed, except this time she danced the opening set with him rather than the second set. No matter how tired they all were, their departure from London the day following the ball was at the scheduled time.

A few days after arriving home from Town, Elizabeth and Jane sat in their shared bedchamber at Longbourn. "Jane, you will be a married woman in a few days!" Elizabeth cried. "I will miss you every day."

"We will stop here after our wedding trip, Lizzy, Alex promised me that the next time we go to Seaview Cottage you and Mary will be with us," Jane reassured her younger sister. Since their parents and Jamie had been ripped away from them, the three sisters had never not slept in the same home even for a single night. Jane had foregone inviting one of her sisters along on her wedding trip. Unlike arranged marriages where the practice was much more prevalent, she and Alex loved one another deeply.

"It will be an exceedingly long month until we see you again, Janie, but do not allow my maudlin thoughts to distract from the joyous occasion. I am genuinely happy for you and Alex; I was being selfish thinking about how much I will miss you. You will be happy, Jane; Alex is one of the best men that I know," Elizabeth stated as she hugged her older sister.

"Unfortunately, it is the way of the world for our gender. We grow up and then leave our childhood homes to cleave ourselves to our husbands. One day it will be your turn, Lizzy and then Mary too will have a new family. Regardless of how far we live from one another, the bonds of sisterhood between us are and always will be unbreakable," Jane stated emphatically.

The two talked well into the night and only fell asleep after midnight.

~~~~~~~/~~~~~~~

Convinced he had killed his former employer, Bennet had ridden hard, this time not halting until he was in Wiltshire. He had remained at an inn in the shire for three days, allowing *his* horse to be well rested, but mainly so he could drink and indulge in some games of chance. He did not win, but neither did he lose much either. As the wins and losses had almost balanced out, he was less than five pounds the poorer when he departed for Somerset.

He arrived in Clevedon, Somerset, six days after his escape. It was a small coastal town in the north of the county and relatively new, founded only ten years earlier. It was being touted as a resort with more visitors than residents at any given time, so new people were rarely noted.

As much as he hated to credit his deceased wife with anything, he followed her example and used some of his stolen funds to pay the lease on a cottage for a year. In addition, he left funds with the landlord to pay the salaries of a maid and man of all work as well as a part time cook for the full year.

In a rare moment of forethought, he pried a floorboard under his bed loose and secreted four hundred pounds in his hiding place to make sure that he would have more than enough money to live on. What Bennet did not know was that he had in fact not killed his former employer and unlike the murder of Fanny, now there was a victim who reported the crime and the perpetrator.

~~~~~~~/~~~~~~~

The night before the wedding, Hattie Phillips, Maddie Gardiner, and Lady Lucas asked Elizabeth to allow them to talk to Jane in private. "As you know, you will be a married woman on the morrow and after the wedding follows the wedding night and the marriage bed," Hattie Phillips opened.

"Our advice to you is simple, never be shy to tell your husband what pleases you and let him know that you want to know what pleases him. As long as it is done in privacy, nothing that you both desire and consent to is wrong," Maddie Gardiner followed.

"You are making a love match, Jane, so never allow anyone to convince you that a woman is not supposed to take pleasure in the marriage act or that she has improper lust. Especially when there is love, never be ashamed of taking as much pleasure as your husband," Lady Lucas added.

"There will be some pain the first time you join with your husband, but it will not be too bad. You can expect a little blood, but there is nothing to be concerned about as it is a normal part of losing your maidenhood. Given how besotted your Alexander is, if you need time when that final barrier is breached, indicate that and I am positive that he will give you as much time as you need before continuing," Hattie Phillips said in summation.

"Do you have any questions, Jane?" Maddie Gardiner asked.

"No thank you, Aunts, I think that you have answered any

questions that I may have had," Jane replied, not being able to stop the blush that suffused her face.

The three ladies kissed Jane goodnight and departed and were replaced by Elizabeth. "Well, did our aunts give you the *talk*?" Jane nodded. "Will you not tell me what they told you?" Elizabeth asked in anticipation.

"No Lizzy, it is not for your ears yet. You will learn what you need to know before your wedding as I did tonight," Jane returned with resolve.

"Well, I just have to wait until then," Elizabeth huffed.

The two sisters prepared for the night for the last time they would be sharing the bedchamber as maiden sisters. After brushing each other's tresses, they climbed into bed. Elizabeth was asleep relatively soon, but it took Jane a few hours as she found it hard to sleep with the excitement of marrying the man she loved above all in not too many hours.

~~~~~~~/~~~~~~~

George Darcy had taught his sons that contrary to the behaviour deemed acceptable by members of the Ton that if they demanded their wives come to them pure, then they needed to be pure as well. He had drummed into his sons' heads that the vows said before God and man on the day of their marriages were meant to be upheld and not treated more like suggestions as many in the Ton did.

He had passed on his disgust of the practice that many outside of their family partook in of keeping a mistress. Thankfully, it was eschewed by the Fitzwilliams and de Bourghs as well. It was the reason so much emphasis had been put on making love matches, and neither George nor Lady Anne Darcy would ever consider an arranged marriage for any of their offspring.

At Netherfield Park, the night before his wedding, George Darcy had the talk with his son Alexander and told him where he could find reference books on the subject at either Darcy House, where the couple would spend an overnight on their way to Seaview Cottage, or at Pemberley. He made sure Alexander understood his wife deserved to take as much pleasure from the marriage act as he did and to always be solicitous of Jane's needs and desires.

"There is no doubt in my mind that you have in Jane the lady that is your perfect mate, my son. Your mother and I could not be prouder of you," George Darcy told his son in summation, his voice thick with emotion.

"That is something I have not doubted for a long time, Father. I want to thank you and mother for being such good parents to me--to all of us," Alexander hugged his father who returned the hug in full measure.

Darcy wished his son well on the morrow and then departed to join his wife in their chambers. Like Jane three miles away, it took Alexander a few hours to finally find sleep.

~~~~~~~/~~~~~~~

Caroline Bingley was not pleased with her establishment. It was a set of apartments a few miles from her brother's home. It had only two bedchambers, a small parlour, and an even smaller dining parlour. She hated her new companion, Mrs. Isabelle Chandler, with a passion. However, she was fully aware she needed to make her brother and sister believe she had changed and was happy with her life.

How she was going to live without Charles covering her overspending was an open question for which she did not have an answer. She was determined to carry out her ruse for as long as was needed for her brother and sister to drop their guard. Once they relaxed, she would find a way to meet William Darcy and if needed compromise him. Once she was married, she would have to find a way to make sure some unfortunate accident befell his older brother.

What Miss Bingley was not aware of was that all three of her servants, as well as Mrs. Chandler, reported to her brother and regardless of whether he relaxed, he would be kept abreast of his sister's machinations. Given how much Caroline disdained servants, she would not be cautious around them as they were invisible to her.

~~~~~~~/~~~~~~~

The morning of her wedding, Miss Jane Bennet awoke with the sunrise even though she had fallen asleep past midnight. She was too excited to be tired as it was the last day she would bear the name Bennet.

Jane loved her family name; she just loved her Alex more. She turned and patted the bed next to her and was not surprised Lizzy was no longer next to her. Given her younger sister's penchant for early morning rambles, even on this day, it was not unexpected. Jane hoped her sister and best friend would be back in time to assist her. She had her lady's maid, but on her wedding day, she wanted Lizzy at her side as she prepared to dress in her childhood chambers for the last time before she became a Darcy.

Elizabeth, knowing Jane would want her to be with her as she prepared for her big day, departed the manor house a half hour before sunrise. As was her wont, she walked through the kitchen breathing in the welcoming aromas of baking bread. As she passed the cook, Elizabeth lifted two warm muffins from the tray on the table that held the cooling items. Cook gave her the gimlet eye as she always did, though not truly objecting to the young miss taking some of the baked items. In fact, the cook always made sure that there were one or two more than needed so she would never have to refuse Miss Elizabeth. The wide smile that accompanied the look of mock censure was a dead giveaway.

Given the time constraints that morning Elizabeth had asked Paul in the stable to saddle Nellie for her. The groom was well aware that when she rode in the early morning Miss Elizabeth sat astride, given the chance of being seen was exceptionally low. Elizabeth mounted Nellie and pointed the mare towards Oakham Mount.

Just before she arrived at the base of the mount, Elizabeth was horrified to see William Darcy dismounting from his stallion, Zeus. Before she could turn away, his stallion betrayed her as he lifted his head in her direction and whinnied. William, who usually looked pleased to see Elizabeth, scowled at her.

"Riding in that fashion is indecent!" William stared at Elizabeth with disapproval clearly written on his countenance.

"You ride this way!" Elizabeth returned as she dismounted. Already embarrassed to be exposed, her courage rose as she was not ready to allow William to lecture her on decorum.

"I am a man! Women are not permitted to ride in that fashion," he insisted.

"Says who?"

"I...society, everyone!"

"Is there a law against my riding in any fashion that I choose?" Elizabeth demanded.

"No, it is a rule of society," William was angry. Did she not know he was worried about her and her reputation? Did she not care about those things?

"Do you follow all rules that the society dictates, Master Darcy?" came the question with a formal address that just upset him more.

"No! Some of society's rules are nonsensical!"

"But I should follow them all even if they are, as you say, *nonsensical*? You hypocrite you! What, I should follow them because I am a weak-minded woman," Elizabeth challenged William as she stood inches away from him, her hands on her hips.

"I...er...that is to say..."

"What *Master* Darcy? What is it you are trying to mumble?"

Darcy recognised how much he had succeeded in raising Elizabeth's ire. Her eyes, one of her most attractive features among many manifest attractions, were flashing as her ire built at his officiousness.

He was about to apologise when she turned on her heel, walked to the mare, placed her foot in the stirrup and with one fluid movement was in the saddle. She pulled Nellie's reins, wheeling her around and almost hitting William, and broke into a gallop as she headed back towards Longbourn. The last thing that William heard from the angry young lady was "Insufferable man!" William knew he would need to make his apologies at his first opportunity; he did not want the young lady he loved angry with him.

Paul was concerned when Miss Elizabeth returned far earlier than he expected her. "Is everything well with Nellie, Miss?" he asked with concern. He could see nothing obvious on the mare.

"All is well with Nellie, thank you, Paul," Elizabeth informed the groom. "I encountered a very pig headed and interfering animal and that cut my enjoyment short!" she said with asperity. "Nothing to do with you or Nellie, Paul, I promise," Elizabeth assured the young groom who had looked concerned. To highlight her point, she presented Paul with the now cool but very fresh muffins that had been wrapped in a serviette in her pocket.

~~~~~~~/~~~~~~~

When William returned to Netherfield and after changing, he entered Alexander's suite to see if he could be of service to his older brother on the morning of his wedding. Alexander immediately saw that his brother was discomposed. "William, what has upset you?"

"Nothing of consequence, Alex. It is your wedding day, and I am here to support you, not burden you with my problems—if there are problems," William tried to obfuscate.

"William, it will help me to think of something else, so I stop counting the seconds until I see Jane walk towards me in the church," Alexander insisted.

After a little more prodding William shared the story with his brother. Alexander's first reaction was a loud guffaw. "William, how many years have you known Lizzy?" Alexander asked when he was done laughing at his chagrined brother—for the moment.

"Almost four years," William replied.

"In that time, how has Lizzy reacted when she is both embarrassed and feels herself lectured to?" Alexander pointed out.

"In a similar fashion as she did earlier today," William

owned.

"So you need to...?" Alexander prompted.

"Apologise profusely!" William said softly.

"Yes, brother, and do not allow her time to stew. Jane told me that once Elizabeth feels slighted or wronged by someone it can take a long time before she forgives. If you are dressed, ride to Longbourn now and make your amends," Alexander advised.

"What if I see Jane before she enters the church?" William tried to procrastinate.

"It is not *you* that she is marrying at ten, William, so I think that you will be safe," Alexander ribbed his brother.

"Will you inform our parents..."

"Inform us of what," George Darcy asked as he, Lady Anne, and his daughters entered Alexander's chambers.

"William put his foot in his mouth with our Lizzy and he needs to go beg her forgiveness," Alexander relayed with glee. A thoroughly embarrassed William was soon on Zeus making the three-mile ride.

~~~~~~~/~~~~~~~

"Lizzy, what vexes you so?" Jane asked her still fuming sister.

"It is your wedding day Jane, I am sorry you noticed my pique," Elizabeth responded with contrition.

"You do not hide your emotions well, sister of mine," Jane pointed out.

Elizabeth gave in and told Jane what had happened with her aborted trip to watch the sunrise from Oakham Mount. "Oh Lizzy, I am sure that he was as embarrassed as you were! Have you not noticed before that William is wont to blurt out things he does not mean when he is uncomfortable?"

"I suppose you are correct..." the sisters were interrupted by Mrs. Hill informing them that Master William Darcy was in the drawing room requesting to speak to Miss Elizabeth. "Tell him I am too bu..."

"Do not complete that sentence, Elizabeth Rose Bennet! I

love you, Lizzy, but you are far too stubborn for your own good at times," Jane interjected. "Please inform William that Lizzy will be there momentarily."

"That was very high-handed, Jane," Elizabeth objected after Mrs. Hill had withdrawn.

"It is my wedding day, Lizzy, and you will not upset the bride before her wedding, will you?" Jane trumped her sister's objections.

With a harrumph, Elizabeth started down the stairs with as much of her bruised dignity as she could muster. "Lizzy, Miss Elizabeth, I am here to apologise for my abominable behaviour. I was surprised to see you and the way you were riding. However, that does not excuse the condescending manner in which I spoke to you," William apologised sincerely.

"You have my forgiveness, William. My behaviour was not above reproach either. For that, I am terribly sorry. I was embarrassed and took it out on you," Elizabeth returned. "I hope that you can forgive me for my sharp and impertinent tongue."

"You have nothing to apologise for Lizzy, but you must know that I would never deny you anything that you requested were it in my power to grant it," William stated as he took Elizabeth's hand and slowly kissed the inside of each of her wrists. Elizabeth blushed profusely. William was incredibly pleased to notice it as to him it signalled that she was not indifferent to him.

~~~~~~~/~~~~~~~

Although Jane would be married from Longbourn's church, the wedding breakfast was being held at Netherfield as that estate's ball room was large enough to accommodate all the expected guests. When Jane walked the short distance to the church, she did not miss the open landau with the four matched white horses waiting near the church's main doors.

That would be the first vehicle in which she would ride after she became Mrs. Alexander Fitzwilliam Darcy. Jane was holding Uncle Frank's arm, as he had the honour of giving her away, while Elizabeth followed closely behind, holding the gown's train off the ground. When they arrived in the vestibule the doors leading into the church were closed. One of the deacons had been on the lookout for the bride and had closed the doors before she arrived.

Annabeth and Lydia, although a little older than the average flower girls, were waiting for them, each with a basket of rose petals. Alexander, who was standing right below the altar, did not miss the opening of the doors as Annabeth and Lydia entered. As the doors closed behind them, the two dropped rose petals behind them.

Next, the doors opened, and Elizabeth started down the aisle. William, who was standing up for his brother, needed the groom to elbow his ribs to close his mouth and stop staring at Elizabeth. With the halo of light behind her, she looked like a dark-haired angel.

Finally, Mr. Pierce, the relatively young parson, gave the signal for the congregants to rise as the vestibule doors swung open. Jane was a vision on her Uncle Frank's arm as they walked stately up the aisle. Now it was William's turn to nudge his brother into action as Mr. Phillips stopped and waited for the mesmerized groom to approach and have his bride's hand placed on his arm.

Lady Anne had to give her daughters a stern look to stifle the giggles that almost escaped their lips, knowing if they allowed their amusement to escape in audible form, they would more than likely set Kitty and Lydia off as well. The look did its job and both girls bit their lips and brought themselves under regulation.

Once Alexander was woken from his stupor, he did a creditable job for the rest of the ceremony. With the vows bespoken, Mr. Piece intoned the final prayers:

"Those whom God hath joined together let no man put asunder.

"Forasmuch as *Alexander* and *Jane* have consented together in holy wedlock and have witnessed the same before God and this company, and thereto have given and pledged their troth each to the other and have declared the same by giving and receiving a Ring, and by joining hands; I pronounce that they be Man and Wife together, In the Name of the Father, the Son, and the Holy Ghost. Amen.

"God the Father, God the Son, God the Holy Ghost, bless, preserve, and keep you; the Lord mercifully with his favour look upon you, and fill you with all spiritual benediction and grace; that ye may so live together in this life, that in the world to come ye may have life everlasting. *Amen.*"

With a returned "Amen" from the congregation it was done, except for the registry. Jane and Alexander followed Mr. Pierce into the vestry and signed the register. Mr. Pierce offered his well wishes and then left the couple alone as he exited a door that led to the rectory.

"Mrs. Darcy! How well that sounds to me, my beloved Jane. You have made me the happiest of men today, my wife," Alexander said as he pulled his bride to him and kissed her soundly.

"Oh Mr. Darcy," Jane needed some air after the deep and passionate kiss they had just shared. "Did I give my permission for you to cease kissing me?" Jane asked saucily as she pulled his head to hers. It was almost ten minutes later when the couple exited the vestry to the amused and knowing looks of their family.

"Why are my sister's lips so swollen?" Annabeth asked in her innocence.

"You will know the answer to that many, many years from now, Sprite," her father responded.

After many hugs and kisses, including an especially long one from Lady Catherine, the rest of the family boarded their carriages. Ever since Elizabeth had set Anne on the road to recovery, the Bennet sisters, and Elizabeth especially, could do no wrong in the lady's eyes, an opinion held by Sir Lewis as well.

Five minutes after the last family conveyance departed Longbourn church, the newlywed Darcys followed them in their open landau. Alexander had a bag full of coins that he and Jane tossed to the tenants and their children that had lined Long-bourn church's drive.

~~~~~~~/~~~~~~~

The wedding breakfast was a blur for Jane and Alexander. They made sure they personally spoke to each of their guests and endured much inane conversation. Thanks to Lady Anne's insistence, they sat for a full quarter of an hour and had something to drink and eat.

"Lizzy," Jane called her sister quietly, "Would you accompany me to the chambers so that I may change out of my wedding gown?"

"Of course, I will help you, Janie. Is it time for you to depart already?" Elizabeth asked softly as they ascended the stairs.

"It is Lizzy. We have a four-hour journey ahead of us until we reach Darcy House, and neither of us desire to leave too late," Jane replied.

"It will not be the same without you, Jane," Elizabeth told her sister as she undid the tiny pearl buttons that went down the back of the gown.

"As we discussed, Lizzy, it is the way of the world. You will still have Mary and the Phillips with you. Do not forget that Gigi and Anna, along with my parents-in-law, will be here until after Twelfth Night. You and Mary will accompany them to Town in January, and we will see each other at Darcy House when Alex and I return from our honeymoon," Jane laid out.

"All of that is known to me, so ignore me, Jane; I am just being silly," Elizabeth stated.

"It is not silly, Lizzy. We three Bennet sisters have not been parted one from another since the time that Mama, Papa, and Jamie were murdered until this very night. We have said this to one another before, but it bears repeating. It is a change for all of us, one that will take some time to get used to, but we will overcome this and move forward with the love and support of those around us. It is how we survived after they went to God; it is how we will get through this as well. Just think, you have all of those who helped you before, and a good number of others." Jane held Elizabeth and rocked her, understanding that this separation brought back memories of losing their parents for her younger sister all over again.

Elizabeth had a good cry and then she felt a lot better. "All will be well, now you go and have the best wedding trip. I love you, Janie," Elizabeth told her sister as she hugged her tightly.

After Elizabeth's eyes were sufficiently dry and evidence of her tears wiped away, the two older Bennet sisters descended the stairs and joined the waiting family members. There were many hugs and kisses and even a few tears. The newlyweds boarded the coach with the last wave to their family. The door was closed, Alexander rapped on the ceiling, and they were off, man and wife to begin their life together.

CHAPTER 11

Thomas Bennet had been in Clevedon for a little over a year when he overheard two men talking about his ex-employer. He decided to listen in; mayhap he would hear who took over from the man as heir, as Bennet knew that the sons were far from coming of age.

"Did you hear what happened to Eagleton of Bliss Hill just outside of Southampton?" the one talker asked the other.

"Has he recovered fully?" the second man asked.

"Yes, it was a long road to recovery. He did not remember what happened to him, until recently."

'He's alive and he has recovered all of his faculties!' an extremely nervous Bennet told himself.

"What befell him?"

"He had hired a tutor for his sons, a Thomas Bennet, who used to teach at Oxford. He felt that with the man's breadth of knowledge, he did not need to check his characters. Eagleton called him to account for tardiness and being in his cups when the man was supposed to be teaching the boys. The man picked up a heavy ornament from the desk and threw it at Eagleton. Evidently, he rifled through the strongbox in the desk and stole one thousand pounds or thereabouts. If that was not bad enough, he stole a horse when he made his escape," the first man recited the story as he knew it.

"Let us hope that the bastard hangs for what he did," the second stated emphatically.

"Bow Street is on the job. Eagleton does not care about the cost; he wants this Bennet caught and brought to justice."

Bennet did not wait to hear more. He hied to his cottage and removed the four hundred pounds from under the floor board. His next stop was the stables, where *his* horse was housed. "I would like to swap my horse for a more docile beast," Bennet told the stable manager as calmly as he could.

"That there be some fine 'orseflesh. Be you sure, Sir?" the bewildered man asked. "It would be a swap; I will not pay extra for 'im."

"Good, make sure the one you give me has tack and you may keep mine. It was made specially for him, so I need a new set," Bennet prevaricated.

Not long after, with his hat pulled low over his eyes, Thomas Bennet was on the nag that he had received in return. The horse he had stolen was far superior to the one he was riding, but he needed to shed anything that tied him to Eagleton and Bliss Hill. That included his name. In what he felt was a twist of irony, he took his brother's first name and the family name of the interfering man that helped steal his estate.

When he arrived at the inn that evening, Mr. James Gardiner was welcomed and given a room for the night. The former Thomas Bennet took a circuitous route in case anyone saw him leave Clevedon. He struck north and then turned west in Hampshire. He turned south again and eventually crossed the border into Dorset. He lingered in a few towns in the county he was in for a day or two, always careful to mention that he was for London. After the first four days of travel, the fugitive had grown tired of all the stops that he needed to make because of the old nag. He had passed a farm and negotiated a price for a gelding. The nag was thrown in for free.

It took a fortnight of riding thither and yon. He eventually reached the town of Croyde in Devon. He rented a room in a boarding house run by a widow and for the first few weeks he very much kept to himself. Bennet was very frustrated that he was no closer to divining a plot to avenge himself on those that stole his estate when one night at the local tavern he overheard a conversation that changed everything for him.

"Wickham, it does no good telling me to go claim my estate in Hertfordshire. I have shown you the entailment documents. Until my cousin Bennet is no longer of this world, I have no rights," the one man told the one he called Wickham with exasperation.

'Could this be? Has my luck turned and I have happened upon the presumptive heir to Longbourn?' The former Thomas Bennet was salivating at the possibilities that ran through his mind.

"Come now Collins, there must be a way!" the one called Wickham exclaimed. "One of them is married to a Darcy, they would have no need for some insignificant estate called Longriver!"

"Longbourn, not Longriver," the man dressed in clerical garb answered.

'I need to think on how to best exploit this information,' Bennet told himself as he left the public house for his room.

~~~~~~~~/~~~~~~~~

After some years of nothing, *the Spaniard's* man contacted Gardiner. He told him he had the two men who had assisted with the murder of the three people in Hertfordshire more than four years ago. Gardiner handed over the agreed price of one thousand pounds and the two bound and gagged, very scared men, looking rather worse for wear, were unceremoniously deposited on his warehouse floor.

Gardiner had one of his footmen remove the gag from one of the two shaking men. "What you tell me next will determine if you are transported or you swing. Do you understand me?" The miscreant nodded his head, one of his eyes swollen shut and numerous contusions visible on his person. "Who hired you to run the Bennet's carriage off the road in '02?" Gardiner demanded.

"It was Tom, guv'nor. Tom Bennet. 'im and 'is missus paid us to 'elp 'im," the man managed.

"Smith, summon the head runner; he needs to hear this from their mouths," Gardiner instructed. He nodded to one of his other men who re-gagged the criminal.

Two hours later, Mr. Johns, the head runner, was sitting across from Gardiner as the two men nursed steaming cups of coffee. "It seems that this Thomas Bennet was not satisfied to murder his brother and family," Johns stated as he took another sip of the black liquid.

"Who else did he murder?" Gardiner asked.

Johns told him about the attempted murder and the theft of Mr. Eagleton near Southampton. "One of my men found that he and the wife had lived in East Meon, Hampshire. It seems after you and your friend evicted him from the estate, they lived there for more than a year, until he disappeared, and she was kicked to death. He must have found out that she was cuckolding him. There are no witnesses to the murder, but given his flight, there is no doubt that he murdered the wife."

"I will cry no tears for the wife, she was in on the plan that led to the death of three people," Gardiner stated with steel in his voice.

"It was from there that he went to Southampton and gained employment at Bliss Hill. So far, we traced him to Clevedon in Somerset. We are not sure why he ran from there as he seemed to keep to himself. My guess is that he discovered by some means that Mr. Eagleton was not dead. He had no memory for a long time after the attack but recovered his memories some months ago after knocking his head hard once again," Johns related.

"Is there no trail from Clevedon?" Gardiner asked hopefully.

"We know he exchanged the stolen horse for another to attempt to hide himself as much as possible. He told the man at the stables that he was for London, so we may assume that is the only location that he will not be in. Given his travels towards the south each time, I would guess that he has done the same now," Johns opined.

"Money is not an object, Mr. Phillips. Mr. George Darcy of Pemberley—the oldest daughter's father-in-law—and I will foot whatever the bill is. Put as many men on this as you are able; he needs to be brought to justice for the misery that he had sown,"

Gardiner informed the head runner.

"In that case, we will flood the area with investigators. Mr. Eagleton is funding five men, but I can send twenty more as you and your friends can pay the costs." With that Johns stood, shook Gardiner's hand, and left the Gardiner and Sons office on a mission.

~~~~~~~/~~~~~~~

Lady Sarah De Melville did not know how to proceed. A few months after she wrote her letters, she had eventually heard back from Ladies Anne and Elaine and they had told her they did not know about Jane's parents, just that they were no longer alive. Lady Sarah had been careful how she asked about Jane as to not raise suspicion, but due to her circumspection, the two friends she wrote to thought she was simply curious like many members of the Ton were about the young lady that had taken a highly eligible bachelor off the marriage mart.

Lady Sarah had not asked about Jane Darcy nee Bennet's looks so neither lady had mentioned that Jane looked eerily like Andrews betrothed, Marie De Melville. The newlyweds and the betrothed couple had not seen one another as Jane had been fatigued after the wedding trip and a month or so later had begun to feel bilious in the mornings.

Andrew and Marie would marry from Broadhurst in early September necessitating the whole family traveling to Essex at the end of August. Lady Anne had sent her friend a letter informing her that her daughter-in-law's sisters were at Pemberley for the summer, to which Lady Sarah sent an invitation including the Miss Bennets.

~~~~~~~/~~~~~~~

The two current and one former Bennet had reunited with hugs and tears when Elizabeth and Mary had arrived at Darcy House a few days after Jane and Alexander returned. Elizabeth and Mary noted that their sister was far more emotional than she had been in the past. Jane had some sort of malady, so she hardly ventured out of Darcy House. By the end of April, Jane felt much better and her sickness had stopped. By then they all knew what the malady was—Jane and Alexander were to be parents.

Not long after Jane started to feel better, the family decamped Town as none cared for London society. The first stops were Longbourn and Netherfield, where they would stay for a fortnight. Before the Darcys departed to Pemberley, Jane had felt the quickening. Elizabeth and Mary accompanied William, with Miss Ponsonby as chaperone, to Pemberley in July.

Jane Darcy was round and heavy with a child and most happy to have her sisters and cousins with her at Pemberley for the summer. After the wonderful wedding trip to Seaview Cottage on a bluff close to Brighton, the newlyweds had returned to Town and participated in the season. Their joining multiple times per day explained the state that Jane was now in, and she was about a month away from her confinement.

It was a few days before the departure to Essex when Jane felt the pains in her back. It seemed a little early, but according to the midwife, within a reasonable time window of the expected date of her final confinement. "If you are entering your confinement, then I am not leaving," Lady Anne stated.

"Mother Anne, I will be well. Alex is here. You cannot miss your godson's, wedding," Jane objected weakly.

"George will go with William, Gigi, and Anna. Both my brother and the De Melvilles will understand. Lizzy and Mary may go as well if they like," Lady Anne replied.

"If Jane is entering her confinement, even if I am not allowed in the birthing room, this is where I want to be. I am sure that Mary feels the same way," Elizabeth stated. Mary nodded her head in agreement. "In addition, Kitty and Lydia are here; we will not leave them alone while we go to the wedding."

Two days later, George Darcy and his three youngest offspring departed for Essex. Meanwhile, Jane was still having back pains but had not commenced actual labour pains yet.

~~~~~~~/~~~~~~~

It did not take Bennet much observation before he understood that the distant cousin was a fool of the first order and the friend was no friend at all. This was confirmed on one night when Bennet joined a game of *Vingt-et-Un*. It pleased Bennet to see that the one named Wickham was at the table, and he was a worse card player than most. He drew a card when he should have held, held when he should draw.

It was not long before Wickham owed Bennet more than ten pounds. As usual, he had no way to pay his debt of honour. "Come have a drink with me and we will call it even," Bennet suggested.

Wickham jumped at the chance both for free drinks and to get out of paying his debt to the older man. "I assume that you wanted to talk to me about something," Wickham probed.

"You are not wrong. Unlike your friend, I see that you are an intelligent man." Bennet could easily tell that this man had an inflated sense of self-worth, so he played into that.

"He is not really my friend, and he is one of the most stupid men that I have ever met. It is a battle to get him to bathe every week or two. He cannot understand why most people run the other way when they are downwind of him. He has his uses though," Wickham admitted.

"I am, James Gardiner," Bennet extended his hand.

"George Wickham," the young man returned.

"It is a coincidence that you and the curate were speaking of Longbourn in Hertfordshire." Bennet finally had a plan; he recognised a fellow resentful man who wanted money without having to earn it. "It just so happens that I know that the master, one Thomas Bennet, is dead and your friend has not been notified as people are trying to steal his inheritance. There are also some daughters left with sizable dowries," Bennet sowed his poison.

Wickham was extremely interested now. All he had to do was relieve Collins of the estate and compromise one of the daughters of the late master, so he could possess the *large* dowry. He missed that had the man really known about the girls and their dowries, he would have known the amount.

"You may have to remove the interlopers by force," Bennet relayed nonchalantly.

"That will not be a problem; I will not allow anyone to steal from Collins," Wickham responded. *'Besides me!'* he added to himself.

Over the next month, Wickham seemed overly interested in Collins's connections and antecedents. Wickham made copious notes and Collins took it as a sign of respect that his lowborn friend admired him, a clergyman.

~~~~~~~/~~~~~~~

On the second day of September, two events of great significance were connected to the Darcys. Lord Hilldale, Andrew Fitzwilliam, married Lady Marie De Melville and Jane Darcy gave birth to a healthy baby boy, securing the future of Pemberley for another generation.

At the wedding and subsequent breakfast at Broadhurst, Lady Elaine was too caught up in her son's wedding celebration to mention that Marie Fitzwilliam and Jane Darcy could have been sisters as they looked so much alike.

At Pemberley, the birth of James Bennet Darcy was being celebrated. Jane was well on her way to recovery and the proud father could not have been happier as he held his son at every opportunity—that is, when Jamie was not in his grandmama's arms with his aunts and cousins waiting for their turn as well.

"He is so handsome, Jane," Elizabeth gushed one day as her sister fed her hungry babe.

"As Mother Anne explained, it will be a year or two before we truly know how he will look, but regardless, he is the most beautiful child to me." Jane shared.

"It is so hard to believe that you are a mother, Jane," Elizabeth stated. "Not that long ago we were just carefree girls."

"You know Lizzy, we have not been that since Mama, Papa, and Jamie were taken from us," Jane said wistfully. "How I would have loved to have them here to see Jamie."

"They are with us; they always will be in here," Elizabeth

touched her heart.

"I know it Lizzy, but at times like these, I miss them so very much. But enough maudlin thoughts, I think this young man is sated and would like his aunt to help him belch." Jane handed the babe to his aunt. Jamie was tall for a babe, a Darcy trait. He had a thick mop of dark hair like his father and for now, he had deep blue eyes.

"He will be tall like his father, grandfather, and Uncle William," Elizabeth opined. "Did Alex send an express to Essex?"

"No, he did not," the beaming father answered as he entered his wife's chambers. "The missive would have passed them on the way home. I sent notes to Longbourn, London, Snowhaven, Rosings, Lucas Lodge, and Broadhurst," Alex informed his wife and sister. "At least now Peter can no longer crow that he produced an heir his first time as a father. He and Charlotte predicted a girl for us."

The next day the rest of the Darcys returned home and were instantly in love with little Jamie. William looked at Elizabeth and prayed that the time left until she came out would pass with all speed.

~~~~~~~/~~~~~~~

Collins could not believe what his friend had told him. According to Wickham, Collins did not have to wait to claim his inheritance; it was already his. As both Wickham and Bennet, known to Wickham as Gardiner, expected, Collins wanted to hear the news from the man himself.

The three sat in a private dining parlour at the inn. After Bennet relayed his story, Collins was flabbergasted. "I will set the magistrate on them for trying to steal what is mine!" Collins blustered. At first, he had been a little sceptical until Mr. Gardiner related that he had known all about his late mother and father. Bennet related things that only an intimate would know. With his greed and desire to rise in society, it was not hard for Bennet to sell the story he had concocted to Collins.

"When can we be off?" Wickham asked keenly.

"Not until after Christmastide," Collins responded. "I am committed until then, and the estate will still be there in January."

Wickham reluctantly agreed; they would depart after Twelfth Night.

~~~~~~~/~~~~~~~

The investigators had fanned out from Clevedon, and a fortnight later one of them found the town where one James Gardiner had arrived. When the horse was described, the man knew he had discovered something significant. Messages were sent to the rest of the men in the field. Soon the search began, starting from the inn. Eventually, they found the next clue—the farmer from whom Bennet had purchased a fresh horse.

After four plus months of extensive searching, the investigators arrived at the town of Croyde in Devon.

CHAPTER 12

A week after Twelfth Night a group of five runners spread out in Croyde. The rest of their number were camped just outside of town. Each of the five had entered the town from different directions and at different times so as not to draw attention to themselves. Their arrival in the town was the day after George Wickham and William Collins departed.

Collins planned to take the post to Southampton, from there to London, and then the last four and twenty miles to Meryton. Wickham had vastly different plans, but he never shared them with the stupid clergyman who would not shut up about himself becoming a landed gentleman. As much as he wanted a fortune he did not have to earn, Wickham craved the respect that would come with being recognised as a gentleman.

The first day Wickham kept his peace, but on the second day, as they approached the town of Knowle St Giles in Somerset, Wickham pleaded illness. Someone alerted the driver, who made an unscheduled stop on the outskirts of the town as it was bypassed by the coach they were on. On one side of the road was a wooded area. Wickham suggested that they pull their trunks out of sight of the road so their belongings would not be molested by a traveller who spied them.

"Come Collins, we crossed a little bridge a few minutes ago so I know there is a stream running through the forest. It would help me recover to drink some fresh water and I need your assistance as I feel weak," Wickham performed for the silly man.

"It is no less than my Christian duty to help my fellow man, no matter how far below my station he might be," was the pompous pronouncement.

Wickham placed his weight on Collins's shoulder to maintain the illusion he was ill. As they approached the stream, George Wickham seemed to make a miraculous recovery. William Collins's eyes were huge as he saw a knife in his friend's hand. "If you were not such a pompous and obsequious fool, I may have had some regrets about ending you, but this will be satisfying after having put up with you all these years."

"B-b-but you are my friend!" Collins cried out as his knees started to buckle with abject fear.

"I was never your friend! I had to put up with your inanities and smell so I would have a place to rest my head, food to eat, and funds for amusement. George Wickham is about to die," Wickham told the now snivelling man malevolently.

"HELP..." Collins started to scream as the knife found his heart. Given the distance from the roadway and as it was a very seldom travelled stretch, no one heard the final word of William Collins, besides his murderer. Collins had fallen forward, and Wickham did not even bother to try and retrieve the murder weapon.

Wickham opened the trunk and changed into the dark clothing that clergymen wore. He did not know if the people he would have to present himself to, knew his victim had been a clergyman. He had used some of the funds he pilfered from Collins to purchase the needed clothing. He checked the purse that he lifted off the body and found that there were just over thirty pounds in it. It was more than enough for the journey and a decent amount if he found a game of cards along the way. He was sure it was not uncommon for a man of the cloth to partake in games of chance.

Dragging the trunk behind him, Wickham walked the mile into Knowle St Giles. He rented a room at the inn in the name of Mr. William Collins. He would have preferred to commence his travels to Hertfordshire, but the landlord informed him that there was a post coach only twice a week, and the next one would depart two days hence. As he did not want to stand out, he paid for the two nights upfront and purchased a ticket for the post to Southampton.

~~~~~~~/~~~~~~~

It did not take the runners long to discover the boarding house where one James Gardiner was residing. One of the five went to the encampment out of town and returned with five more men. The leader did not want to importune the landlady and cause a commotion in her house, so he placed two men to watch the entrance and two more at the rear of the house for the night.

Bennet was pleased with himself. He would have his revenge. He was sure that Wickham would compromise one of the two remaining unmarried brats at the very least and Phillips and Gardiner would have to deal with the very stupid heir who would try and claim the estate as his own. As was his wont, he joined the widow and the other lodgers to break his fast a little after nine.

By midday, he was feeling thirsty, so he decided to take a ride to the tavern situated in the other end of town. He exited the rear door and headed to the small stables that the widow maintained for her tenants. He was half way to his destination when a man holding a cocked pistol stepped in front of him.

"If you are trying to rob me, I do not have more than two pounds on my person," Bennet said as he reached for his purse.

"Thomas Bennet!" Came from behind him as he froze when he heard his real name used.

"I-I have never heard that name, I am…" he tried to prevaricate as he felt his arms grasped by a man on either side.

"Yes, you thought yourself so clever when you, a man with no honour at all, assumed a new name. First using the Christian name of the brother you murdered was not enough, but then you had the temerity to use the last name of an eminently honourable man." The leader of the runners holding Bennet felt nothing but disdain for the murderer.

"You have no proof that I murdered my pampered brother," Bennet blustered.

"As Mr. Eagleton can testify against you, we do not need it; there is more than enough evidence to have you swing. However, Mr. Gardiner is acquainted with the two criminals who assisted your murder of his friends and their son. Enough talk; you are for Newgate and the Old Bailey in London." The man who had spoken nodded to his men who dragged the quaking man toward a cart.

The landlady and some of the tenants had seen Mr. Gardiner accosted and filed out of the house. "Why are you dragging poor Mr. Gardiner away?" the landlady demanded arms akimbo.

"We are Bow Street Runners. This man is in fact Thomas Bennet who murdered four people about which we know. He also stands accused of attempted murder and theft!" one of the runners stated as he showed the landlady the warrant for the apprehension of Thomas Bennet.

The landlady blanched. "I gave succour to a murderer!" she exclaimed.

"You did not know what he was, madam," the lead runner allowed.

Bennet knew that even if he had not been trussed up like a holiday goose before roasting, that with all the men who seemed to materialise out of thin air, he would have no opportunity to escape. '*I should have left the county!*' Bennet berated himself. '*At least I will get my revenge thanks to Wickham and Collins!*' The knowledge that he would hurt those who, in his mind, had done so to him, gave Bennet a small measure of solace.

~~~~~~~/~~~~~~~

Wickham arrived in London two days after leaving the little town in Somerset. He felt a lot better about himself without the pompous curate to tell him that as the son of a steward he was not much higher than a servant. Even though he had promised himself that he would stay away from trouble in London, he made his way to Seven Dials and the first gambling hell he found just happened to be the one owned by one Juan Antonio Álvarez, *the Spaniard.*

Wickham still had over twenty pounds left. He had joined a game in Southampton and lost ten pounds and had the good sense to stop before he lost too much. As he drank more of the cheap swill that the establishment served, his card playing, not good at the best of times, deteriorated. He kept on upping his wagers to try and recoup his losses but never did.

By the time he was too far in his cups to play any longer, Wickham had turned his twenty pounds into over three hundred pounds of debt. If he were sober, he would have tried to slip out unobtrusively, like he had done before when he owed money. He woke up the next morning on the floor of a windowless room with a headache that felt like a herd of galloping horses when a bucket of cold water was emptied onto him.

"Hey! Why would you do that?" Wickham croaked, his throat feeling like a parched desert.

"'Cause it is time to pay what ya owe!" the man holding the bucket returned.

"How much do I owe?" Wickham remembered extraordinarily little of the previous night's entertainment.

"Over three 'undred pounds!" Was the last answer that Wickham wanted to hear.

"I do not have that." Wickham knew his charms would be meaningless to these men. They would sooner slit his throat than look at him.

"Then I will take it from your hide," a second, much larger man stated menacingly.

Wickham was sure they would rather collect than kill him and lose any chance of recovering the debt. "I am on my way to Hertfordshire to claim my inheritance, it is the estate of Longbourn near Meryton. My name is William Collins, I am the heir to the estate. My information is that the previous master is deceased. Allow me to leave with a half crown to pay post and get a meal and once I am installed as master, I will pay you five hundred pounds."

'*What is it with promises related to that estate?*' the big man asked himself. "You have a fortnight to make good on your debt Mr. Collins. We have eyes everywhere; if you want to live, do not try to run out on your debt!"

Wickham felt a chill run down his spine. He had no doubt the man meant every word that he said. The big man threw a half crown at Wickham's feet and wordlessly, with his man following close behind, walked out of the room leaving the door open.

~~~~~~~/~~~~~~~

Chained up and lying on the bed of a wagon, Bennet had never experienced such an uncomfortable journey. Four days after they departed Devon, Bennet could tell they had entered the environs of London. There was no mistaking the smells and sounds of the capital city.

Thomas Bennet regretted the straits in which he now found himself. No regret was spared for any of his actions that had led to this point, but rather for finally being caught and having to face the consequences of said actions. He did not care one whit for the victims of his crimes. How could he, when in his mind he was the victim of being treated badly by everyone.

The cart trundled through the enormous gates that led to a courtyard at Newgate. The gates were closed after the final pair of outriders passed them. The cart came to a halt and a man unlocked Bennet's chains from the ring on the side of the cart. "Is this Thomas Bennet?" One of the runners asked. Bennet looked up to see the hated Edward Gardiner looking at him with complete disdain.

"Yes, that is the murderer. The same man my friend Phillips and I evicted from Longbourn. I understand that one set of murders was not enough for you Bennet. You next murdered your wife and then you tried to murder your employer. It will be my pleasure to watch you swing soon enough!" Gardiner spat out. Bennet for some reason looked smug, but Gardiner was in no mood to try and interpret what it was that made the murderer look so.

"You stole my estate!" Bennet spat back.

"How could anyone take what was not yours to begin with? Did you not realise as soon as you murdered your brother that you lost all claim to his property?" Gardiner turned and was about to walk away.

"It is only a pity that the three brats were not in the carriage that night!" Bennet shot a vituperative barb.

Gardiner, not usually a violent man, wheeled and planted his fist into Bennet's jaw. He turned away after having the satisfaction of seeing blood pouring from the criminal's face. There was something in the look Bennet had given him that put Gardiner on alert for trouble. He decided to write an express to Phillips as soon as he reached Gracechurch Street.

~~~~~~~/~~~~~~~

Wickham had just enough money left to hire a gig in Meryton to take him and his trunk the one mile to Longbourn. As the little vehicle turned into the drive, Wickham became more excited. An express rider was coming up the drive towards the road that Wickham had just turned off, but Wickham thought nothing of it.

The one thing he was sorry about was he had not ordered cards in London before he lost his money at the tables. He hoped the people he was to hoodwink would not think it out of the ordinary that a *poor curate* did not have calling cards. A groom held the horse still while Wickham alighted. He knocked on the front door.

Mr. Hill opened the door and looked at the man standing without and waited for him to talk. "Mr. William Collins at your service," Wickham intoned. "I am the new master of this estate."

Mr. Hill did not flinch at the presumptive man in front of him. "Please wait here, Mr. Collins." As he waited in the entrance hall, Wickham heard the dulcet tones of female voices coming from one of the rooms further down.

The butler knocked on a door and disappeared within. A minute later he returned. "Please follow me, Mr. Collins."

They entered a study where a man was sitting behind the desk, standing when he saw the visitor following behind Mr. Hill. "Mr. William Collins sir," Hill announced.

"I am Frank Phillips, the interim master of the estate." Phillips did not offer his hand to shake but pointed to one of the chairs before the desk. "Mr. Hill says you claim to be the master of this estate. You are not Mr. Thomas Bennet so how is it you feel that you are the master here?" Phillips was good at taking the measure of a man and everything about this raised his hackles.

"I was led to believe that Thomas Bennet is dead and there are those here trying to deny me my rightful inheritance," Wickham stated. For the first time he did not feel as confident as he had when he arrived.

"Was the man that told you this lie, because it was a bald-faced lie, a James Gardiner perchance?" Phillips asked.

"Yes, how would you know that?" asked a confused Wickham.

"Because that man is in fact Thomas Bennet." Phillips reached for a miniature in the desk drawer. He handed it to the man sitting opposite, glad to see the veneer of confidence had slipped somewhat. "Is this the man you know as Gardiner?"

"Yes, that is he," Wickham owned. "Why would he send me here on a fool's errand?" Wickham was starting to feel extremely nervous. If he as Collins was not to be master, where would he get the money to repay the dangerous men to whom he now owed the five hundred pounds?

Phillips handed the man he knew as Collins a copy of the document that Bennet had signed, relinquishing control of Longbourn. He did not miss how the colour drained out of the man sitting opposite him. "What are your intentions with Longbourn?" Phillips asked.

"I would sell a part of it to raise some capital for estate improvement," Wickham lied. He wished now that he had not spoiled his chance of receiving a gentleman's education from Mr. Darcy as it would have become useful to know what to say about

estate management. He had hated that his father served the Darcys and at the time refused to learn from his father.

"I am afraid that even when you do *eventually* inherit, that
you will not be allowed to do that. Have you not read the articles
of the entailment?" Phillips asked. '*Another one who wants to
drain the estate of resources, no doubt a profligate gambler like Bennet!'* Phillips surmised to himself.

"Then I am sure I could withdraw funds from the estate accounts for my purpose," Wickham hoped.

"You really should read the document that lays out the
terms of the entailment. The new master, *when* he inherits, is
only entitled to money earned *after* he takes over the estate,
all funds earned prior to that date are divided among the late
master's daughters," Phillips informed the man who by now
was not looking happy at all. He decided to send an express to
Gardiner and have the money paid to house Bennet at Newgate
with a delayed trial while he would have the man sitting opposite him investigated. "As you can see, until we receive a death
certificate and one of the named trustees sees his dead body or
thirty years from the date that the document was signed have
passed, you do not inherit anything. Until such time, you are not
welcome here I am afraid."

"B-but I am family!" Things were going from bad to worse
for Wickham. Not only was there no inheritance now or for the
foreseeable future, but he was not welcomed to reside at the
estate. "I used the last of my money to travel hither. As a poor
curate, it took all that I had." Wickham tried to play on the man's
sympathies.

"Here is five pounds Mr. Collins, but I hope that you understand with young ladies under my roof I will not allow a man
not known to us to reside in the same house. Mayhap one of the
vicars in the area needs a curate." Phillips rang the bell. "Mr. Hill,
please see that Mr. Collins is transported into Meryton; he is leaving now."

As if in a stupor, Wickham was shown out. The groom that
had met the gig when he arrived brought a trap around and

loaded the trunk; they were soon on their way toward the market town. *'I will have to keep watch and compromise one of the girls. One of them married a Darcy, so they must have large dowries!'* Wickham schemed to himself.

~~~~~~~/~~~~~~~

Caroline Bingley did not know what had gone wrong with her brilliant plan. For almost a year she had saved as much of her money as she could. When she had enough, her plan had been to hire a carriage that would take her to the little town of Meryton in Hertfordshire to find and compromise Mr. William Darcy.

Once she was married, he would want to take his bride to see his ancestral home. There she would arrange for Mr. Alexander Darcy and the whelp, that she had heard he had sired, to meet with an accident, so she could have her desire fulfilled and become the mistress of Pemberley.

She had acted the part to perfection, in her opinion, of the demure and contrite woman her brother and sister expected her to be. So how was it that they had discovered her plans and she was now the permanent resident of an asylum for the insane in the wilds of Scotland?

If her servants had not been invisible to her, she would have noticed that every time she ranted on about her plans when she was alone, there was a servant within an earshot. As she did not ascribe any intelligence to servants, even had she noted their presence, she would not have worried that they would understand what she was planning.

Her maid had been with her when she went to hire the coach and men that would take her to her destination. It was only on the third day of travel that Miss Bingley noted that the weather seemed to get colder, not warmer as she would expect when traveling south. On the fourth day, her carriage arrived at a dark and forbidding structure. When she alighted, she saw the high walls and realised that she was not in Hertfordshire. None of her screaming and attempted scratching helped.

The restrained woman had been pushed into a chamber

with two high, narrow, and barred windows. There was a narrow bed against one wall with a table and a single chair. There was a missive waiting for her on the table.

Sister,

As much as it grieves me, for the safety of others and yourself, I have done what I warned you I would do if you did not get over your delusions. Neither Louisa nor myself were fooled by your attempted obfuscation.

You will not see us again; this will be your home for the rest of your days. I pray that you find a measure of peace,

Charles.

After reading the letter, Miss Bingley tore it into many tiny pieces as she ranted and raved about how she would escape and get her revenge. Her brother had refused to send her to Bedlam to be on display like a wild animal in the Menagerie, so he chose an extremely secure private facility in the Scottish Highlands where, regardless of what she told herself, the only way that Miss Bingley would depart would be in a coffin.

CHAPTER 13

Newgate prison was a living hell for Bennet. He had no money to bribe the guards for better treatment so he was in a louse infested communal cell with almost twenty other men. The stench was pungent enough to make a man retch. The cell was so crowded that Bennet practically had to sleep standing up. For the first time in his life, he started to experience regret over his actions.

One morning he was dragged out of the cell, placed in irons, and pushed into a room with a table and a chair on either side. The guard forced Bennet to sit in one chair and then ran a chain around the connecting chain between the irons on his ankles and locked it to a ring fixed into the floor. Even without the numerous guards close by escape was impossible.

Edward Gardiner walked into the room and sat down, waving the guard out of the room. The man took up station just outside the door. "Come to gloat, have you?" Bennet spat out bitterly.

"That is nothing less than you deserve, but no, Bennet, that is not my purpose today. When I was here last, I felt you were too smug, somehow you had managed to cause some mischief and then lo and behold, a man claiming to be William Collins shows up with a tale of a James Gardiner who told him that Longbourn was being stolen from him. As we know you used that name and he came from the same town where you were apprehended, it is not hard to guess this was your futile attempt at revenge," Gardiner informed Bennet.

"You thought nothing of stealing my estate from me!" Bennet spat.

"Do we need to go over this again Bennet? You know full

well that you murdered your brother, his wife, and his son in a vain attempt to sell Longbourn to pay your debts and have more money to waste on your debauched habits. Ironically, when you hang, then Collins will be able to inherit. We suspect there is something not right with the man, so we have paid for your trial to be delayed. In the meanwhile, I hope that you enjoy Newgate's hospitality!" Gardiner enjoyed seeing the look of horror on Bennet's face.

"Being in that gaol cell is worse than death; at least have me moved to a cell on my own," Bennet begged. "Wait, you said Collins. Was Wickham not with him?"

"Do you think any of us who know about your despicable actions would pay a single coin for your comfort? If you do, not only are you a criminal but insane. You are a disgrace to all of the Bennets who came before you!" Gardiner stood, but then reconsidered his words. He did not tell Bennet, but he would have him transferred to a solitary cell as it was important to keep the reprobate alive for now. Gardiner rapped on the door ignoring the mention of another man. It was opened by a guard and Gardiner walked out never looking back at the snivelling man chained to the floor. He proceeded to the warden's office.

"Mr. Humphries, thank you for allowing me to see that snivelling murderer. As much as I do not want him to have any sort of comfort, it suits my purposes that he does not die yet. I will pay for him to have a solitary cell and for some of the cheapest wine possible. In addition, let him have one meal a day. If he asks, please have none of your men inform him that this was paid for by me or any other," Gardiner requested of the warden.

"We can do that for you Mr. Gardiner; it will cost ten pounds a month," the warden returned.

"Agreed!" Gardiner handed the man the amount for the first month sure that half of it went directly in the warden's pocket, but it was worth it to keep Bennet alive—for now. He hoped a second month would not be needed.

"When Bennet was dragged back to his cell, he was confused when they passed the communal cesspool he had been in and was pushed into a small, but by Newgate's standards clean, individual cell. The thing that caught his eye was not the food on the table but the bottle of wine. Bennet drank the contents of the bottle, no matter how vile it tasted, like a man finding an oasis after days of thirst in the desert. Bennet did not know what had changed, but he did not care. He had begun to shake after days without a drink, he even remembered to eat the food that was on the table. For the first time since he was arrested, Bennet slept well on the straw mattress in the corner.

~~~~~~~~/~~~~~~~~

After his first night at the Cock and Bull Inn in Meryton, Wickham tried to gain some intelligence about the Bennets of Longbourn. Unfortunately for him, no one except the Phillips and Lucas families knew about Thomas Bennet's capture and incarceration. In addition, Wickham had no idea that a Darcy lived in the area, so he did not feel the need to mention his connection, tentative as it was, to that family.

As usual, Wickham was overconfident in his abilities to charm and manipulate. It did not enter his consciousness that the man he spoke to at Longbourn was suspicious of him. He proceeded with his plan as if there were no possibility that anyone would not believe that he was William Collins.

He found out the master of the estate before Bennet had been murdered along with two members of his family in '02. Now Wickham was trying to steal the same estate from the dead clergyman. Furthermore, Bennet, the one who had sent him on this fool's errand, was suspected of being behind the murders. Some two years ago, Bennet and his wife, both universally disliked in the neighbourhood, had left as suddenly as they had arrived, abandoning their two young daughters when they departed.

Wickham mentioned to a man he had purchased a pint of ale for that he heard that the Bennet girls had large dowries. The man had laughed and told him that if he considered two thousand pounds a large dowry, then his information was correct.

Thankfully, Phillips had continued his late friend's policy of not disclosing the truth of the girl's dowries.

The amount was a big setback. It seemed there was nothing that the man, Gardiner or Bennet, whatever his true name was, had told him that was true. Wickham was still confused. Why would a high and mighty Darcy prig marry one who had only two thousand pounds and seemingly no notable connections? There was no answer when processed through the filter of his grasping greed that he could divine to explain this anomaly. He did discover that the oldest remaining Miss Bennet liked to ramble around the countryside in the early morning hours.

Two thousand was far less than he expected to gain in a dowry, but it would have to do. He was petrified of the *Spaniard's* men, not doubting that things would not go well for him if he did not pay up. He learned that the paltry sum was in fact the largest dowry of any woman in the area. As much as he hated rising with the sun, based on what he learnt, he knew he must if he was to learn which paths the lady took on her rambles.

~~~~~~~/~~~~~~~

What Wickham could not have known was that his questions about Longbourn and the Bennets were reported to Phillips the same day, especially his questions about the girls' dowries. The reported inquiries added to Phillips's misgivings about the man. On receiving the reports regarding Mr. Collins's questioning, Phillips dug out a report that James Bennet had commissioned to investigate the heir presumptive in case something disastrous happened and he lost his son before Jamie reached his majority and thereby ending the entail.

The report described the man as sycophantic to his betters while showing unwarranted pomposity to those he felt beneath him. The writer of the report mentioned that the man did not seem to enjoy bathing as he usually had a very pungent smell about him.

Phillips allowed that his standards of cleanliness may have been improved, but he saw nothing of the character that was described. His feeling that there could very well be foul play afoot was raised beyond a mere unfounded visceral reaction to the man he had met with. That evening after dinner, he asked his daughters and wards to give him their attention.

"You remember I told you about the man who said he was William Collins, and he was here to claim the estate?" Phillips asked. All four young ladies nodded. "He has been asking questions about all of you that have raised my suspicion that he is not the man he tries to portray himself as. Until we know what he is about, no more solitary rambles, Lizzy." He raised his hand to stay the protest that was about to be mounted. "You will still be allowed to walk, but only with a footman or a groom, even when you ride. That goes for all of you."

"When do the Darcys arrive from Town?" Hattie asked.

"William will return to Netherfield two days hence and the rest of the family, yes including Jane, will arrive a few days later," Phillips informed his family. No one missed the blush that Lizzy, who would be seventeen in a little more than a month, sported at the mention of William's impending return.

At the mention of William, Elizabeth remembered their conversation, as she had many times since they had spoken during her visit to Darcy House during the little season that had just passed.

Elizabeth had been reading the latest volume of Cowper's work in the library at Darcy House when she became aware she was no longer alone. When she looked up, she found William standing nearby, staring at her in the way that he did often. She feared his staring was to find fault with her, so she decided it was time to give free rein to her impertinence.

"William, do I have a blemish? Do you look at me with censure as you did that day you discovered me riding astride?" she had asked pointedly.

"No Lizzy, I thought you knew. I stare at you because you are the most beautiful woman in the world to me, both inside and out, and I love you. I have for a long time. If my face looks strange, it is because I do not know your feelings and am nervous that they are not

returned in full measure. I would only want you to accept me if your feelings match mine for you," William told her.

Elizabeth had been in love with William for an exceptionally long time; since she was fourteen in fact. Since his face was inscrutable much of the time, she had detected no look that conveyed special regard. She had remembered Jane telling her that she was sure that William had tender feelings for Elizabeth. Not seeing them, or not being able to identify them herself, Elizabeth had discounted her older sister's opinion.

"What fools we have been, William," Elizabeth had laughed. She saw the hurt look on William's face and assumed he thought she was laughing at his declaration of love. "William, I love you too! Even though Jane told me you had tender feelings for me, you hid them effectively and I thought it was my love that was unrequited. That is what caused my mirth; the pair of us were at cross purposes while both feeling the same about one another."

"You love me, Lizzy?" William seemed to need reassurance.

"Yes, I do, most ardently!" Elizabeth had returned.

"If I were not worried that someone would walk in, I would kiss you. I am so relieved. I too thought that you did not feel love for me," William released a breath he had been holding.

"You meant romantic love..." Elizabeth teased as she arched an eyebrow at William. Her tease resulted in one of the simple revealing smiles that made William look even more handsome than usual.

She was snapped out of her reverie as Phillips was waiting for an answer. "I was wool gathering; please repeat your questions, Uncle Frank," Elizabeth requested as she blushed anew.

"I asked if I had your word of honour that you will follow what I have laid out until this Collins problem is resolved," Phillips repeated. Based on the fact that William had informed him of his intent to request a courtship with Lizzy as soon as she came out, Phillips had a good idea where his ward's mind had been engaged.

"Yes, Uncle, I swear to follow the rules for our safety." Yes, the two days until William returned could not pass fast enough.

~~~~~~~/~~~~~~~

William was pining for Elizabeth and knew he would not feel whole until he was in her company again. "Mother and Father, I will ride to Netherfield in the morning," William informed his parents.

"Are we missing someone terribly?" Major Richard Fitzwilliam ribbed his cousin, knowing exactly why he would want to accelerate his return to the estate.

"Richard makes a good point, William, it is only one day earlier than you planned to return," Lady Anne stated. "If however, you feel you would prefer not to wait, you will not be missing anything of consequence here on the morrow."

"I agree with your mother, William," George Darcy added. "It is your choice. You have attained your majority and are master of your own estate after all. We will see you there in a few days."

"Lizzy will be happy to see you," Jane Darcy informed her brother-in-law. Jane was the only one with whom an ecstatic Elizabeth had shared the details of the conversation between herself and William that day in the library.

"Are you sure we do not need William here until we are ready to depart for Netherfield?" Alexander asked with a deadpan expression.

"Alex, there is no need to tease your brother so!" Lady Anne admonished her older son playfully.

"Sorry, Mother," Alexander grinned as he was not sorry at all, especially when he had caused a look of horror on his younger brother's face.

"Do you object to having company on your ride, cousin?" the Major asked.

"You are more than welcome, Richard," William replied.

"I assume you will want to depart at some ungodly hour, so Aunt Anne, would you be willing to have this soldier hosted at Darcy House tonight?"

"You know you do not have to request that, Richard; you are

always welcome," Lady Anne replied. She liked all three of her nephews very well, but she always had a soft spot for Richard Fitzwilliam.

~~~~~~~/~~~~~~~

George Wickham rose before the sunrise and made his way towards Longbourn. He hid behind some trees where he had a good view of the house. His patience was rewarded when just after sunrise a very pretty young lady, who he assumed to be Miss Bennet, walked out of the house through what he assumed to be the kitchen door,

Rather than walk as he expected she would, she seemed to be waiting for something as she munched on something warm. Wickham could see the tendrils of steam rising from whatever it was she was eating. He did not have to wait too long; a footman joined her.

Much to his vexation, she was not walking unaccompanied as he had been informed, she would. The footman was not a small man, and it was a complication he had not foreseen. As much as he wanted to get it over with that morning, he knew he was not ready for the complication that her being escorted presented.

As she had neared the trees where he was hidden, she had stopped and looked toward where Wickham hid behind the trees. Wickham was sure she could not see him, but to be safe he backed up into the trees some more. She had soon started walking again and had not repeated the same again for the rest of the walk. The effect was that Wickham allowed a greater distance between himself and his quarry than he would have otherwise done.

At least the time was not a complete waste; he was able to follow at a discreet distance and see the route she took. He knew there was no guarantee she would follow the same path on the morrow, but nevertheless he wanted to be prepared. Given the distance at which the footman followed, Wickham identified a few spots where she would not be able to see her escort and the footman would be vulnerable to a surprise attack.

After more than a half hour, she walked up a hill. Twenty minutes later she returned; her dark tresses revealed as her bonnet swung from her hand. Rather than a simple compromise, given the beauty he saw before him, he decided that bedding her would not be unpleasant. If only she had a larger dowry!

~~~~~~~/~~~~~~~~

Elizabeth was pleased that her uncle had demanded that she take a footman. She found Tom's company very pleasant. He stayed back a little so she still had the illusion that she was enjoying a solitary ramble. When she approached the stand of trees a little after she exited the kitchen garden, Elizabeth had the feeling that she was being observed.

Elizabeth stopped, as did Tom. She looked towards the trees and thought she saw a flash of colour, but she was not sure if it was a bird or some other small animal. Not seeing anything more, Elizabeth resumed her ramble.

She had left later than she liked to, so she was not in time to see the sunrise from Oakham Mount, but she walked the path to summit nonetheless. She looked wistfully at Netherfield, knowing that William would be back in two days. How she missed the man she loved so very much.

He had told her that after her come out it would be her choice, a courtship or betrothal. She had no doubt he was the man for her, so she was not inclined to waste time on an unnecessary courtship. Unlike a lot of women on their wedding day, she knew William Darcy well.

Yes, he could be officious sometimes, but it happened when he was afraid for one that he loved. He respected her as much as she respected him, so even if he had a lapse from time to time when he became worried, he was the man—the *only* man—she would ever agree to marry.

She removed her bonnet and twirled it in her left hand as she and Tom descended from the hill. She was so deep in thought about the man of her dreams that she was not aware of being watched.

CHAPTER 14

As Major Richard Fitzwilliam had predicted, William Darcy roused him hours before the dawn. Within half an hour, regardless of his cousin's complaints about the time of day, actually more like night, William was atop Zeus ready for the ride to Netherfield and waiting for his cousin to mount his horse so the ride could commence.

"Do you really think if we had a decent night's sleep that you would not get to see Lizzy today?" the Major asked.

"That is not..." William stopped himself as he knew he was about to prevaricate, and he abhorred deception. "I miss her! We declared our love for one another you know."

"When?"

"After Twelfth Night before the Phillipses returned to Longbourn. We had a misunderstanding; do you know that she thought I stared at her to find fault?"

"That I can well believe with the way you used to stare at her with that inscrutable mask you put in place. Sometimes you made it seem that you were the heir being chased by every debutante of the Ton. I never understood that as you had Alex to take the bulk of the attention, well before he married the angelic Jane, that is." The Major paused as he thought about something. "You were at Andrew's wedding. Does my new sister-in-law remind you of someone?"

"Yes, you are correct, it is Jane! I thought about that at the wedding but as usual, my head was with Lizzy, as well as hoping the newest Darcy would be born with no complications for babe or mother," William remembered.

The two rode on without talking for some miles. There was more than enough light to ride safely and having made the ride to and from Netherfield more times than he cared to remember; William knew the road like the back of his hand.

"You are lucky that you have Netherfield, and do not have to worry that Lizzy only has two thousand," the Major stated as they left the inn halfway to their destination where they had rested and watered their horses some. "Unlike you, I am a poor second son without an estate and must marry for money. Not too many second sons have a father who purchased an estate for him."

"You are good at keeping secrets are you not, Richard?" William asked with a sly grin. The Major nodded. "The three Bennet sisters each have around thirty thousand pounds!"

"How? Just what you and Alex need!"

"I intend to have the settlement state that Lizzy's dowry remains under her control just as Alex did with Jane's. By the way, you are fooling no one with that *poor second son* act. You think I do not know that you have saved most of your pay and allowance since you were inducted into the army? It is common knowledge that after you met Gardiner you took your funds from the four percents and placed them with Gardiner and Sons. Father, Alex, and I have all invested with him and if your returns are anything like ours, you will be able to purchase an estate when you finally decide to resign from the army," William enjoyed the look on his cousin's face as Richard realised that his affairs were not as private as he had hoped.

The two cousins, who were best of friends and as close as brothers, rode on. They neared Meryton at the break of dawn.

~~~~~~~/~~~~~~~

Wickham left the Cock and Bull as the first light of dawn was showing itself in the eastern sky. He crossed the road to make his way out of the town and towards Longbourn when he heard two horses on the main street behind him. He did not bother to look at the riders as he knew no one connected to him was in the area.

After walking the mile to Longbourn's land, for what he

told himself was the final time, he hid in the stand of trees so he could see the rear of the house and his quarry when she exited the house. This time she exited before sunrise and again waited for the groom. Wickham saw her share something with the servants. '*Such weakness to share with a servant! It will be all the easier to compromise this one. I think I will have my way with her so there can be no question,*' Wickham told himself lecherously.

He watched with anticipation as she struck out using the same path as the previous day; the only difference was the footman was a little further back. As soon as he was sure she was indeed following the path he expected, Wickham melted back into the trees and headed for where the path made a sharp turn. He found a nice thick piece of a branch and hid next to the path behind a tree.

~~~~~~~/~~~~~~~

Elizabeth was not paying much attention to her surroundings. It was a cold winter day, but she did not notice that either. Her thoughts were all about William and the fact that he would return on the morrow. He was almost six years older than her, the same difference between Jane and Alex, in her mind the perfect age difference.

She hoped he would come straight to Longbourn before he went to Netherfield on the morrow, mayhap even meet her on her walk. As she passed the sharp turn in the path, she thought she heard a rustling of the underbrush, but she dismissed it as her imagination of a small animal like the previous day.

As she progressed a few yards, she did not miss the sound of a thwack and a groan. She turned and ran back to the corner. Tom was lying on the ground, seemingly unconscious and a man she did not remember ever seeing before standing over him.

"What on earth do you think that you are doing?" Elizabeth cried.

"Is that a way to greet your cousin and the rightful owner of Longbourn? William Collins at your service." Wickham gave a mocking bow.

"You ridiculous man, why did you accost Tom?" Elizabeth was too angry to be scared.

"He would have been in the way when I compromise you dear cousin," Wickham said as he approached the angry woman who was backing up. "I need funds and your paltry two thousand will have to do."

"Compromising me will get you nothing!" Elizabeth shot back.

"You lie, what would a young girl know about men's business?" Wickham returned.

"Before my father was murdered, he placed safeguards so no fortune hunter could compromise us. If my guardian plus one of the other designated do not approve *beforehand,* not one penny will be released, you dunderhead!" Elizabeth allowed her temper to get the better of her.

"In that case, I will ransom you and still ruin you just for the trouble you are causing me." Wickham's demeanour became menacing as he reached for his quarry.

"Unhand Miss Bennet, Wickham," William yelled as he and Richard approached on their horses.

Wickham froze as he heard his name. He whirled around, grabbing the young lady placing her between him and the horsemen. What were Darcy and Fitzwilliam doing here? He pulled a knife out of his boot but as he did the lady raked down his shin with the heel of her walking boot and stomped on his foot with all of her might.

Wickham dropped the knife and at the same time, he managed to push the young lady towards the two horsemen. Elizabeth hit the ground hard, her head connecting with a rock that was protruding from the dirt. Wickham turned and attempted his escape. As if by silent communication, William jumped off his horse and went to Elizabeth while his cousin kicked his horse's flanks and went after Wickham.

William was distraught; Elizabeth was breathing but there was much blood where her head had hit the piece of rock and she was not moving. William took her in his arms, tears of despair running down his cheeks, and stood. He called Zeus to him as he mounted with one hand, the other arm holding his beloved. As soon as he was on his mount, he turned his horse toward Long-bourn and was soon going as fast as he could while still holding Elizabeth to his chest.

Wickham felt like he had been hit by a runaway carriage as Richard Fitzwilliam ran him down with his horse before he reached the tree line. Wickham was awake, but he could not feel his legs and no matter how much he willed himself to stand, his limbs would not obey him. He could feel pain above his waist, but for some reason, below it, there was nothing.

The Major rolled the miscreant over with his boot. He saw the rock where Wickham had struck his back in the initial fall and suspected that the man's back was broken. "W-why can I feel nothing below my waist? My legs, I cannot move them," Wickham wailed confirming what Major Fitzwilliam suspected.

"Your back is broken, you miserable wastrel. What would make you attack Miss Bennet? What has she ever done to you? Never mind, we will get answers soon enough." The Major picked Wickham up like he was a sack of potatoes and secured him to his horse behind his saddle. He mounted and turned toward Longbourn.

~~~~~~~~/~~~~~~~~

As soon as Hattie Phillips spied William Darcy riding up to the manor house with Elizabeth clutched to his chest, she knew something was very wrong. "William, what happened to Lizzy?" she asked with much concern.

"She hit her head; I must ride to Mr. Jones at once," William reported as he handed Elizabeth to a footman and a groom as carefully as he could. It was then that Hattie Phillips saw the blood.

"Hill have her placed on her bed and have your wife attend me immediately," Mrs. Phillips instructed. "Also summon my husband; he is at Lucas Lodge this morning."

Within a minute a groom was riding at speed toward Lucas Lodge. As he left Major Richard Fitzwilliam rode up with the unconscious criminal tied to his horse. "Where can I have this useless piece of garbage placed and guarded?" he asked.

It was then that Hattie Phillips saw the captive's face. "Why is Mr. Collins tied to your horse Richard?" she asked.

"His name is not Collins; it was he who attacked Lizzy and the footman with her. The footman was coming to as I returned here and said he can return by himself. This useless waste of a man is George Wickham," Richard stated emphatically.

"Frank suspected the man was not who he said he was; that is why he is with Sir William this morning," Hattie Phillips informed the Major.

"When he wakes, we will get answers. How is Lizzy? Has someone summoned the doctor?"

"I am on my way to see my niece now, and William rode to Mr. Jones," Hattie Phillips answered, as she turned and rushed back into the house. When she entered, she found three very worried young ladies.

"What happened to Lizzy?" Mary asked, with much concern.

"As of now, I know no more than you. She was hurt somehow, and I am on my way to help Hill tend to her now. William has gone for Mr. Jones." With that, Mrs. Phillips made her way up the stairs to Elizabeth's chamber.

~~~~~~~/~~~~~~~

Frank Phillips and Sir William had just commenced their discussion of what to do about the man that Phillips strongly suspected was an imposter when Lady Lucas burst into the study without knocking. "Lizzy had been hurt. A groom rode from Longbourn," Lady Lucas reported.

"I must leave immediately," Phillips stood.

"And I will accompany you," Sir William insisted.

Only a few minutes had passed before their horses were brought to the front of the house and the two men were on their way to Longbourn.

~~~~~~~/~~~~~~~

With the assistance of Elizabeth's maid, Mrs. Hill had changed the miss into a nightgown and washed her wound as well as they could. When they dried the area where she had been bleeding. Hattie Phillips was happy to see that it was not a deep wound.

What concerned Mrs. Phillips was that Elizabeth's breathing was shallow, and she had shown no signs of waking since being brought home. She heard feet running up the stairs, and from the sound of it, they were the feet of a man or men. Mr. Jones entered the chamber and William would have as well if his cousin had not restrained him.

For William, waiting in the hall while his beloved was examined by Mr. Jones seemed like an eternity. While he was pacing up and down the hall Phillips and Sir William arrived. "William, what happened to Lizzy?" Phillips demanded.

His cousin explained, as William was not ready to talk to anyone until he heard from Mr. Jones. Once everything that was known was explained, Phillips almost collapsed into a chair in the hallway. "This is all my fault. I suspected he was not who he said, I should have had him followed. The girls would have been safe if I had sent that damned letter to their uncle and not held onto it!" Phillips bemoaned.

"Firstly, Wickham has been bedevilling my family for years, so if anyone bears blame it is us for not dealing with him long ago," William told Phillips.

"Were you not with me this morning asking for my help with the man that called himself Collins...wait what uncle?" asked a bewildered Sir William.

"When James Bennet brought his wife here, they were already married, correct?" Sir William nodded. "You only ever knew her as Mrs. Bennet or Priscilla, is that also not correct? She never discussed her antecedents and would say that she had no family besides her Bennet family when asked about her parents;

do you remember William?" Phillips reminded his friend.

"Yes, but what of it," Sir William asked, looking more confused than before.

"Good Lord, that is why Jane and Marie look like they could be sisters," Richard Fitzwilliam hit his own head as the realisation hit.

"What are you talking about Richard?" Darcy wanted to know.

"Mr. Phillips, the late Mrs. Bennet was the late Lady Priscilla De Melville, was she not?" Phillips nodded his head. "That makes the Bennet sisters the current earl's nieces, so he is in fact their closest blood relative!" Before Phillips could explain why James Bennet had instructed him not to contact Lord Jersey, Mr. Jones joined them in the hall.

"I stitched up the laceration, it was long but thankfully not deep. There is so much we do not understand about the brain and what happens when it receives a bad blow as it seems this one has. All we can do is wait, watch, and pray that she does not develop a fever. The sooner she awakens, the better; only time will tell," the physician and apothecary in one reported.

"Would it help if I write to my father and request that he send our physician from London?" William asked.

"It cannot hurt, and another opinion could be most valuable. She needs to be watched at all times and she needs nourishment and to drink. I have left an invalid feeder and Mrs. Hill is well aware how to use it," Jones concluded. No one noticed that Mrs. Phillips had exited Elizabeth's chambers.

"It is time to post the letter with a cover from you, Frank," Hattie Phillips said simply.

"It will go by express within the hour with one to Gardiner," Phillips stated without emotion.

"We need to send one to Darcy House," William stated.

"And Matlock and de Bourgh Houses," the major added.

"I suggest that whoever needs to write a letter does so now so the rider can be dispatched to London as soon as may be," Phillips said.

William verbalised what the other men were thinking, and said, "Once we are done with the letters, we need to continue the discussion we started before Mr. Jones's report." Phillips nodded.

~~~~~~~/~~~~~~~

An hour later, one of Longbourn's grooms was on his way to Town with five missives. Mrs. Phillips and Elizabeth's maid were sitting with an unconscious Elizabeth making sure that they dripped some water and broth into her mouth every now and again.

The men were seated around the table in the dining parlour. It was driving William mad that there was not much he could do to help his Elizabeth. As they were about to start the continuation of the conversation from the upstairs hall, Mr. Hill cleared his throat to make them aware of his presence and informed them that the injured captive was awake.

The four men walked into the chamber where Tom had taken up a station as self-appointed guard. Besides an egg sized lump on his head, Tom was well. Phillips nodded to him, and the footman left the chamber and stood in the hall outside of the door.

"How did you know to call yourself William Collins?" Phillips took on the role of an inquisitor without any preamble.

Wickham knew that he was not long for the world one way or another, being scared of Richard Fitzwilliam and knowing Fitzwilliam could make whatever time he had left very painful he decided to answer the questions honestly. "I lived with Collins for some years in Croyde, Devon, where he used to be a curate," Wickham answered.

"So you left him there and decided to steal his inheritance?" Phillips pressed.

"Partly, true; I did not leave him there," Wickham owned.

"I do not understand," Phillips was a little confused.

"When Gardiner or Bennet, or whatever his name is..." Wickham started to explain.

"It is Bennet. Gardiner was no more his name than Collins is yours," Phillips interjected.

"Yes, well when *Bennet* told us his tale, Collins waited until mid-January to depart from Croyde. The second day of travel I sent him to the God who he attempted to serve," Wickham related dispassionately.

"You murdered him, assumed his identity and then came here to try to claim the estate. Why did you attack my niece?" Phillips wanted more answers.

"I owe money to dangerous men, as I could get nothing from the estate, I wanted to compromise her for her dowry so I could pay the five hundred pounds I owe to *the Spaniard*."

"It would have got you naught," Phillips informed Wickham.

"Yes, she informed me of that, so I was going to take her for ransom and return her ruined for the trouble," Wickham related as if it was an everyday occurrence.

"You bloody bastard!" William Darcy roared. "If you were not going to expire soon, I would kill you myself.

"So she is your piece of muslin, is she? If I hurt a Darcy as I die, so much the better." Wickham started to cough up bright red bubbles as he fell silent.

"Tom, Mr. Jones now," Phillips called.

Mr. Jones examined the man and when he lifted his shirt, his whole abdomen was almost purple. "He has massive internal bleeding; he will be gone within the next hour or two," Mr. Jones reported. Wickham slipped back into unconsciousness and took his final breath within a half hour.

~~~~~~~/~~~~~~~

"Mama, Papa, Jamie! How is it that I can see you," Elizabeth asked in wonder.

"My darling girl, what fine ladies you and your sisters are becoming. We are so proud of you. As much as we want to see you again, Lizzy, it is not your time yet," Priscilla Bennet told her second daughter.

"Where am I?" Elizabeth asked as she looked around. She could

not make out anything, almost as if she were in the clouds that she would watch in the sky on a windy day.

"This is the in-between place, Lizzy," James Bennet told his daughter.

"I do not understand," a confused Elizabeth told her family members. She tried to walk towards them, to hug and hold them, but she could get no closer than the point she stood at now, about two yards from them.

"You know where you are, Lizzy," Jamie told her. "You just have to allow yourself to acknowledge in your heart what your head already knows."

"It is the place between life and death," Elizabeth said tentatively. "Is it my choice to make, whether I join you or go back?"

"In a way it is, Lizzy," her mother told her. "It is your choice whether or not you fight for your life or give up. It is His decision what ultimately happens to you. I need you to fight, Lizzy, fight with all that you are."

"You do not want me to stay with you, Mama?" Elizabeth cried as tears rolled down her cheeks.

William was sitting next to Elizabeth when he saw tears start to fall from her eyes. He did not understand how she could be crying while unconscious, but he prayed that it was a good sign.

"My darling girl, there is nothing that Mama, Jamie, and I want more than to be reunited with you and your sisters, but we cannot be selfish. One day when He decides it is your time, we will see you again. Do you remember how you and your sisters felt after we were murdered?" Elizabeth nodded.

William saw Elizabeth's head move, almost like she was nodding. He had a footman summon Mr. Jones. "Lizzy was crying and then her head moved, what could that mean?" William asked.

"As I told you earlier Mr. Darcy, there is very little that we know about brain injuries, all we can do is hope that it is a good sign," Mr. Jones responded.

"You know Jane and Mary, even though Jane is as happy as can be with her Alex and little Jamie, they will not be able to get over

another loss, especially not you, that is why you have to fight to wake up and go back to them," her mother explained to Elizabeth.

"I like my nephew's name," Jamie teased, "I could not have chosen better myself."

"If I give up, I will be selfish too...WILLIAM! I love him, I cannot leave him, I have to fight!" Elizabeth realised.

"You see Lizzy, you have much to live for, as much as we loved seeing you, it is time for us to go now. Remember our love for you and your sisters is everlasting..." As her mother said the last word, she, along with Elizabeth's father and brother faded away into the cloud, and then everything went black again.

"Look, you see, she is still again," Mr. Jones told William as he picked up Elizabeth's dainty wrist to take her pulse. "Hmm, that is better, it feels stronger to me, and her breathing is stronger as well. The next few days will tell." Mr. Jones stood and placed his hand on William's shoulder. "We have to have faith that she will be well, Son. All we can do is pray that it is not her time to be with her parents and Jamie."

Mrs. Phillips sat down in the chair next to William. "William, you have to sleep." She raised her hand to stay the protest on his lips. "You will be no good to our girl if you too get sick. Off with you young man, Mrs. Hill prepared the blue guest chambers for you."

"Goodnight Aunt Hattie." William stood and obeyed, he was so tired he felt himself swaying but he steadied himself and made his way to the guest suite. He encountered Mary in the hall in her nightgown and robe.

"Mary, why are you not asleep?" William asked tiredly.

"I had to find out how Lizzy is doing," Mary cried.

"Aunt Hattie just kicked me out and commanded me to go sleep. Lizzy moved a little earlier but seems to rest well now. Mr. Jones had seen some encouraging signs," William told the worried young lady.

"Thank you, William. Do you think Jane will be here in the morning?" Mary asked.

"I do not think wild horses would be able to keep her away.

I expect many arrivals in the next several hours," William surmised. He did not mention the De Melville connection, as he did not feel it was his place to make that particular disclosure. Mary gave him a shy hug and retired to her chamber. William was asleep a half hour later.

CHAPTER 15

The Darcys were preparing for bed when Killion brought the salver to his master. "George, who would send an express now?" a worried Lady Anne asked.

"Good Lord, no!" George Darcy exclaimed.

"What is it, George? Are William and Richard well?" Lady Anne was now very much in fear that there was terrible news.

"It is Lizzy, she was attacked by George Wickham, and she is not in a good way. We need to leave before the first light. Anne, we have to tell Jane now, we cannot keep this from her and Alex," George Darcy exclaimed.

"You have the right of it, George; come, let us go to Alex and Jane's suite." Lady Anne and George Darcy put on their robes and made the way to the suite a few doors down from the master suite. They found Alex's valet exiting the suite and told him to inform his master that they needed to see him and Mrs. Darcy right away. Alex opened the door almost immediately.

Jane did not miss the looks on her parents-in-law's faces. "Mother Anne, Father George, what is it?"

"Lizzy was hurt today; Jane, it is serious," George Darcy told his daughter-in-law as gently as he could. "We will depart for Longbourn at first light."

"What happened?" Alex asked. His father handed him the missive.

"That bast…sorry, Jane and Mother. If he is not dead by the time we get there, I will do it myself!"

"It cannot be helped, but we need to have our personal servants pack tonight so we may depart with no delay in the morning," Lady Anne stated. "Have a footman go directly to Mr.

Bartholomew with a request he be here in the morning so he may journey with us to attend to Lizzy."

Not long after the message was delivered to the Darcys, similar messages were received at Matlock House, where Lord Andrew and Lady Marie Fitzwilliam were in residence, de Bourgh House, and Gracechurch Street. Similar arrangements were made at all three houses for the earliest possible departure for Hertfordshire.

~~~~~~~/~~~~~~~

The last letter delivered was the thick one to Jersey House on St. James square. The butler, knowing that his master would not like to be disturbed at night with an express from an unknown man, placed it in the centre of the Earl's desk, so it would be the first thing that he would see in the morning.

The next morning, as he was wont to do, the Earl of Jersey rose early. He preferred country hours to those most kept in Town. He seated himself at his desk and spied the express. It was rather bulky. Lord Cyril broke the seat and saw that there was a missive wrapped around an envelope addressed to him. He did not recognise either writer's handwriting. As he sipped his morning coffee, he started to read.

February 5, 1807
Longbourn, Hertfordshire
My Lord,
There is no easy way to tell you this. Your sister Priscilla, her husband James, and their oldest, a son Jamie, were all murdered in April '02.

"Brandson! **Brandson**!" Lord Cyril yelled for his butler. The normally inscrutable man entered the Earl's study looking worried. "When did this arrive?" he demanded holding up the express.

"After you and the Countess were abed last night, my Lord," the butler returned.

"Why did you not wake me, Brandson?" Lord Cyril demanded.

"It was your orders that I was following my Lord; you gave me express instructions..." the butler tried to explain.

"You are correct, Brandson, I did issue those orders. You may go." The Earl waved his butler away and reread the opening sentence of the letter. It was too late; he would never see Priscilla again. He proceeded to read the rest of the accompanying letter.

You have three nieces, Jane, who is Mrs. Alexander Darcy, Elizabeth, who God willing will be seventeen soon, and Mary, fourteen. I was under incontrovertible instructions from the late James Bennet to not contact you unless both her and his wife were no longer alive, and it was a dire situation.

Elizabeth was attacked by a blackguard, who is now thankfully in hell, and as of the time of my writing this, she has not regained consciousness. If you desire to be of service to your nieces and meet them, I will answer any questions that you may have.

Sincerely,

Frank Phillips, Esq.

The guilt was crushing as the Earl opened the letter from his late brother-in-law. Would his dear sister still be alive if not for his father's abominable pride? Why did he adhere to a pledge he should never have made, even after his father passed away? It was guilt and cowardice; he should not have acted thusly. He could not change the past but would do all within his power to help Priscilla's daughters now.

May 1799

Longbourn, Hertfordshire

Lord Jersey,

I am loath to write to you after the pain that your father caused, and that you perpetuated after his death, to my most beloved wife. If you are reading this then the worst has occurred and both myself and my beloved are no longer among the living.

I instructed my solicitor not to post this letter except in dire circumstances. As you are reading my words, something has occurred. I hope that you will do your duty to your nephew and nieces and not treat them with the disgusting pride and arrogance that I received from your father.

James Bennet

Reading the letter made the Earl's feelings of shame and guilt palpable. He rang for his butler and told the man to ask the Countess to join him. When Lady Sarah entered the study and saw her husband's pallor, she was genuinely concerned.

"Cyril, what has occurred?" Lady Sarah asked. Her husband silently handed her the two letters. "I am so sorry that your sister is no longer with us, Cyril. We must go to Hertfordshire, and we will take our physician with us!"

"Yes, Sarah, we must go as soon as may be; I will not fail Priscilla after her death as I did in her life!" Lord Cyril stated emphatically. "The one thing that I do not know is how our nieces will receive us once they are informed of the truth about the way their mother was treated first by my father and then by myself."

"All we can do is apologise most sincerely and pray that they are more interested in the future than the past. And Cyril," Lady Sarah looked at her husband and waited until he met her eyes, "no remonstrating with this Mr. Phillips that he did not send the letter earlier, he was honouring your late brother's wishes."

As the packing was being done for the family to travel, a note was received from Mr. Bartholomew's housekeeper informing Lady Sarah that the doctor had departed with the Darcys some hours previously. Less than two hours later, the De Melvilles were on the road to Meryton and the estate of Longbourn.

~~~~~~~/~~~~~~~

After sleeping barely two hours, William returned to Elizabeth's side and spent the rest of the night sitting by her side. To him, it seemed like she was sleeping comfortably, but he had no way of knowing, and not being able to help his beloved Elizabeth was gutting him.

"William, you have been with our Lizzy most of the night. I thought I sent you to bed some eight hours ago! Allow Miss Ponsonby and me to sit with her. You need to sleep. You will be no good to anyone if you make yourself sick too," Hattie Phillips instructed.

"I will go soon, Aunt Hattie, you have my word," an exhausted William replied.

"You will sleep a minimum of four hours, William!" Hattie Phillips ordered. "I will make sure that Carstens is aware. He will wake you by ten, and then you will have some food. Understand, William?"

"You have my word of honour," William said as he leaned over and kissed Lizzy on the forehead. He walked out of the chamber reluctantly and fell onto the bed that was ready for his use and was asleep within minutes.

Hattie and Miss Ponsonby noticed as Elizabeth became restless. "Please wake Mr. Jones," Hattie Phillips requested Miss Ponsonby.

Elizabeth could see the three figures again! They seemed to float above her, but they were indistinct. She could not talk to them, nor they to her. They were simply watching her, saying a final goodbye. She was not in a cloud this time; she was lying down in a bed, and she had just felt lips on her forehead. Elizabeth felt that the person who had kissed her was someone extremely important to her. William!

'I have to get back to William and my sisters!' Elizabeth told herself. As she made that final decision, the three faded away completely and Elizabeth for the first time believed all would be well.

By the time Mr. Jones arrived and just before Mrs. Phillips was about to send Miss Ponsonby to summon William Darcy, Elizabeth calmed and returned to her peaceful state. "I am sorry that I had you woken, Mr. Jones, but Lizzy got agitated, but her agitation subsided as quickly as it had commenced," Mrs. Phillips informed the medical man.

"She has no fever," Mr. Jones reported as he placed the back of his hand against Elizabeth's forehead. "She seems as well as she can be under the circumstances."

"The poor girl. Thank goodness that the vile man is no more!" Mrs. Phillips exclaimed vehemently.

Just then Major Richard Fitzwilliam walked into the sickroom. After accompanying Sir William back to Lucas Lodge and filling in some more background information about the miscreant, the Major had made his way to Netherfield. He had warned the Nichols to expect an influx of visitors soon. By the time he rode away from Netherfield Park, maids and footmen were swarming over all the available chambers to make them ready.

"How is our Lizzy this morning?" The Major asked. "Where is William? I would have thought he would be here at her side."

"You just missed him, Richard. I ordered him to sleep; he looked haggard," Hattie Phillips reported.

"I would have liked to see my great, big, tall cousin ordered around like an errant child," Richard Fitzwilliam chuckled.

"I can do the same for you if you like, Richard."

"Unlike William I *did* sleep last night, Aunt," the Major returned and left the chambers before he got himself into trouble again.

~~~~~~~/~~~~~~~

Just before ten in the morning, the Darcy, Fitzwilliam, and De Bourgh carriages arrived, almost simultaneously, at Longbourn. The Darcy equipages were between the Fitzwilliam's in front and the De Bourgh's behind them. At almost the same time, Alexander Darcy and Lord Andrew Fitzwilliam helped their wives out of their respective carriages.

The two couples stared at one another, as the rest of the occupants of the various carriages exited. Lord Andrew, Viscount Hilldale, had suspected that Marie and Jane looked similar, but the two looked like they could have been twin sisters. Alexander, who had spent little time in Marie's company, looked from his wife to his cousin's wife in amazement, not believing what he was seeing.

The two couples closed the distance with eyes still locked on one another. "You must be my cousin, Marie," Jane surmised. "I would love to find out why we look like one another, but I must see Lizzy."

"Of course, my love," Alexander nodded to his cousin as they turned and walked in, past Mr. Hill who could not credit what he was seeing.

"My goodness, Anne, our daughters look like they could be twin sisters!" Lady Elaine exclaimed to her sister-in-law.

"I think I understand why Sarah wrote that letter to us. Do you think that the Priscilla who was Jane's mother was Lady Priscilla De Melville as was?" Lady Anne surmised.

"If you are correct, then I would expect to see the De Melvilles here," Lady Catherine conjectured.

"If someone has informed them, I understand there was a major split in the family when Priscilla De Melville defied her father," Lady Anne shared. As the arriving party entered the house, the Gardiner carriage halted on the doorstep. Mrs. Gardiner directed the nursemaids to take the children to the nursery while she and her husband went to wait in the drawing room.

Anne de Bourgh made a beeline for the younger Darcy couple and followed them into the house. As Alexander, Jane, and Anne stepped onto the landing outside Lizzy's chambers, William stepped out of the chamber he had been using while at Longbourn. "Jane, it is so good that you are here!" William exclaimed, "you too, Andrew."

"Jane!" Mary flew into her older sister's open arms. "I am so worried about Lizzy." The tears that had been threatening since hearing of what had befallen her sister spilled out of Jane's eyes, as she clutched her younger sister to herself.

As the five entered the bedchamber, William saw Lizzy stir. She was fighting to open her eyes. William went around the bed and took Elizabeth's left hand in his, while Jane and Mary grasped her other hand. Miss Ponsonby unobtrusively slipped out of the room to make more space.

"Lizzy, I am here," Jane told her sister. "Please wake up, dearest. Little Jamie wants to see his aunt, please dearest."

"Lizzy, please come back to me, I love you and I care not who knows. I beseech you, Lizzy," William pleaded.

"O-only if y-y-you say i-it again," Elizabeth croaked out as her eyes fluttered open.

William assisted her to sit as the older family members

congregated in the hall outside the chamber. He lovingly held a glass of water as Elizabeth took a few sips. "I will tell you I love you as many times as you are willing to hear it, Lizzy. We were so very worried for you!" William told her softly as she took sips of water.

"W-where is the man t-that said he was the h-heir to Longbourn?" Elizabeth asked.

"He will never bother you or any other again," William informed her. "He murdered Longbourn's heir, and his name was Wickham."

George and Alexander got thunderous looks on their countenances as William mentioned the blackguard's name. "Wickham has been sent to Hades where he belongs," the Major stated dispassionately from behind his Darcy uncle and cousin.

"I know that everyone wants to talk to Miss Lizzy," Mr. Jones said as he and Mr. Bartholomew entered Elizabeth's chamber "but please allow us some time to examine the patient and then we will report back to all of you shortly." William looked like he was about to argue when Elizabeth arched an eyebrow at him, and he followed the rest out of the chamber. It left the two doctors, Jane, Anne de Bourgh who refused to leave her friend's side, Miss Ponsonby, and Elizabeth's maid inside once the door was closed.

"Let us withdraw to the drawing room; I am sure that you all have many questions." Phillips turned to lead the rest down the stairs when he was halted by the lady who looked just like Jane and the late Priscilla Bennet. Once everyone was seated in the drawing room, the two nursemaids handed little Lewis to Charlotte and little Jamie to Alexander. First Marie was introduced to the four Phillipses, Mr. & Mrs. Gardiner, and Mary Bennet.

"How is it that you look so much like my late Mama and Jane," Mary blurted out. "I apologise your Ladyship, but the resemblance is striking.

"No apology is needed, Miss Mary; it is the same question that I have had since I met your oldest sister upon our arrival.

"There is a simple explanation," Phillips stated. "Priscilla Bennet was Lady Priscilla De Melville before she married your father, Mary. She was sister to Lady Marie's father."

"How can that be?" Lady Marie asked in shock. "Father has never spoken about a sister, nor did grandfather before he passed away." No one noticed the newcomers standing at the door to the drawing room.

"That is because I was a coward, Daughter, and did not stand up to my father's unreasonable dictates long before today," Lord Cyril said as he, Lady Sarah, Lord Wesley, and Lady Loretta entered the drawing room. He had requested that the butler not disturb his oldest as she was speaking when they arrived. "Your grandfather placed too much store in rank and perceived wealth and tried to deny my sister's marriage to the man she loved."

"So even without Jane's marriage to Alex and yours to Andrew, you and the three Bennet sisters are first cousins," Phillips informed the stunned Viscountess.

"If we had a family by blood, why were we not told about them before, Uncle Frank?" Mary enquired. Before he could answer, Jane Darcy and the two doctors entered the drawing room.

"Miss Lizzy, I should say Miss Bennet, will be well. She will need much rest for the next few weeks, and she will suffer from severe headaches. She refuses to take laudanum, so headache powers and the occasional sleeping draught will have to suffice," Mr. Jones reported.

"From our examination and the fact that the young lady is awake barely four and twenty hours after her injury, the chances that there is any internal damage to the skull and brain are negligible," Mr. Bartholomew added.

"You know Lizzy will chafe at the restrictions of having to stay abed," Jane Darcy pointed out.

"You are correct Miss J…I mean Mrs. Darcy, but it is very important that she not move much until her headaches are all but gone," Mr. Jones informed them.

"She was incredibly lucky as whatever it was she struck with her head, from examining the gash that my colleague stitched, was not a sharp object. In my opinion, it was more of a glancing blow than a penetrating wound. Had the object breached Miss Bennet's skull, the outcome could have been vastly different," Mr. Bartholomew told the assembled family.

A worried Georgiana had been silent, but asked, "When may I see Lizzy?"

"She is asleep again, Gigi, but if you want to go sit with her, you will see her when she wakes," Jane told her sister-in-law.

"Mama, I will go with Gigi, but I would like to go to the nursery first to inform Lyddie and Anna that Lizzy will be well," Kitty requested of Hattie Phillips who nodded her permission. The two medical men withdrew to the small dining parlour to have some sustenance.

"Before we hear more about the De Melville connection, what was that wastrel George Wickham doing here?" George Darcy insisted.

Between Phillips, William, and Richard, the assembled party was informed of how Bennet had set Collins and Wickham on a path towards Longbourn to try and get some measure of revenge against those he claimed *stole* Longbourn from him. Wickham's confession that he had murdered Collins in an attempt to supplant him as heir to Longbourn was explained. Phillips relayed his suspicions that the man was looking for any way to get money from the estate and Wickham's debts had driven his need for funds.

William and Richard retold how they came upon Wickham's attempt to violate Elizabeth and the way the coward pushed her in his vain attempt to escape capture ending with Richard running the blackguard down with his charger. Richard received many pats on the back during the retelling.

"How did my sister, brother-in-law, and nephew lose their lives?" Lord Cyril asked.

Phillips and Gardiner told of the murders and how Fanny and Thomas Bennet just *happened* to be in the area days after. Phillips relayed how upset Bennet had been to discover that due to the entail he could not sell the property.

Gardiner recounted how they had eventually contacted the holder of Bennet's debts and purchased them and called them in, giving Bennet the choice between Marshalsea or leaving Longbourn forever. Phillips relayed how the Bennets had abandoned their two daughters without a thought and left as soon as they could with the money they were allowed to take with them.

Lastly, Gardiner spoke about the search for Bennet and his crimes after he left Longbourn. He informed all how *the Spaniard's* men had found the two accomplices and they had sworn affidavits against Bennet in return for permanent transportation rather than hanging and that Bennet was currently being held at Newgate. "Now that there is not an issue with a legitimate heir, I will send an express to my solicitor to have the trial held as soon as may be," Gardiner added at the end of his recitation. Gardiner saw Phillips shake his head imperceptibly. They would need to talk to see why his friend did not want him to dispatch the express.

"What will happen to Longbourn now?" George Darcy asked.

"According to the entail, if there are no more male heirs, and there *are* no others, then James Bennet's will decides the disposition of the estate. His will states that it is to be left to his surviving children if it comes to pass that there is no male heir. This ends the entail of the male heir but leaves in place the entail making it impossible to break up or sell any of the estate to a person not a Bennet by blood," Phillips answered comprehensively.

"It should be left to Lizzy and Mary as I have no need for the estate, as one day, hopefully many years from now, my husband will be master of a somewhat larger one," Jane said as she looked at her father-in-law with warmth.

"And Lizzy will not need it, as we have Netherfield," William said raising many eyebrows at his bold declaration. "However, before that decision is made, I will canvass her opinion on the matter."

"Mr. Phillips, I understand that my late brother-in-law restricted you to contacting me except in a very grave situation,"

Lord Cyril stated.

"Yes, my Lord, and it is Phillips."

"My niece called you Uncle. Phillips, how were you related to Bennet?" Lord Cyril asked.

"I am not, but after we evicted Thomas and Fanny Bennet, I, along with Gardiner here, Sir William Lucas, who you will meet soon enough, and George Darcy all become guardians of the three sisters," Phillips replied. "I know you are a blood relative, but James Bennet was furious at you, not for any slight or hurt directed at himself, but for the way that your father and you hurt his beloved Priscilla. He could forgive anything, but not that."

"It shames me that I behaved in such a cowardly way. I hid behind honour when the truth is I was afraid of the upbraiding, a much deserved one, that Priscilla would unleash if I ever approached her again after waiting so long. It is my greatest regret that I did not stand up to my domineering and arrogant father," Lord Cyril said in contrition.

"Uncle, there is nothing that we can do about the past, only the present and future. I think we should all take Lizzy's philosophy: only remember the past as that remembrance gives you pleasure," Mary said as she smiled at her newly discovered uncle.

"It seems that I have some wise nieces," Lord Cyril observed. Turning to William, in the same way his three nieces did, he arched an eyebrow. "As the closest living male relative, is there something that you would like to ask me young Darcy?"

"Not yet my Lord; I need to ask the lady first. You will find out soon enough that the lady in question does not take kindly to officious arranging of her life without being consulted. She can flay you with her tongue when she is angry," William stated shuddering as he remembered how angry Lizzy had been with him before his brother's wedding.

"Then she is very much like the Priscilla that I remember before she married," Lady Sarah smiled.

William informed all the arrivals that Netherfield was prepared to host all of them. The Gardiners elected to remain at

Longbourn, also Anne de Bourgh refused to leave the estate until her friend was once more up and about.

CHAPTER 16

"I am very happy to meet my cousins," Jane stated as she sat in the drawing room at Netherfield. "I agree with Lizzy's philosophy that Mary repeated at Longbourn, however, your Lordship, how am I to forgive and forget the way you treated my mother? She was the best mother in the world to me, my brother, and my sisters. Your father disowned her because my father was not high enough for him, and then you chose to do the same."

"While I seek forgiveness for my cowardly and thoughtless actions, I am not asking you to forget, Mrs. Darcy. At this time you do not trust me; I understand that. All I ask is that you give me a chance to show you that I have learnt from my past actions, or inaction as it was in this case," Lord Cyril postulated. "If I had more of a backbone, I would have made contact with your mother even while my father was alive, but I failed my sister; I will not fail her daughters."

Lord Wesley looked at his father with disappointment. He then added his opinion when he said, "Father, you know well it is not only our cousins and aunt and uncle you failed. You robbed us of knowing our cousins for many years, years that we can never get back."

"Son, I am well aware of my failings and as your cousin Mary stated so eloquently, there is naught that I can do to change any of my past behaviour. You have no idea how it hurt my dear mother that my father cut contact with Priscilla. I wish there were a way to go back and make different decisions, but I cannot." Lord Cyril stated contritely.

"Believe me when I tell you that your father has agonised over this for years. It does not change the fact that you were all denied knowing one another or meeting Priscilla, who was a good friend to me before she was disowned. Mayhap we sometimes take the commandment *to honour thy mother and father too far*," Lady Sarah opined.

"People make mistakes, Jane," Lady Anne, who had been quiet up to that point, told her daughter-in-law. "Is not forgiveness one of the central tenets of our belief as Christians?"

"Yes, Mother Anne, it is," Jane owned. "Do not expect me to call you 'Uncle' yet, your Lordship, but am willing to move forward from here and will try not to look to the past too much."

"If you are done with maudlin subjects, did William make a very public declaration to our Lizzy when she awoke?" Lady Catherine asked.

"From what I hear, she made the declaration right back, Mother Cat," Charlotte de Bourgh stated.

"My wife has the right of it," Peter de Bourgh declared. "It seems that a romantic heart is beating in the chest of our staid cousin." Peter grinned.

"You know full well that my brother is not staid, Peter," Alexander defended his absent brother. "He is shy and not gregarious like you, Cousin, but he is as romantic, if not more so, than any of us!"

"Seeing Marie and Jane sitting next to one another, I see Priscilla when she was their age. She would have loved to see little Jamie enter the world, Jane," Lady Elaine stated sadly. Like Lady Sarah, she had been a friend of Lady Priscilla De Melville. They had gone to school together and lost touch before the debacle of her being disowned. Each one had assumed the other did not desire further contact.

Lord Cyril was not the only one who felt guilty that they had not maintained the connection with Priscilla Bennet. At least the others had paid penance for some years now as they looked after their friend's children, without knowing that they were hers.

~~~~~~~/~~~~~~~

Elizabeth still had a severe headache, but other than that she was starting to recuperate. The morning following her waking up, she had a good nourishing breakfast. She was very happy when William joined her in her chambers just after she had been washed and changed. Anne, Miss Ponsonby, and her maid were present for the sake of propriety, even though Elizabeth decided she would not mind being compromised and having to marry William right away.

As if reading his adoptive niece's mind, Phillips joined the two immediately after he broke his fast. "I am for London with Gardiner this morning, but I wanted to talk to you two before I depart. You both made a very public declaration last night. Are you both sure that it is what you want?" he asked the couple after asking the three ladies to give them some privacy.

"Anne, please stay," Elizabeth reached for her friend, "you are family so there is no reason for you to leave." Anne sat down with a big smile on her face.

"As long as Anne's presence is acceptable to William as well." Phillips looked at William who nodded his head as he reached for and took Elizabeth's hand. "As I was saying, what the two of you said last night was before many witnesses. More than that, anyone that knows the two of you has no doubt that you are formed for each other. You will be seventeen in under two months Lizzy, if you are both sure, my fellow guardians agree that William may ask the question he desires to now. If you become betrothed today, the only stipulation is that the wedding be after Lizzy makes her curtsy before the Queen a sennight before her birthday." Phillips looked at William again. "Would you like five minutes alone with Lizzy, William?" The dimple-revealing smile was the only answer that Phillips needed as he and Anne de Bourgh stood and vacated the bedchamber. The door was not closed all the way.

Elizabeth sat up as much as she could in the bed as William went down on one knee. That caused both to laugh. William's head was at the level of the bed, so all Elizabeth could see was his head and the hand that still held her own. A grinning William seated himself back in the chair next to the bed.

"William, please do not cause me to laugh; it hurts my head too much," Elizabeth told him.

"My aim here is not to cause you pain, Lizzy. In fact, I hope to engender the opposite." William cleared his throat. "Lizzy, Elizabeth Rose Bennet, my ardent love for you is not the work of a moment, but of long duration. There could never be anyone else that I want to walk life's paths with besides you. You are the most beautiful woman of my acquaintance, but your beauty is not skin deep; it is infused in your character, your very being.

"I love your charitable nature. Most grasping ladies would have jumped at being able to add to their portion if they had a share of your late brother's legacy, but you suggested dowering your cousins and the rest for charity. I am but a second son, but I know that has never been an impediment for you. My family has loved you since the day that they met you and you are already a sister of the heart to Gigi and Anna.

"Please make me the happiest man in the world and agree to be my partner, my helpmate, my wife." William poured his heart out to his beloved Elizabeth.

"I have loved you almost since the day we met, William. No one will be able to say that my love is born of gratitude for saving me from that vile man. For not a few years now, I have known that if I did not marry you, I would never settle for anyone else. So yes, William, and for all eternity, yes, I will marry you." Elizabeth said the words that made her betrothed glow with pleasure.

William did not want to do anything to cause his betrothed to move too much so he leaned forward in question, seeing her close her eyes with anticipation, he brushed his lips on hers for the first, albeit chaste, kiss. He drew his head back; he would wait until her headaches had subsided and then they would be able to kiss as he wanted, and from her look of longing, so did Elizabeth.

There was a knock on the door and Phillips and Anne slowly entered the bedchamber. The looks on both members of the newly betrothed couple's faces said all. "Is there something that you need to ask me William?" Phillips asked.

"I have requested Lizzy's hand in marriage, and she had granted my most ardent desire in agreeing to marry me," William fairly gushed.

"In that case let me be the first to wish you both joy and confer my hearty consent and blessing." Phillips had barely completed his statement before Anne de Bourgh's effusions began.

"If you ever mistreat my friend, William..." she stated with mock severity. "Oh, I know you never will; I am so happy for both of you. I knew how it would be! Lizzy is your perfect match, Cousin."

"You are almost as happy as I am, Anne," Elizabeth smiled. No one missed that neither one of the couple had relinquished the other's hand.

"Before I depart for London, there is something I must impart to you." Phillips became more serious. "You have an uncle, aunt, and cousins that you never knew about. He is Lord Cyril De Melville, the Earl of Jersey, and is your late mother's brother." Seeing the look of absolute surprise, Phillips explained it all to Elizabeth.

"If that is how that man treated my mama, then I have no desire to know him!" Elizabeth stated angrily.

"Lizzy, I beg you to remember your own philosophy about the past," Phillips entreated. "I have spoken to the Earl, and he is full of regret and shame about his father's and his own past actions. He has openly acknowledged this was a case when the son should not have honoured the dictates of the father, but as you well know he cannot change the past.

"It was your father's wishes that stopped me sending the letter right after the murders, I see in hindsight that I should have sent it right away, as you would have been living under your true uncle's protection these past years and would never have had to live in the same house with the murderers for even a day." Phillips regretted his error in judgement.

"I will think on it, Uncle Frank, and then make a decision. It may take me a while to reconcile myself to his Lordship and forgive him for hurting Mama," Elizabeth allowed.

"You know, technically, I need to ask the Earl for permission to marry you as he is your closest male blood relative," William grinned, seeing the look of horror on his betrothed's face. "He heard about our declarations yesterday my love, I promise you, he will not deny my petition."

"Where is that man who tried to attack me, William? He claimed to be some sort of cousin, but I remember you using another name before I became unconscious," Elizabeth asked with trepidation.

"His name *was* George Wickham, and he is no longer among the living," William replied.

"You did not…" Elizabeth did not want to say the words.

"No love, I did not, Richard's charger knocked him down and his fall was a lot more severe than yours," William related.

"Wait! I remember that name. Was that not the man that you and Alex ran off Pemberley's lands on one of our visits?" Elizabeth recalled.

"Yes, Lizzy, the very same wastrel," William confirmed. "He has been buried in a potter's field so you will never have to think about him again."

"Lizzy, I do want to prepare you for somewhat of a shock. The Earl's oldest daughter, Lady Marie, is the one who is married to Andrew. You know how closely Jane resembles your late mother?" Phillips asked. Elizabeth nodded. "Lady Marie and Jane look like they could be twin sisters, their resemblance is so close."

"Thank you for telling me, Uncle Frank. Please do not berate yourself about not contacting my mama's brother sooner; you simply did what Papa instructed you to do," Elizabeth said, thereby absolving Phillips of the guilt he was feeling.

"When you think about the Earl, remember that he was following the dictates of his father," William interjected.

"Gardiner and I will depart for London not long after the Netherfield party arrives," Phillips informed.

"May I ask what business you have in London, Uncle Frank?" Elizabeth asked. Seeing her uncle looking somewhat uncomfortable she started to retract her question. "That was impertinent of me…" Phillips held up his hand to stay her.

"Bennet is in Newgate. We had delayed the trial until we discovered if the man claiming to be the heir was genuine, as those questions have all been answered, there is no reason to delay any longer," Phillips relayed dispassionately. Elizabeth had questions about how and where Bennet was apprehended and was pleased he would finally be called to account for murdering her father, mother, and brother.

Hearing the sounds of arriving carriages, Phillips and William left to welcome the arriving family as they were replaced with Madeline Gardiner, who joined Anne de Bourgh in Elizabeth's bedchamber.

~~~~~~~/~~~~~~~

If Elizabeth had not been warned that Lady Marie Fitzwilliam resembled Jane and her mother so closely, she would have thought that she was seeing things. What she had been told was accurate; the two women looked like twins. A young man and a lady were standing next to Lady Marie.

"Lizzy, do you feel up to meeting some cousins?" Jane asked.

"I am, Jane. Although technically this is the second time they will be our cousins," Elizabeth jested.

"Miss Bennet is correct; we are cousins by marriage and blood," Lady Marie responded.

"As we are double cousins; I think we can do away with formality do you not? I am Elizabeth or, as you heard Jane call me, Lizzy," Elizabeth said welcomingly. She may not be ready to forgive the father, but her cousins were blameless.

"In that case, Lizzy, I am Marie, this handsome young man is my brother, Wesley. We all call him Wes and hiding behind him is Loretta who is called Retta," Marie introduced her siblings.

"Am I correct that you found out about us at the same time that we were told about you?" Elizabeth asked.

All three siblings nodded. "Our mother would like to meet

you if that is agreeable to you," Wesley requested on behalf of his mother. Having been told that his late sister's middle daughter was slow to forgive, Lord Cyril made the wise decision not to request an introduction yet.

"It would be a pleasure to meet your mother," Elizabeth agreed. Loretta stepped out and returned with an elegant looking lady, who was very fashionably dressed, but nothing ostentatious.

"Mother, this is our cousin, Lizzy, Miss Bennet. Lizzy, this is our mother Lady Sarah De Melville, Countess of Jersey," Wesley had the honour of making the introduction.

"As my children seem to be on familiar name terms with you, I would be pleased if you will call me Aunt Sarah," the Countess requested.

"I am happy to meet you, Aunt Sarah. Are you not one of the patronesses of Almack's?" Elizabeth greeted her new aunt.

"It is particularly good to see you starting to recover, Elizabeth. When we received Mr. Phillips' missive with the one from your late father we feared the worst. Yes, I am one of the patronesses so you, like your sisters, will receive as many vouchers to attend as you wish, if you wish to experience it that is." Lady Sarah paused and decided to carry on having heard that Elizabeth preferred straight talk. "My husband understands that you may be justifiably angry with him, so he will not request an introduction until you feel ready to meet him."

"Please, let the Earl know that I appreciate being able to wait until I feel it is right, Aunt Sarah," Elizabeth felt relieved that the Earl would not force his presence on her. It was a point in his favour.

Just then, William and the rest of the Darcys crowded into the bedchamber. Anne slipped out to give them more room, very sure she knew what news was about to be shared. Lady Sarah and her children were about to exit as well when Elizabeth requested that they remain. William stood next to his betrothed and looked at the assembled family in her bedchamber. He looked at Elizabeth, who gave him a quick nod of her head.

"It is my pleasure to inform you that before you arrived, I requested Lizzy's hand in marriage and she made me the happiest of men by accepting me," William said with pride. There was a cacophony of well wishes as everyone wanted to wish the couple well. Elizabeth raised an eyebrow in question.

"Yes, your uncle, I mean the Earl, did not object in the least," William whispered, so only Elizabeth would hear. That was another point in the man's favour, as he did not exercise the authority that he had.

"Lizzy, I am so excited for you and William," Georgiana gushed. "Have you decided on a date yet?"

"Uncle Frank said not before I make my curtsy before the Queen in early March," Elizabeth shared.

"What about on your birthday, Lizzy?" William suggested, "I looked at a calendar, it is a Tuesday."

"There you go, Gigi, we have a date," Elizabeth told her sister of the heart.

"Am I too old to be the flower girl?" Annabeth asked her mother.

"I am afraid so my love, but if Lizzy would like, the youngest Gardiner girl, May, is just the right age," Lady Anne informed her youngest.

"Where do you want to marry from, Lizzy?" William asked.

"I had thought to follow Jane's example and marry from somewhere else as our parents are not here. My mind has changed; I believe that Mama, Papa, and Jamie are here looking out for us, so I would like to marry from Longbourn," Elizabeth responded. She remembered part of the dream she had while unconscious and honestly believed her parents and brother's presence would always be with them.

"It is a great pity that I do not have a third son for Mary to marry so that I would have all three of you as daughters," George Darcy stated as he leant down to kiss his newest daughter on the forehead.

"No you do not, Father George." The Darcy patriarch was well pleased to be thusly addressed by his secretly favourite Bennet sister. "However, Uncle Reggie and Aunt Elaine do have an unmarried son," Elizabeth joked.

"No matchmaking, Lizzy," came a mock indignant voice from the hallway as the Major poked his head into the chamber. "Do *not* put any ideas into mother's head, she is like a dog with a bone; she will not let the subject rest."

"Of what are you talking, my son?" Lady Elaine asked as she came to congratulate her nephew and niece-to-be. Once William had requested that his family join him in Elizabeth's bedchamber, Phillips informed the rest, of the momentous news of that day.

"It is a pity that Netherfield is so far from Pemberley," Jane said wistfully. "I suppose we will see each other in Town."

"This is as good a time as any to tell you," George Darcy stated. "Jane and Lizzy, you know of Bennington Fields do you not?" Both sisters nodded. "The family is for the New World and when the estate came on the market, I purchased it as a satellite estate. How would you and Alex like to live at, and manage, the Fields until the day arrives for you to move to Pemberley, Jane?"

Alexander looked at his wife and saw the way her face lit up with joy. "That is an excellent idea, Father; we cannot thank you enough."

It had been an exciting day so far, but it was taking its toll on Elizabeth, whose head told her that it was time to rest. Jane elected to remain in her sister's bedchamber and sit with her while she slept along with Elizabeth's lady's maid. The rest headed back to the drawing room.

~~~~~~~/~~~~~~~

The men met in the west parlour while their ladies and offspring were in the drawing room. Phillips informed them that they were to London to have the delay in Bennet's trial lifted. "Why not just write a missive?" Lewis de Bourgh asked.

"Gardiner was going to, but I want to look into that criminal's eyes when I tell him how his revenge failed," Phillips explained.

"In that case, may I accompany you?" Lord Cyril requested. "If we need to overnight, we can use Jersey House. I too want to see the man who murdered my sister and part of her family!"

Thus it was decided. The three men would depart after the midday meal.

CHAPTER 17

The three men arrived at Newgate prison in the late afternoon. Gardiner requested that Bennet be placed in a room where they could meet with him. A half hour later one of the guards directed them to a room where a sullen Bennet was shackled to a ring in the table. "What do you want here," Bennet spat. "And who is this man?"

"I am the brother of the woman that you murdered," Lord Cyril informed Bennet.

"Fanny did not have a brother," Bennet was confused, at least he did not remember a brother.

"Not your murdered wife's brother. I am Lord Cyril De Melville brother of Priscilla Bennet that you murdered!" the Earl practically yelled at Bennet.

"What should I care who you are. These idiotic men need me alive so the heir that I sent to Longbourn cannot inherit." Bennet laughed, but it sounded more like a cackle.

"That is just it, we are here to tell you that we no longer need you alive!" Phillips exclaimed as Bennet blanched. "Thanks to you the entail concerning male heirs is broken."

"W-what d-do y-you mean?" Bennet asked all bravado gone.

"You sent two men towards Longbourn, one was Collins, the late heir presumptive, and the second one was a lascivious fortune hunter, George Wickham. You told them of massive dowries to get Wickham interested and hoping he would hurt one of the sisters." Gardiner recounted.

"The late heir? Did you have him murdered?" Bennet wanted to know.

"Do you think we are like you? Wickham murdered Collins

on the way to Longbourn. Wickham then tried to pass himself off as Collins to acquire the estate, also to pay debts to *the Spaniard*, so you have that and being a murderer in common," Phillips stated.

"We wanted to see your face when we told you that your attempted revenge failed. You will be in the Old Bailey on the morrow, and if things go according to the way we expect, you will swing the next morning!" Gardiner told the now shaking man.

"You are very lucky that you are safe in gaol!" Lord Cyril glared at the cowering man. "I would have you feel the pain that you inflicted before ending your waste of a life!"

"We will see you in court in the morning, Bennet. You will receive no more wine, of any quality, and enjoy being back in the communal cell." Gardiner followed the two others out of the room as they heard invectives and abuses yelled by the criminal Bennet at them.

~~~~~~~~/~~~~~~~~

Bennet's case was heard at nine in the morning. By ten, he was convicted on all charges and sentenced to the ultimate penalty to be carried out that same day. Given the speed of his trial, Bennet was able to make the early afternoon hanging.

The three men watched as Bennet was dragged to the gallows begging for his life and still trying to blame everyone but himself. He was forced to stand above the trapdoor as the hangman placed the noose and tightened it whereupon the howling man soiled himself. The pastor said a short prayer and the lever was pulled. Thomas Bennet would never hurt another living being again.

Lord Cyril, Gardiner, and Phillips were satisfied that the story of Thomas Bennet was at an end. None of the men applauded the loss of a life, but for someone who had committed multiple murders and other crimes, this was a fitting end. The men returned to Jersey House, had a small meal, and spent the evening in quiet reflection. Early the next morning they departed for Hertfordshire.

~~~~~~~/~~~~~~~

Lord Cyril kept his word and did not force his company on his niece Elizabeth. At the same time, his wife and children all became close to the Bennets and former Bennets. Loretta became part of the close friendship circle that Mary and Georgiana enjoyed. Wesley and Marie got much closer with Jane and Elizabeth.

Each time she saw Jane and Marie together, Elizabeth had to remind herself it was not an illusion created by the blow to her head that she had experienced. To her doctors' pleasure, Elizabeth seemed to be recovering much faster than they expected. By a sennight after the attack, her headaches were all but gone. The improvement was so rapid that Mr. Bartholomew said goodbye and returned to his practice in London.

Jane bestowed her complete forgiveness on her uncle four days after the three men returned from Town. He was joyful when the next day, Jane followed Mary's example and called him Uncle Cyril.

The day that the doctor returned to London, Jane, Alexander, Anne, and of course William visited Elizabeth in her bedchamber.

"Jane, you have forgiven Lord Cyril and now call him 'uncle' like Mary does, do you not?" Elizabeth asked.

"I have Lizzy. I looked to your philosophy, but it was more than that. I see genuine regret for his actions in our uncle. How would any of us wilfully go against a promise made to a parent? It is up to you, but you may want to meet him and judge for yourself," Jane advised.

"You may be right, Jane. I think it is time to meet my uncle. You do not hold it against me that I have taken my time do you, Marie?" Elizabeth asked her cousin.

"You needed to decide on your own. Papa knows that had someone forced any of you ladies, there would never have been a genuine relationship between him and his nieces. Jane did not forgive him right away and nobody held that against her," Marie replied.

"I, for one, am very happy that your *whole* family came to Longbourn," Anne blushed. No one had missed how much time Wesley and Anne spent in one another's company talking quietly and not noticing any other in the room.

"Anne, you are only pleased since a certain Viscount is here," Elizabeth teased her friend.

"Lizzy," Anne batted Elizbeth's hand but never refuted what had been said.

"Never have I seen you blush with such colour, Anne, I wonder what had caused your change in colour," William added to his betrothed's tease.

"Little brother, do you not remember how fearsome our cousin can be when you rile her?" Alexander grinned.

Anne looked like she was about to swat William when Elizabeth distracted her betrothed. "William, rather than embarrass your cousin, would you ask unc—Lord Cyril if he is willing to attend me?" William left the chamber after kissing Elizabeth's hand.

When William returned with the tentative looking Earl, Elizabeth's other three visitors stood and vacated the bedchamber. William looked at his beloved who shook her head to his unspoken question whether he should join the others. He sat in his chair as he took one of Elizabeth's hands in his.

"Your Lordsh...Uncle, it is time for me to join my sisters and move forward. I forgive you as my sisters have, but not because they did. Having spoken to William and my sisters I believe that your contrition is genuine and as Jane pointed out, none of us can know how we would have reacted in a similar situation with immense pressure from an honoured parent. I am Elizabeth Rose, named, as I now understand, after both of my grandmothers," Elizabeth stated as she drew strength from her hand connected to William.

"It is not just regret that I feel, but deep guilt and shame as well Miss Benn..." Lord Cyril started when Elizabeth interjected.

"Elizabeth or Lizzy if you please, Uncle Cyril," she told him with an arched eyebrow, just like his sister Priscilla used to do.

"Thank you, Lizzy. Your mother used to do the same with her eyebrow," he reminisced.

"That is where all three of us inherited the trait from," Elizabeth informed her uncle.

"My guilt is the greatest because I knew that the separation from your mother broke my mother's heart. If only I had dared to go against my father," he stated with anguish.

"Now is not the time to look back, but to move forward. There is no point remonstrating over the past as none of us can change it. It took almost seventeen years to meet you and your family, so I do not want to waste any more time on recriminations that are counterproductive. I know you are our only male blood relative; you will not make us leave Longbourn will you," Elizabeth asked.

"First, Lizzy, would that not be irrelevant to you considering that you are to marry in March, and I assume will be moving to Netherfield Park? Even were that not true, as it is not for Mary, I will not exert any authority over you and your sisters. It seems that Phillips, Gardiner, and Sir William have been remarkably effective guardians so there is no need for me to insert myself just because I am capable to do so. I will do nothing that I am not specifically requested to do," Lord Cyril promised.

More than anything else, her uncle's speech convinced Elizabeth of the rectitude of allowing him to be part of her life.

~~~~~~~/~~~~~~~

For the first time since being confined to her bed, Mr. Jones agreed that Elizabeth could descend the stairs the next day to be with everyone, if she first went a full four and twenty hours without any serious headache. She promised Mr. Jones if she felt fatigued, she would return to her bed and rest.

When she woke up that morning with nary a headache, Elizabeth could barely contain her excitement. For the first time in over a week, Elizabeth had her maid dress her in a day dress.

Once she was ready, William was waiting for her outside of her chamber being as solicitous as he always was.

"Do you need me to assist you down the stairs, Lizzy?" William asked.

"The bannister will help steady me, as long as I have your arm to hold with my other hand," Elizabeth replied.

"You are so beautiful, Lizzy, it is a joyful day now that you are out of your bed, and so much sooner than the doctors predicted," William almost gushed with joy.

On entering the breakfast parlour, all four Phillips were most pleased to see Elizabeth on her feet again. William steered his fiancée to a seat and proceeded to fill a plate for her. Not long after they broke their fasts, there was the sound of carriages from the drive. Not many minutes later the six Darcys staying at Netherfield were shown into the drawing room.

"You are out of bed," Georgiana stated the obvious as she took a seat next to her soon-to-be sister.

"As you see, Gigi. No more headaches for the last day," Elizabeth informed the rest. William knew that Jane and Alexander had news to share that would excite Elizabeth, so he made room for Jane to sit next to her younger sister on the settee.

"You look so good, Lizzy," Annabeth said after she planted a kiss on Elizabeth's cheek. "Mama, may I go spend time with Kitty and Lydia?"

"You may, Anna," Lady Anne acquiesced.

"Yes, Kitty and Lydia, you are free to go," Hattie Phillips waved her excited daughters away.

"Lizzy, you know how we have bemoaned the fact that we will be separated by more than two days of travel given where we both will live?" Jane asked, with one of her serene smiles that gave nothing away.

"Yes, you and I have discussed that many times," Elizabeth replied, somewhat confused as to Jane's purpose.

"Did you know that the Bennington's have left the neighbourhood for the New World?" Jane prodded.

"I had heard talk of that yes, but what has that to do—wait.

Who purchased Bennington Fields?" Elizabeth asked, starting to suspect why Jane was asking what she was not daring to believe that it could be so.

"My father purchased it as a sateli…" Alexander only got so far before Elizabeth understood what she was being told.

"Jane, you and Alex, and my nephew are going to live at the Fields, are you not?" Elizabeth fairly bounced on her seat, luckily not triggering any significant pains in her head.

"Yes, sister dearest, we will be your neighbours!" Jane confirmed.

"Thank you, Mother Anne and Father George, you know not what your generosity has done for us!" Tears of joy rolled down Elizabeth's cheeks.

"It will be hard not to see little Jamie as much," Lady Anne said with a sad smile thinking about her grandson being far away from Pemberley. "However, we will see all of you during the seasons and we will have to make *long* stops in Hertfordshire to and from London."

"It is not like we will not be visiting Pemberley during the summertime," Alexander pointed out.

"The boy is correct, Anne, we will see both of our sons and their families often," George Darcy agreed. The truth was that hardly a month would go by between seeing one another if things were planned correctly and Darcys loved to make plans.

"When did you find out that you were moving to Bennington Fields?" Elizabeth asked suspiciously.

"The doctors asked us to hold off exciting you too much, Lizzy. You know I would not have withheld this news from you for any other reason," Jane explained.

"They only told me last night after you were asleep," William owned. "They knew I would not be able to keep such a secret from you, my Lizzy."

"In that case, I forgive you for not telling me, Janey. I would have done the same if the roles were reversed," Elizabeth agreed.

"Now Elizabeth, some more news, of the less pleasant variety," Phillips informed his niece. Phillips informed Elizabeth of the reason Wickham had come to Longbourn, the murder of the heir and the capture, trial, and hanging of Thomas Bennet.

"I am sorry for the other people the murderer hurt, but I can never repine the fact that justice was served when our parents and Jamie's murderer was dispatched. He deserved far less than the clean execution he received! Given how she behaved, and you say that she was aware of the plan to steal Longbourn, I feel no sympathy for Fanny Bennet," Elizabeth stated with vehemence. "Do Kitty and Lyddie know that both of their former parents are no more?"

"They were told, and they showed no more sympathy for the pair than you did now," Hattie Phillips revealed. "It was, I believe, a relief to know that there is no chance they will ever encounter the two who abandoned them ever again."

"Now back to more pleasant things. We have a wedding and a wedding breakfast to plan," Jane said as she changed the subject to a decidedly more pleasant topic.

"Speaking of weddings, or possible ones, is it just me who has noticed Wes and Anne?" Elizabeth smiled.

"No Lizzy, we have all taken note of them," Lady Anne noted. "Sarah has not said a word as she was afraid that Wes would wait a good number of years before he found a lady who captured his interest. Like my sons, he had no desire to marry for wealth and connections as is the fashion among the Ton, although Anne has both."

"Has Aunt Cat noticed? Or is she too busy making sure that little Lewis never touches the ground," Georgiana asked.

"Gigi, your aunt misses *nothing*," Lady Anne laughed. "She will not interfere but will allow the two to reach any decisions they make on their own. We all convinced my brother Lewis not to interrogate Wes yet. You know how protective your uncle is of his *baby* girl."

"Wes would be a particularly good match for my niece," George Darcy opined. "They will do very well together, if it comes to pass."

"We are going to view the estate this afternoon, Lizzy, it is a pity that you are not allowed out of the house yet," Jane informed her younger sister. "I know you must be itching to walk or ride again. I remember when we were younger how Mama had to practically secure you to your bed when you were ill."

"Mr. Jones told me that once I have been pain free for five days complete, he will allow short excursions outside. The longer I go without any adverse reactions, the more I will be allowed to do. As much as I would like to accompany all of you today, my task is to get completely well. It would not do to not to be healthy enough to walk down the aisle after all," Elizabeth said as she looked out of the window wistfully.

As the Darcys were preparing to go to view Bennington Fields, Georgiana and Annabeth requested, and were granted, permission to remain at Longbourn. A few minutes after four of the Darcys departed, the rest of the Netherfield party arrived.

~~~~~~~/~~~~~~~

Bennington Fields was less than three miles north of Longbourn and about the same size as Netherfield Park. Oakham Mount stood between the two estates. The Bennington family had kept the estate in good order and the house had been well maintained with all the modern conveniences and a kitchen that had been redesigned with all new equipment barely more than a year previously.

The three senior staff were all family. The butler and housekeeper were Mr. and Mrs. Mason. The steward was a Mr. Mason also, and brother of the butler. He had been sent to Oxford by the previous master as he had shown a keen aptitude for estate management. The estate brought in more than William's estate with a clear five thousand pounds per annum.

"Mother and Father, this is perfect, you have our deepest gratitude," Alexander spoke for himself and his wife.

"We knew you and Jane would be happy being close to William and Lizzy, but it was not all altruistic. Running your own estate without me in the next room will be good training for when you take over Pemberley one day. Also, it was a good investment. The family was keen to sell so they did so below market," George Darcy informed the grateful couple.

"Also one day, if you give Jamie a brother, he will have a good estate and not have to seek a profession if he chooses not to," Lady Anne added.

"Is this estate entailed?" Jane asked knowing how much trouble the entail on Longbourn had caused.

"It is but it has nothing to do with gender. Once you and Alexander are mistress and master of Pemberley, you are free to will it to any of your children, even if you have only daughters after Jamie. The entail is like the new one on Longbourn, the estate cannot be broken up or sold to one who is not a Darcy by blood," George Darcy explained.

"When will we move in, Alex?" Jane asked.

"I was thinking perhaps after Lizzy and William's wedding. We can return to Pemberley and supervise the packing and then on our return we will take up residence here. What say you, Jane?" Jane enjoyed the fact that her husband would always consult her.

"That sounds like a perfect plan, husband," Jane returned.

When the four made the short ride back to Longbourn, Jane reported all that she saw at the Fields to her sisters and the assembled family members with enthusiasm. Even baby Jamie seemed to babble his approval.

CHAPTER 18

March 1807

Two days before Elizabeth's birthday, there was to be a betrothal and birthday ball at Netherfield Park. The ball was organised down to the last detail. The families would all depart for London as soon as Elizabeth and Anne returned from their curtsies before the Queen.

Elizabeth was extremely happy that she, like her older sister before her, was marrying for love, the deepest kind she could imagine. William was her perfect match. Adding to Elizabeth's happiness, Jane and Alex would be ensconced at Bennington Fields by the time that she and William returned from their wedding trip. As the weather in March still tended to be chilly in the north, rather than her first choice of the Lake District, their wedding trip would be to Seaview Cottage near Brighton. William had promised his betrothed they would go to Lake View House near Lake Windemere in July or August, when they would be at Pemberley.

There were no residual problems from Elizabeth's injury, and she could walk and ride to her heart's content, the only difference being that besides two footmen, William insisted on accompanying her as well when she rambled or rode. At first, she thought the demands officious until she saw it was done because of the depth of his love for her and he could not countenance her being harmed again.

With the impending marriage of Elizabeth to William, it was agreed unanimously that Mary would become the heiress of Longbourn. With the land that had been recently purchased using some of the money invested by Uncle Edward Gardiner,

Longbourn was not much smaller than Bennington Fields.

Any doubt about breaking the entail regarding male inheritance was removed when runners found the corpse of the former curate William Collins outside Knowle St Giles in Somerset as Wickham had enumerated before his demise. Thankfully, Wickham had hidden the late clergyman's trunk near the body and there was ample evidence within to identify the late William Collins.

The Phillips family would continue to reside at Longbourn until Mary married or reached her majority. Not long after the attack on Elizabeth, Kitty had changed her name to Kate. She was tired of the constant reminder of the lady who gave birth to her and given her the name she had chosen on a whim. Both Phillips sisters had all but erased the terrible memories of their birth parents from their minds.

Since all three of James and Priscilla Bennet's daughters had forgiven their uncle, the family had become close. Once Elizabeth was able to travel, she and Mary had come to London and resided at Jersey House with the De Melvilles for almost three weeks. Georgiana, Annabeth, Kate, and Lydia had joined them there and they had all became remarkably close to Lady Loretta, who they all called Retta.

Of Lord Wesley, Viscount Westmore, not much was seen during the day as he spent much of his time at de Bourgh house courting Anne or squiring her to events in London. A week before the ball, Wesley proposed to and was accepted by Anne. He was approved by Sir Lewis with Lady Catherine's happy agreement. There was no doubt that Wesley loved and respected their daughter and she him. The couple would marry in three months from Rosings.

When Lady Anne heard that her niece was betrothed, she spoke to William and Elizabeth who insisted that the ball honour the newly betrothed couple as well as them. So it was that the upcoming ball was set to celebrate two betrothals. At first, Anne and Wesley tried to demure as they did not want to impose on their cousins' time to celebrate. Elizabeth made short work of convincing her friend that it was her desire as much as anyone's, so it was decided.

The night before the return to Hertfordshire for the betrothal ball and wedding, Elizabeth and William were sitting in the Darcy House library together with Mrs. Annesley sitting opposite where she could see them but not hear what was being said. While Elizabeth resided at Darcy House, William had been a resident at Matlock House. "I anxiously wait for these four days to pass until we are married! We, my sisters and I, have endured so much since the murders of the rest of our family and even worse, having to put up with the murderers living at Longbourn! If it were not for the Phillipses, Gardiners, Lucases, and your family William, our lives would have been hell on earth. The fact that you and I love each other as we do is a testament to the lives Mama and Papa would have wanted for me," Elizabeth stated as she looked into the fire. "I do not mean to be maudlin, William, but as happy as I feel with our impending nuptials, I cannot but help think of those who will not be here to celebrate our wedding with us."

"Your feelings do you credit, my love. I would hate to know how I would be feeling if my parents and my older brother were not here to celebrate with us. Had I not had the supportive family I have around me, I can only imagine that my life, and my outlook on life, would have been vastly different. It just shows how strong you are that you have endured everything that you have and are still a wonderful, intelligent, compassionate, and charitable lady. And on top of that, the perfect life partner for me. Never forget that I love you with all that I am, Lizzy, not even when God calls me home will I stop loving you," William said as he squeezed his beloved Elizabeth's hand.

"Enough maudlin thoughts from both of us William, the day after tomorrow I get to dance with you for three sets at our betrothal ball! I have always enjoyed dancing with you at the monthly assemblies in Meryton, but I am looking forward to tomorrow more than any other dance as it is the last one that either of us will have as single people. It pleases me that Gigi,

Mary, Retta, and Kate are allowed to attend. Luckily, there are more than enough male members of the family and close friends so that they will not have to sit out too many dances before supper." Elizabeth changed the subject to a more pleasant one.

"Poor Annabeth and Lydia, they so much wanted to attend as well but could not convince their mothers. At least they will be able to spend the night together, as Lydia will be at Netherfield with Anna," William stated.

"After all Jane has told me about Seaview Cottage, I am much in anticipation of our wedding trip. Did you know, William, that I have never seen the ocean before?" Elizabeth asked.

"No my love, I was not aware of that fact. We will be at Seaview for a full three weeks, so not only will you get to see the ocean, but if the sea water is not too cold, we will swim in it," William promised. "Did Jane tell you about the secluded beach at Seaview?"

"Yes, she did, William, I am looking forward to whatever you have planned for that particular location," Elizabeth answered as she blushed deeply.

"It is time for me to return to Matlock house. I will see you on the morrow, my love." William stood and extended his hand to help Elizabeth stand as well.

"If only you did not have to live in a separate house," Elizabeth said wistfully.

"In no time at all, my love, we will be sleeping in the same house, in fact, in the same bedchamber," William told Elizabeth as they both felt much pleasure at the prospect of sharing a bedchamber.

Elizabeth walked William to the front door and hoping nobody was looking he gave his fiancée a quick kiss on the cheek before taking his leave. Even after the butler closed the front door Elizabeth stood where she was, looking at the spot where her William had just been standing.

~~~~~~~/~~~~~~~

The morning before the ball, Ladies Anne, Sarah, Catherine, and Elaine accompanied Anne de Bourgh and Elizabeth to

St. James Palace to make their curtsies before the Queen. Ladies Anne and Sarah were the sponsors for Elizabeth while Ladies Catherine and Elaine had the honour of presenting Anne. In the end, after so much preparation and practice, it was all over in mere minutes. The wait in the antechamber was about an hour before the Lord Chamberlain summoned Anne and then Elizabeth to enter the main chamber where the Queen and some of her daughters were seated, all looking bored.

It was almost an anti-climax after all of the practise to have the deed completed so fast. Miss Elizabeth Bennett and Miss Anne de Bourgh were now official members of London society. Elizabeth could not wait to return to Darcy house in order to divest herself of the gaudy hooped gown Queen Charlotte mandated would be worn by all debutants. It was the last thing that had to be done before their departure. Anne was no less keen to return to de Bourgh house for the same reason.

Lady Sarah had offered the two vouchers to Almack's, but both demurred. The primary function of Almack's was, after all, to act as a high-class marriage mart and neither of the newest members of society needed any help in that area much to the chagrin of many mothers of unmarried daughters who lamented that two eligible bachelors were out of their reach, even if one of them happened to be a second son.

Word had spread that not only was Miss Bennet the sister of the younger Mrs. Darcy, but that she was regarded as another daughter by the Darcy parents, even before her wedding, It was also now known she was the niece of the Earl and Countess of Jersey. Anyone who had thoughts of trying to denigrate the lady out of spite and jealousy gave up the idea as soon as they thought about it, given the formidable connections the lady claimed. Additionally, it was clear that both Bennet sisters were well connected to both the houses of Matlock and de Bourgh, which further disincentivised any rudeness or snubbing to be directed at Miss Bennet.

When they returned home, all the trunks were packed and as soon as the ladies changed into travel attire, the coaches departed for Hertfordshire.

~~~~~~~/~~~~~~~~

When Elizabeth had descended the stairs, all dressed in her finery for the ball, the vision of beauty that William saw stole his breath away. Her ball gown was hunter green velvet. Her hair was up with some curls hanging down her neck. She was wearing an emerald necklace that William recognised as part of the Darcy collection. There were dainty emerald and diamond earbobs that completed the ensemble.

William had always known that Elizabeth was beautiful, but never more so than the vision standing before him. Jane and Mary, resplendent in their gowns as well, descended the stairs behind Elizabeth. Before the receiving line formed, the de Bourgh, De Melville, Phillips, Gardiner, and Lucas families assembled in the largest drawing room at Netherfield.

William had invited his friend Charles Bingley along with Mr. and Mrs. Hurst, who were staying at the inn due to the lack of space at Netherfield, to join them before the start of the ball. It was the first time that Bingley had met Miss Phillips having only arrived that morning. She was not the traditional blonde that until that point had caught his eye. She was very pretty in her own way, certainly not a classic beauty. William shared that she was among the group of younger ladies permitted to attend the ball and would depart after supper. Bingley requested an introduction which William and Lizzy effected.

"Miss Phillips, if it is not taken, may I request the honour of the supper set?" Bingley asked.

Kate looked at her father for approval. Phillips knew of Bingley from William and was well aware he was a close friend of William's and had heard only good about the young man, so he gave his daughter a nod. "I will be happy to reserve that set for you Mr. Bingley," Kate blushed becomingly.

Bingley was pleased to be granted the set he requested. He would have tried for the first set if he had not seen Miss Phillips' father's name on her card for that set.

After an aperitif, the receiving line formed. It had been decided that rather than have an inordinately long receiving line that the two couples along with the hosts would form part of the receiving line. As the de Bourghs were co-hosting the ball, they made up the other part of the receiving line. It took close to an hour for all of the invited guests to arrive. Thankfully, unlike in Town, no one was rude enough to be what they considered *fashionably* late.

<div align="center">~~~~~~~/~~~~~~~</div>

William and Elizabeth along with Wesley and Anne stood at the top of the line. They were followed by Alexander and Jane, Peter and Charlotte, and then fathers with their daughters before the rest of the guests who chose to join the first. The musicians played three bars to warn the dancers that the set was about to begin. The first was a quadrille, so the first four couples made up the first grouping of the dance. Elizabeth and William were lost in one another's eyes and did not need to talk as they were communicating silently far more than they would have been able to with words.

William would have danced every set with Lizzy if his mother and aunt had not squelched his plan. He settled for the first, supper, and final sets. Even though the activity was not his favourite, William danced each set. Thankfully, with the younger members allowed to participate until the end of supper, the next four sets before the supper set were with his sister, Retta, Kate, and Mary.

When William came to collect her for the supper set, no one missed the way Elizabeth's countenance lit up to match the look of love that her betrothed was directing at her. Those from London who did know the families intimately were left with no doubts that another love match had been made, which seemed the be the fashion among the Darcys and their extended family.

"Are you enjoying the ball?" Elizabeth asked as the dance brought her back together with William.

"Never have I enjoyed a ball more," William owned just before they went down the line. "I have never danced with the lady who owns my heart at a London ball before, so mayhap that has something to do with it," he told Elizabeth with his dimples on display for all to see when they reached the end of the line and took each other's hand once again.

"It is most pleasing to hear you articulate that, William," Elizabeth stated as she arched her eyebrow. "What would it say if that was not true when you were dancing with the woman you are to marry in less than two days?" she teased.

"I will dance every set as you charged me to do, but not one is with a single lady not a member of our family," William informed his beloved proudly. They separated and went down the line once again.

"Although you are fulfilling your pledge, you know that is not what I meant," Elizabeth told William when they came back together.

"Then my lady should have been more exact in her instructions," William pointed out.

"You are lucky I love you so very much, exasperating man," Elizabeth bantered with mock indignation.

The music ended and William seated Elizabeth at a table with Jane, Charlotte, Anne, Kate, and Georgiana while he joined their partners in making a plate for their partners. While William was selecting food he knew his betrothed liked, Bingley stood next to him.

"Kate, Miss Phillips, is five and ten is she not?" Bingley asked softly.

"She is, why do you ask. You know she will not come out for another two years or so," William warned. "Also, she is not exactly your type and if you meddle with her, you will have a lot of angry family members after you, me included!"

"That is just it, I do not care how she looks, my intentions are completely honourable. She fascinates me and if I need to, I will prove my constancy for however many years it takes until she comes out. Do not worry Darcy, I do not fancy myself in love. I would like to get to know her better though." Darcy saw the sincerity in Bingley's speech.

"Recently, I heard of an estate near mine. Haye Park's ten-ant left at the end of the lease. It is a small estate, less than two thousand per annum, but a good one where you can learn if you are so inclined," William shared. "Ask Mr. Phillips about it; I believe that he is the leasing agent for the owners."

"That sounds like a good situation; I will look into it. It is close enough to Town for me to take care of my interests in partnership with Mr. Gardiner." Bingley was thankful for the information. Regardless of the estate's size, he would be happy living in the same neighbourhood as his friend.

After some of the ladies exhibited after supper, the highlight a collaboration between Jane, Elizabeth, and Mary, the younger ladies left for their bedchambers thanking their parents profusely for allowing them to partake.

The rest of the night sped by. Thankfully, the final dance was the waltz. Both betrothed couples had nothing to repine as each man held the lady of choice as close as he could without causing a scandal. By the time Elizabeth's head rested on her pillow in her bedchamber at Longbourn, the first light of dawn was visible in the east.

~~~~~~~/~~~~~~~

The night before her wedding to the love of her life, Elizabeth was joined by Jane, who had requested the honour of giving her younger sister *The Talk*. Elizabeth was not really nervous about the wedding night, in fact, she could not wait, but Jane's words were a comfort and dispensed without any traces of nervousness.

Elizabeth liked how Jane explained that pleasure in the act of joining was something to be striven for rather than lying still as some opined. Wanting to please as much as wanting to be pleased only heightened the experience. When Jane was done, she asked if her sister had any questions.

"In a book that I found, it stated that it can be painful the first time. Is that true?" Elizabeth blushed deeply.

"When the barrier of your maidenhead is breached, there will be some pain. With William so solicitous of your feelings, if need be, I am sure he will stop until the pain has subsided. Be prepared that there will be a little blood. It is normal and is not indicative of a problem," Jane replied.

"Thank you, Jane, as Mama could not give me the information I needed, it is only right that it should be you," Elizabeth stated wistfully as she felt a longing for her mother. The closer to her wedding day, the stronger the longing became.

"I missed Mama not being at my wedding too, Lizzy. I am sure she, Papa, and Jamie will be smiling on your union on the morrow. Their presence is everywhere here at Longbourn," Jane told her sister. The sisters had a good cry as they comforted one another they missed their mother not being with them on the eve of this most special of days.

~~~~~~~~/~~~~~~~~

The next morning Elizabeth was attended by Jane and Mary while her maid helped her into the cream satin wedding dress. The jewellery she wore was her mother's pearl necklace, the same one Jane had worn on her wedding, and Mary would one day wear at hers. When they were ready, the three sisters descended the stairs.

Uncle Frank, Aunt Hattie, and their daughters were waiting for Elizabeth in the entrance hall. Uncle Cyril and Aunt Sarah were also present. Uncle Frank would walk Elizabeth half way down the aisle and at that point Uncle Cyril would take over and walk her the rest of the way.

"How beautiful you look, Lizzy," Lydia gushed. "I will miss you!"

"After my wedding trip, I will be but three miles away, Lyddie," Elizabeth returned.

"It is time, Lizzy," Lord Cyril informed the bride as he offered her his arm.

As Jane was standing up with her sister, she remained behind with her sister and uncles when the rest of the party walked to the church. Five minutes later the four started Elizabeth's walk toward the church and the ceremony that would cause her to resign the name Bennet.

~~~~~~~~/~~~~~~~~

William had woken much earlier than he needed to on the morning of his wedding. He waited an hour before he rang for his valet. It was still earlier than he needed to be up, but it was a more reasonable time in the morning. He soaked in the steaming bath and then had his valet shave him. He applied his spice and sandalwood cologne, the one he was aware that Elizabeth preferred on him.

Once he was dressed, he made his way to the dining parlour, while for the most part, the house still slept. All he had was a cup of coffee and a warm roll with butter. He had too much nervous energy to have a big appetite.

As he was still an innocent, his father and Alexander had spoken to him the night before. Yes, it had been mortifying, but was nonetheless informative. He could not wait to get to the church and marry his beloved Elizabeth. By half after seven, everyone had eaten and an hour later they all departed for Longbourn's church.

William rode in a carriage with his parents, Alexander, and his sisters. Jane was at Longbourn as she was standing up with Elizabeth while Alexander was fulfilling the office for William. The wedding was set for half after nine. The church filled rapidly with a good mix of family and guests from both London and the area of Meryton.

William saw the residents of Longbourn, and Lady Sarah take their seats and he knew his waiting was almost over.

~~~~~~~/~~~~~~~

When Elizabeth, Jane, Phillips, and Lord Jersey arrived in the vestibule, The Earl entered the church to take up the station half way up the aisle. Madeline Gardiner was awaiting them; she was holding May Gardiner's hand. The girl of four was holding a basket full of petals. One of the doors leading into the church opened and May, with her mother watching closely, made the walk up the aisle, dutifully dropping rose petals.

When the door opened again, Jane entered the church and made the stately walk toward the altar. Once Jane was standing opposite her husband, both doors were opened, and the pastor asked the congregation to stand.

William held his breath as Phillips escorted his niece into the church and then handed her to the Earl who brought her toward the altar. Elizabeth was a vision; her dress was not ostentatious, but how it suited her. William descended the steps and Lord Cyril handed Elizabeth to her groom, kissed his niece on the forehead and joined his wife and family in the pews.

The bride and groom took their positions before the pastor who indicated the congregation should be seated. Even though William and Elizabeth were lost in one another's eyes, they were aware of what was happening and managed to give the appropriate answers, even if once or twice to the amusement of their witnesses, Jane or Alexander had to prod them a little. Before they knew it, the clergyman announced them, man and wife. In the vestry, with their brother and sister as witnesses, the registry was signed, and it was done. A second Bennet sister was a Mrs. Darcy.

On re-entering the church, the newlyweds were mobbed by their family and closest friends who wanted to bestow their well wishes. The family all then departed for Netherfield where the wedding breakfast was being held. Elizabeth and William followed them out a few minutes later after expressing their love with some passionate kisses in the vestibule.

The open chaise and four that George Darcy had gifted them, one of his less extravagant gifts, was waiting for them outside the church. Once the newlyweds took their seats, the driver flicked the reins, and the horses started forward. The Hills, Longbourn's servants, and tenants lined the drive to wish the former Miss Bennet and her husband well. William and Elizabeth tossed coins to them, much to the delight of the recipients.

Once the chaise turned onto the road to Meryton, Elizabeth leaned back into her husband's welcoming arms. "You do know do you not William, that neither I nor my sisters would have survived living with Thomas and Fanny Bennet without all of the love and support that we received from so many, you and your family chief among them," Elizabeth reminisced.

"You and your sisters are the strongest women that I have ever had the pleasure to meet Lizzy, you would have overcome them," William opined.

"Possibly, but we would not have been the same people that we are today. The support that we had from all of our loved ones was the difference between existing with and surviving when things were at their worst," Elizabeth stated emphatically.

As they rode toward their future life and the waiting family and friends waiting to celebrate their union, the newest Mr. and Mrs. Darcy revelled in their mutual love of the most ardent kind.

EPILOGUE

Four year old, Bennet George Darcy, called Ben, could not contain his excitement. Grandpapa George and Grandmama Anne would be arriving at Netherfield by late afternoon, and he wanted nothing more than to have his grandparents see him ride his new pony. He was more excited about his pony than he had been when Mama had gifted him a sister almost one year ago.

It was rather disappointing that Priscilla could not play with him yet as she could only crawl and Nurse did not chase her around Netherfield's park as Miss Ponsonby did him. Mama and Papa always told him that Nurse, who was also his governess, was not so young any longer and he needed to slow down but, even if she was older, Miss Ponsonby always caught her charge.

"Ben," Elizabeth called her son as she held Priscilla, who to William's delight looked like a miniature Elizabeth, as she tried to put her whole fist into her mouth while she drooled a river. "Grandmother and grandfather will not be here for another two hours."

"Aw, I wanna see them now. And Aunts Gigi and Anna," Ben whined, as a four year old was wont to do.

"Aunt Jane, Uncle Alex, Jamie, and little George will be here soon. Look, I see their carriage in the drive," Elizabeth pointed from her seat in the shade of the trees. She sat in the park near to the drive.

George Alexander Darcy had been born three years after his older brother Jamie and at almost three looked a lot like his namesake. Jane was with child again; she hoped that this time she would have a daughter.

When Elizabeth thought back on the five years since her marriage, she could not remember happier years in her life, other than when her mother, father, and brother Jamie had been alive.

No one had seen it coming when Richard Fitzwilliam, a colonel, proposed to Mary Bennet and she accepted two years previously. They had quietly fallen in love and courted without most of the family noticing what was happening in front of them. Knowing that Mary was the last Bennet, Richard had volunteered, after seeking his parent's approval, to change his name to Fitzwilliam-Bennet. All three Bennet sisters had cried tears of joy to know that the name Bennet would live on at Longbourn.

The Earl and Countess of Matlock had been joyous when Richard had resigned from the army and sold his commission to take up the mantle of master of Longbourn. A year and a half after the wedding, James Bennet IV was born. The couple had decided that their first son would be plain Bennet while any subsequent children would be Fitzwilliam-Bennets. Mary was with child once again.

Charles Bingley, who had become a great friend to all four Darcys living in the neighbourhood had made an offer for Haye Park and had owned it for almost four years now. When she turned eighteen, he had offered for Kate Phillips; they had been married for close to two years and Kate was expecting her first child. Bingley split his time between managing Haye Park and managing his partnership with Edward Gardiner.

Bingley no longer had business in Scarborough as he sold his stake in the carriage works in order to purchase the estate. With Mary having inherited Longbourn, Lydia, who was being courted by the Lucas heir, lived with the Bingleys at their estate.

Elizabeth's Aunt and Uncle Phillips had been gifted Purvis Lodge when it was purchased by the three former Bennet sisters as a gift. George Darcy had provided half of the purchase price. Frank Phillips retired from the active practice of law and was able to spend more time with his good friend Sir William Lucas.

Gigi had been courted by the Marquess of Birchington, Lord Sedgewick Rhys-Davies, and heir to the Dukedom of Bedford. The two had met in Gigi's third season and had become friends over their mutual love of music. He had proposed, and she accepted him a month earlier. Shy little Gigi would be a Marchioness in two months and a Duchess someday in the future.

Annabeth would be coming out in the upcoming little season. Lydia Phillips would take her curtsy on the same day and the best friends would share a coming-out ball at Darcy House. As talented as her older sister was on the pianoforte, Anna who used to rebel against being made to attend her music lessons, was by far the most proficient in the family.

Lord and Lady Westmore, Wes and Anne De Melville, were as happy as a couple not named Darcy could be. They lived at Westmore in Essex when not in Town for the season and had a daughter, Sarah-Kate, who would be three soon; Anne was with child again.

Anne De Melville had never had any health issues since Lizzy started her exercising those many years ago, and to this day Elizabeth and Anne were the closest of friends.

After little Lewis, Charlotte and Peter had gifted the four grandparents with twins—a boy and a girl. Jackson and Maria de Bourgh were a little older than three and the babe of the family, Cathy, had arrived three months previously.

Lady Catherine had finished a year of mourning for her beloved Lewis some four months previously. It had been the only sadness for the extended family when Sir Lewis's heart had failed him. Lady Catherine was much loved by her grandchildren and when she was not visiting her brother or sister, she split her time between her children's homes.

The relationship between the Earl of Jersey and his late sister's daughters had deepened over the years. Lord Cyril and Lady Sarah were adopted as grandparents to the children of all three former Bennet sisters' children. Retta had come out the same year as Gigi and she had become betrothed to the son of a gentleman from Wiltshire. He was heir to his father's estate, but it was not a large estate and had an income of less than three thousand pounds per annum. The family was not well known and had relations in trade.

Lord Cyril had not repeated his father's folly and as soon as he saw that his daughter's suitor loved her deeply, he welcomed the young man with open arms. Since the wedding, his daughter's in-laws had been guests in Town and at Broadhurst many times and there existed a close relationship between both sides of the family. Lord Cyril De Melville knew that his late mother and sister would have heartily approved of his improvement.

Jane came to sit with Elizabeth as the Darcy brothers talked horseflesh off to the side while the cousins ran around as fast as they could. "Look, Mary and Richard have arrived," Jane pointed to the Bennet carriage as it pulled up the drive. "I am looking forward to seeing little James again."

"Is it not perfect that the master after Richard will be James Bennet?" Elizabeth asked.

"Yes. I am sure that Papa would be very pleased to know that," Jane reflected.

"My belief is that he does know," Mary stated as she joined her sisters.

"Mary, how are you?" Elizabeth asked as her sister, heavy with child, lowered herself onto a padded chair.

"My feet are far more swollen than they were with little James," Mary reported. "I see my husband has joined yours playing with our children. Sometimes I wonder if our husbands are not little boys in adult sized bodies!"

"Members of the Ton have asked me if I bewitched William. They cannot believe that my husband is the same stoic and sometimes dour man that they knew five years ago. He loves to play with Ben using toy soldiers. All three of us have made exceeding felicitous matches," Elizabeth stated as she derived pleasure watching her husband and his brother's rough house with the children. All three of the men were careful in the extreme so none of the children were hurt by accident when playing with them. The three sisters watched as Ben demanded that his papa, uncles, and cousins follow him to the stables to view his new pony gifted to him by Grandpapa.

"Thank goodness between the three estates we have more than enough space for everyone, Jane said. "I know the Darcys and Fitzwilliams arrive this afternoon, when do Uncle Cyril, Aunt Sarah, Retta, and Simon arrive?"

"As far as I know on the morrow, as they were all going to meet at Rosings and then travel with the de Bourghs. Uncle Edward and Aunt Maddie are staying at Purvis Lodge. They will also arrive on the morrow," Elizabeth informed her sisters.

"Did you hear what happened to Charles' sister?" Mary asked.

"What happened to Louisa?" Jane was concerned. She had grown close to Louisa Hurst in the last five years.

"Not Louisa, the other one that we never met, Caroline. You remember the one who is committed to the asylum in Scotland?" Her older sisters nodded. "She somehow pilfered a bottle of laudanum and drank the whole of it thinking it was wine. She did not survive. Charles only mourned for one week, to him, his sister was lost many years ago," Mary informed her sisters.

"Any loss of life is sad," Elizabeth said thoughtfully, "but at least that tortured soul is at peace now."

"Mary, when will you enter your confinement?" Jane asked as she rubbed her own swollen belly.

"In two to three months, and you, Jane?" Mary responded.

"Three to four months," Jane replied. "You know Lizzy, it is the one thing that we have never managed to do together. I wonder if we will ever all be with child at the same time," Jane stated slyly, looking at Elizabeth.

"How could you tell Jane? I have only missed two months' worth of courses. I only told William about my suspicion two days ago. We will wait for me to miss my next course before we call Mr. Jones to confirm my state," Elizabeth related.

"Can you believe that we all live such good and fulfilling lives after what *that man* and his wife took from us?" Jane asked, as she thought about her missing parents and brother.

"Look at the damage that he attempted to cause when he sent that criminal here to harm us. He almost succeeded with our Lizzy. I thank God every day, for over five years after the attack, that Lizzy made a complete recovery," Mary added.

"After my wedding, on the ride to Netherfield for the wedding breakfast, I told William that we survived that man, but it is more than that. We did not only survived, but we thrived in spite of his attempts to harm us. We have always been surrounded by love. First from Mama, Papa, and Jamie, and then by all of our protectors that led us to the men we are married to and who we love to distract.

"I have thought about this when I have had time to reflect on the past, which is not often, that the love that surrounded us was too strong to be penetrated by their actions. Yes, they tried to break through the walls of the bubble, and they may have even damaged it a little, but it *never* broke," Elizabeth stated thoughtfully. "That is why I say we did a lot more than just survive those two. It is also why we are always surrounded by love. Mama and Papa sowed the seeds of love and it never left us. It will be with us forever and as William says, this type of love transcends death and the ages."

Jane and Mary could not agree more with Elizabeth's sentiments. The three former Bennets stood and linked arm-in-arm and walked toward where the children, young and old, were extolling Ben's pony and his skill as a rider.

The End

BOOKS BY THIS AUTHOR

A Change Of Fortunes

What if, unlike canon, the Bennets had sons? Could it be, if both father and mother prayed to God and begged for a son that their prayers would be answered? If the prayers were granted how would the parents be different and what kind of life would the family have? What will the consequences of their decisions be?

In many Pride and Prejudice variations the Bennet parents are portrayed as borderline neglectful with Mr. Bennet caring only about making fun of others, reading and drinking his port while shutting himself away in his study. Mrs. Bennet is often shown as flighty, unintelligent and a character to make sport of. The Bennet parent's marriage is often shown as a mistake where there is no love; could there be love there that has been stifled due to circumstances?

In this book, some of those traits are present, but we see what a different set of circumstances and decisions do to the parents and the family as a whole. Most of the characters from canon are here along with some new characters to help broaden the story. The normal villains are present with one added who is not normally a villain per se and I trust that you, my dear reader, will like the way that they are all 'rewarded' in my story.

We find a much stronger and more resolute Bingley. Jane Bennet is serene, but not without a steely resolve. I feel that both need to be portrayed with more strength of character for the purposes of this book. Sit back, relax and enjoy and my hope is that you will be suitably entertained.

The Hypocrite

The Hypocrite is a low angst, sweet and clean tale about the relationship dynamics between Fitzwilliam Darcy and Elizabeth Bennet after his disastrous and insult laden proposal at Hunsford. How does our heroine react to his proposal and the behaviour that she has witnessed from Darcy up to that point in the story?

The traditional villains from Pride and Prejudice that we all love to hate make an appearance in my story BUT they are not the focus. Other than Miss Bingley, whose character provides the small amount of angst in this tale, they play a small role and are dealt with quickly. If dear reader you are looking for an angst filled tale rife with dastardly attempts to disrupt ODC then I am sorry to say, you will not find that in my book.

This story is about the consequences of the decisions made by the characters portrayed within. Along with Darcy and Elizabeth, we examine the trajectory of the supporting character's lives around them. How are they affected by decisions taken by ODC coupled with the decisions that they make themselves? How do the decisions taken by members of the Bingley/Hurst family affect them and their lives?

The Bennets are assumed to be extremely wealthy for the purposes of my tale, the source of that wealth is explained during the telling of this story. The wealth, like so much in this story is a consequence of decisions made Thomas Bennet and Edward Gardiner.

If you like a sweet and clean, low angst story, then dear reader, sit back, pour yourself a glass of your favourite drink and read, because this book is for you.

The Duke's Daughter: Omnibus Edition

Part 1: Lady Elizbeth Bennet is the Daughter of Lord Thomas and Lady Sarah Bennet, the Duke and Duchess of Hertfordshire. She is quick to judge and anger and very slow to forgive. Fitzwilliam Darcy has learnt to rely on his own judgement above all others. Once he believes that something is a certain way, he does not allow anyone to change his mind. He ignored his mother and the result was the Ramsgate debacle, but he had not learnt his lesson yet.

He mistakes information that her heard from his Aunt about her parson's relatives and with assumptions and his failure to listen to his friends the Bingleys, he makes a huge mistake and faces a very angry Lady Elizabeth Bennet.

Part 2: At the end of Part 1, William Darcy saved Lady Elizabeth Bennet's life, but at what cost? After a short look into the future, part 2 picks up from the point that Part 1 ended. We find out very soon what William's fate is. We also follow the villains as they plot their revenge and try to find new ways to get money that they do not deserve.

Elizabeth finally admitted that she loved William the morning that he was shot, is it too late or will love find a way? As there always are in life, there are highs and lows and this second part of three gives us a window into the ups and downs that affect our couple and their extended family.

Part 3: In part 2, the Duke's Daughter became a Duchess. We follow ODC as they continue their married life as they deal with the vagaries of life. We left the villains preparing to sail from Bundoran to execute their dastardly plan. We find out if they are successful or if they fail.

In this final part of the Duke's Daughter series, we get a good idea what the future holds for the characters that we have followed through the first two books in the series.

The Discarded Daughter - Omnibus Edition

All 4 books in the Discarded Daughter series are combined into a single book. They are available individually, in both Kindle and paperback format.

The story is about the life of Elizabeth Bennet who is kidnapped and discarded at an exceedingly early age. It tells the tale of her life with the family that takes her in and loved her as a true daughter.

We follow not only Elizbeth's life, her trials and tribulations, but that of the family that lost her and all of those around her, immediate and extended family, and the effect that she has on their lives. There is love, villains, hurt, and happiness as we watch Elizabeth grow into an exceptional young woman.

If you are looking for a story that only concentrates on our heroine, then this is not for you.

www.ingramcontent.com/pod-product-compliance
Lightning Source LLC
Chambersburg PA
CBHW051506260626
47162CB00008B/2845